SHE FELT SIMON TENSE...

THEY'D JUST PASSED THROUGH the halo of one gas lamp and into the next stretch of darkness when two men stepped out of the shadows of a doorway and into the empty street.

"Just keep walking," Simon said softly.

She kept her head down, but her eyes up as they drew closer to the pair. They'd almost passed them when the men stepped in their way. Elizabeth's heart stuttered.

"What's your hurry?" one said.

Simon tried to guide her off the curb, but the other stepped that way to block them.

"You ain't even sayin' hello?" the skinnier of the two said with a broad smile that revealed two missing teeth.

"We don't want any trouble," Simon said, managing to keep his upper class accent under wraps.

The skinny one laughed and elbowed his friend. "He don't want no trouble?"

The other one laughed and then abruptly added, "I'm afraid you've found it, mate."

"Simon Cross is so smoking that it turns off my higher cognitive functions...Adventuring through time with these two characters is a real treat, and I would happily follow them for another twelve or so books."

SM Reine, author of *Death's Hand*

MONIQUE MARTIN

A Rip in Time

Out of Time Series
Book #7

Cover Photo: Karen Wunderman
Cover Design and Interior Layout and Formatting: TERyvisions

ISBN 10: 0984660798
ISBN 13: 978-0-9846607-9-7

For more information, please contact
writtenbymonique@gmail.com
Or visit: www.moniquemartin.weebly.com

ACKNOWLEDGEMENTS

THIS BOOK WOULD NOT have been possible without the help and support of many people. I would like to take this opportunity to thank Robin without whom this book wouldn't have been nearly as much fun to write or half as much fun to read, Michael, Mom & George, Dad & Anne, Eddie & Carole, Melissa, JM, Cynthia, Lyndsay, Laura, the Council, and the Diaspora.

I'd also like to thank the thousands of people who help preserve the past through books, websites, museums and sheer will.

A Rip in Time

(Out of Time Book #7)

Monique Martin

CHAPTER ONE

FOR THE BRIEFEST MOMENT, the world stopped. Before Elizabeth could put a name to the feeling that sank to the pit of her stomach, it stuttered and restarted.

Chalking it up to fatigue, she shook off the last remnants of the fuzzy-headedness that always came with traveling in time and looked around her living room. It was, as she knew it would be, exactly as they'd left it. In the room, in the present, nothing had changed, no time had even elapsed. The odd disconnect between the busy streets of Cairo and the quiet of their home made the last few weeks they'd spent in Egypt feel like a dream.

But the men on either side of her were a stark reminder that it had been no dream. The bruises on Simon's face had yet to fully fade away, and the worry in his eyes had taken up permanent residence. And Jack; his smile for her was as real as the sling supporting the arm that had been shot just days before.

Appearing distracted for a moment, Simon then focused on her and squeezed her hand. "All right?"

She nodded. He let go, closed the watch and slipped it into his pocket.

He glanced at Jack, all business now. "I want to leave here in less than an hour. Can you manage?"

Jack nodded and slid his arm from its sling. He worked it around in a small circle, wincing as he did. "Yeah."

They'd made plans as they rode away from Shepheard's Hotel in Cairo to a secluded spot where they could make their return to the present. Elizabeth hadn't liked it then and she didn't like it now. But there was no arguing with the logic of it. They weren't safe here. Not as long as Katherine Vale was out there.

Jack glanced at Elizabeth and then back to Simon. "I'll be back before an hour's up."

"Good," Simon said curtly before heading for the kitchen.

Jack lingered for a moment and gave Elizabeth a comforting smile, but it wasn't one she could return.

Gosh, she hated this. She was tired and hungry and there was still sand in places sand should never be. She wanted to take a bath and then sleep through the weekend. But none of that was going to be. They were home, but they weren't staying there. Not even for an hour.

Jack's smile grew even kinder. "Don't worry. We'll figure it out."

Elizabeth nodded quickly and he gave her arm a comforting squeeze as he passed her heading for the front door.

Don't worry, she thought as he left. That wasn't likely. Not for any of them.

There was nothing quite like having a murdering psychopath on the loose, one who hated your very guts, to foster a healthy sense of worry.

At first she'd hoped they might be safe at home. Peter Travers from the Council had deactivated the device that tracked the watches and Katherine Vale had no idea where or when she and Simon lived. But she was resourceful and evil, and that was a very bad combination. Elizabeth quickly realized that finding them wouldn't exactly take a Holmesian effort.

She and Simon had made no attempt to hide who they were. They'd used their real names and in the twenty-first century finding someone was as easy as opening a web browser. Everything they did, who they were, was saved in perpetuity in the ether. Heck, even the university had their pictures and names emblazoned on its website. Finding them would be child's play.

The only thing working in their favor was that Vale hated Charles Graham even more than she hated them. She'd spent every waking moment since escaping from Bedlam trying to kill him. First, she'd tried to murder his great grandfather in 1906 San Francisco. When that had failed, thanks to Simon and Elizabeth, she'd set out again in search of Graham himself.

Graham was no idiot though, and went on the run, forcing Vale to try any means to find him, including trying to summon the goddess Sekhmet in 1920s Cairo. Once again, Simon and Elizabeth were there to stop her.

But had they really? They'd saved the day, but all they'd really managed to do was to delay her a bit longer and make sure her hatred for them grew that much more. And now she was out there, somewhere, plotting her revenge and Elizabeth knew that she and Simon would be playing a role in her Spectacle of Crazy whether they liked it or not.

"Elizabeth?" Simon called from the kitchen. "We don't exactly have time to waste."

She started and turned to look at him on the other side of the pass-through window that linked the two rooms. "Sorry. I'll pack."

Simon closed the drawer he'd been rummaging through. "Keep it light. We want to able to stay on the move easily."

She nodded and swallowed down how much she hated that. She hated running. Even though it was the smart thing to do, the only thing to do when a lunatic was out there hunting you, she bristled at the idea of it and wondered if it would ever end.

Simon rejoined her in the living room, pocketing a small key as he did. "It won't be forever," he said, as though he'd read her mind.

"I know," Elizabeth said, even though she didn't. With a sigh, she started for the stairs. Simon caught her hand in his as she passed.

"It will be all right," he said.

"Promise?"

She'd said it playfully, but Simon's eyes grew dark. She knew he couldn't promise her that any more than he could promise to stop the tide, and yet he would because she needed him to.

"Yes," he said.

Elizabeth knew that one word wasn't a false assurance made just to quiet her fears. It was a promise he meant to keep. No matter what the cost.

Elizabeth pulled their luggage out from an upstairs closet and stared down at it. Somehow, going on the run and their Tumi luggage set didn't seem to go together. They needed something "on the runnier."

She rolled the Tumi aside and dug around in the closet. There weren't many choices. Most of their traveling was done by unconventional methods and was to places that steamer trunks were less likely to stand out. Heck, they had two trunks downstairs in the living room filled with 1920s clothes and a few more in the garage, but they were hardly helpful. What they needed was something light and maneuverable, like a duffle bag, but Simon wasn't the duffle bag type.

After a little more searching she found not one, but two duffle bags resting on the very top shelves in the very back of the closet. Odd, she thought. She'd never noticed them before.

She pulled the small stepladder over to the shelves and started to climb, but a wave of dizziness overtook her and she gripped the edges of the shelves for balance. It passed quickly enough, but when she opened her eyes she had an odd sense of disorientation. It was as though she were in a dream, a strange sensation of being in her home, but at the same time it wasn't her home. The feeling lasted only for a few moments and she shook her head and the feeling passed.

Clearly, she needed a nap stat. But there was no time to rest yet. She climbed up to the top step. One bag was floppy and empty, but the other was heavy, perhaps half-full. Dropping it to the floor, she climbed down and then knelt next to it.

Her heart beat a little faster as she unzipped it.

Inside she found a first aid kit, tablets to make water potable, an all-purpose tool, two space blankets, a tarp, four rolls of duct tape, flashlights, and extra batteries. Maybe she shouldn't have suggested they start watching the Walking Dead, she thought. When she found the big Bowie knife, the gun with two extra clips and ten thousand dollars cash, she was sure of it.

"Ah, good," Simon said behind her. "You found it."

Elizabeth looked at him dumbly.

Simon arched an eyebrow. "I live in California," he said in answer to her unasked question. "There are earthquakes, forest fires and riots. And, need I add, you."

He took the 9mm clip out of her hand and put it back in the bag and zipped it up. "Having a go bag seemed like a good idea."

Elizabeth was still trying to come to terms with Simon having a go bag when he reached out a hand to help her up.

"About that packing…"

Elizabeth winnowed their clothes down to the mere essentials. Jack returned as promised, and the three of them were ready to head out. They needed to stop at the bank to get the additional cash Simon had squirreled away in their safety deposit box. After that, they'd head east and find an out of the way hotel to stay in for the night. Then, they'd come up with a plan.

They knew they couldn't stay on the run, that they'd have to take the fight to Katherine Vale, find her before she found them, but they had nothing to go on. They had no way to contact the Council and it wasn't exactly the sort to be listed in the Yellow Pages under Organizations, Secret. Not to mention that they might be the very ones behind all of this.

Simon lifted both duffle bags. "Ready?"

Jack nodded and slung his bag over his good shoulder.

Elizabeth could see the effort it took. "Let me."

She held out her hands to take his bag, but Jack just smiled. "And lose my man card? Come on, kid."

A knock on the front door stopped Elizabeth's argument, and the three of them froze for a second before she looked to Simon.

He nodded toward the hallway, urging her to hide there. She ignored him and tiptoed over to the fireplace and picked up a poker. Simon glared at her, but the knock at the door came again and pulled his attention away.

Jack unholstered his gun and took up a position behind the door. Simon edged closer and tried to peer through the side windows, but couldn't see anything. Carefully, he moved in front of the door and looked out of the peep hole.

Elizabeth saw his shoulders rise and fall and heard the exhalation of breath, both relieved and annoyed.

He waved for Jack to stand down and then yanked open the door.

Standing nervously on the front steps was a slight, balding man with black-rimmed glasses. He offered them a faltering smile that Simon did not return.

"Travers."

Chapter Two

Peter Travers clutched his briefcase to his chest like a shield against Simon's glare. While he was relieved they didn't have to track down the Council now, a knock on the door from a Council member was never a harbinger of anything remotely good.

The man's thin lips quivered as he tried again to smile. Not finding one in return, he leaned to the side, peering around to see Elizabeth. "Mrs. Cross," he said in that thin, squeaky voice of his.

"Mr. Travers," Elizabeth said. "Come in."

Travers looked up nervously at Simon for permission. Simon lingered in place for a moment, blocking his path. Unfortunately, as loath as he was to let this weaselly little man into their home, they would need his help if they were to find Katherine Vale.

Travers cleared his throat and kept his gaze down as he turned his body sideways and inched past Simon and into the foyer.

Simon heard Jack's low, amused chuckle in the background.

"Thank you," Travers said. "I—I was hoping I'd catch you."

Simon closed the door and turned to face him. "Were you?"

"Y-yes," Travers stammered anxiously as he pushed his glasses back up onto his nose. "I know what happened in Egypt, with, uhm—"

Simon strode forward, quickly closing the small distance between them. He'd never trusted the Council, and with damn good reason. He'd suspected someone in the so-called Shadow Council, a mysterious and corrupt group inside the Council proper, was responsible for Katherine Vale's untimely appearance in Cairo. And Travers, well, his truth was never the whole truth and the parts that were missing seemed inclined to get them killed.

"And just how do you know that? Did you send her?"

"Vale?" Travers squeaked. "Oh my goodness, no. I—I don't know who was responsible for that, but we have bigger problems, I'm afraid."

"That's a habit with you guys, isn't it?" Jack said.

Travers turned, startled, and then smiled broadly in recognition. "Oh! Mr. Wells. I've been looking forward to meeting you."

Although Jack's body language was casual as he leaned against the wall, Simon was pleased to note that he still had his gun in hand. Jack pushed himself off the wall and shifted his eyes anxiously from Travers to Elizabeth and back again. "Yeah?"

"I'm a bit of a World War II nut," Travers said with a blush crawling up his neck. "Models and things mostly. They're not very good, but a chance to speak to a real live OSS man…"

Jack stared back at him blankly.

Before Travers could begin to gush, Simon forced him back on topic. "Mr. Travers."

"Oh, sorry. Right—"

"Do you know where Katherine Vale is?" Elizabeth asked abruptly.

Simon had planned on being a bit more circumspect in his questions, but leave it to Elizabeth to cut to the very heart of the matter.

Travers blinked at her directness, but the forthright question seemed to pull him back to himself and the seriousness of the situation. He straightened his back and stood as tall as his little frame would allow.

"I do."

Simon waited a moment. "And are you going to tell us?"

"I'd rather show you."

Simon's eyes narrowed. "And why on earth should we trust you?"

Travers' small round face wrinkled in thought as he took off his glasses. "No reason at all, I suppose," he said softly before sliding his spectacles back onto his face. "But I sincerely hope you do. Without your help, I shudder to think of the consequences."

Simon glanced over at Elizabeth and recognized her expression. She was already standing on the lip of the frying pan, planning her swan dive down into the fire.

She, Jack and Simon exchanged glances, but in the end, Simon knew they had little choice. If they were ever to rest again, they had to find Katherine Vale. If that meant going along with Travers for now, they simply could not say no.

"And just where will you be taking us?" Simon asked.

"San Francisco." Travers' nervous smile returned. "HQ. The… the headquarters for the Council for Temporal Studies."

ELIZABETH KNEW SHE SHOULDN'T be excited by it all. They were traveling with a man they didn't really trust to a city where they'd nearly been killed to see a woman who wanted them dead. It had "last trip you'll ever take" written all over it. Despite that, Elizabeth was relieved to be going, relieved to be doing something, anything, other than running. Of course, Simon had pointed out that they were running, just into the jaws of death instead of away from them, but she knew deep down he felt the same way. A life on the run was no life at all.

The charter flight took less than two hours, and before they knew it she, Simon and Jack were riding in the back of a town car through the streets of San Francisco. It brought back an onslaught of memories.

She'd often wondered what happened to the Eldridges and Gerald, and Max and Teddy. They'd long since passed by now, but she liked to think of them out there alive and happy, somewhere, somewhen.

The last time they'd been in San Francisco, the city had been destroyed by the Great Earthquake and was in the process of being engulfed by dozens of enormous fires. The city that passed by her window showed no scars. It had risen, literally, from the ashes, and was born again.

As they turned down Market Street, Elizabeth took heart in the courage of the city. It, like them, had been knocked down, but it wasn't out. And neither were they.

Elizabeth slipped her hand over Simon's as it rested on his thigh. He turned to her, and she could see the ghosts of their past reflected in his eyes.

"I'm glad we're going to San Francisco *together* this time," she said with a wry smile.

Simon laughed, half humorous and half self-deprecating. "I won't make that mistake again, I assure you."

The old Elizabeth would have taken that to mean that he wouldn't "let" her run off on her own again, and she would have bristled like a prized colt at the inference. But this Elizabeth knew better. She knew that wasn't what he meant. It meant he trusted her. Completely.

Elizabeth leaned in to kiss him, but before she could, Travers' little Piglet voice interrupted them.

"We're here!"

Simon's discontented sigh made her giggle. She pecked his cheek and then stepped out as the chauffeur opened the door.

They'd stopped in front of an imposing building with large Corinthian columns that looked like a bank or a museum. A detailed frieze with carvings representing the signs of the zodiac wrapped around the top of the building. She recognized all of them immediately except for the one in the center—a boy, robes around his waist, standing inside a circle—until she read the words carved beneath him.

"The Aion Society," she read aloud.

"Clever," Simon said modestly impressed, but trying not to be.

"What am I missing?" Jack said.

"Aion was a god of time during the Hellenic period," Simon explained. "The more popularly known Chronos represented a more linear way of thinking—past, present and future—each discrete from the other. Aion, on the other hand, symbolizes eternity, a perception of time stretching out infinitely in all directions."

Jack nodded. "Got it. *Dr. Who*. Timey-wimey stuff."

Simon frowned and Elizabeth couldn't stop her laugh. "Watch the show, get the joke," she told her husband as he held the door open for her.

The inside of the building was as austere as the outside, and she'd been right about it resembling a museum. Inside were displays and glass cases and even a few tourists.

"The Aion Society's mission," Travers said in his best tour guide voice as he led them through the main lobby area, "is to preserve history for future generations. Our collection is quite eclectic."

Elizabeth and the others peered into a few displays as they passed. Were all of these things from Council missions? Was something from one of their trips here somewhere? One of Sebastian's?

"This way," Travers said as he led them out of the main floor and back behind closed doors.

"The collection?" Elizabeth asked.

Travers pressed the button for the elevator. "A combination of artifacts obtained by the Council, and some through more traditional means. It serves as a good cover. We acquire large sums of period money, clothing and the like. That might appear somewhat suspicious without the society's 'collection'."

"That's all very interesting," Simon said, "but that is not why we've come here."

"No," Travers agreed. "It's not."

The elevator dinged and the doors opened. A large man in a dark suit waited inside for them and held the door open.

"After you," Travers said.

Elizabeth looked at Simon, but she knew they hadn't come all this way to bug out now, and she walked ahead of him into the elevator. Travers and Jack followed.

"Sorry, sir," the big man said as he held his hand out to stop Jack. "You'll have to leave that here." He indicated Jack's holstered gun. How he'd even noticed it beneath Jack's coat, she didn't know.

Jack frowned and glanced at Simon who arched an eyebrow and nodded. Jack unholstered the gun, flipped it in his hand and held it out handle first.

The man waved to a pretty young woman at a nearby desk. She came over and smiled at Jack who smiled back broadly. Elizabeth could see him trying to come up with angle.

The woman laughed lightly, but was otherwise unfazed by Jack's charm. "Your gun, Mr. Wells."

"Oh," Jack said. "Right."

She smiled and took the gun, handing Jack a numbered ticket in return like a coat check girl.

She stepped back out of the way and Jack tilted his head to get one last admiring look before slipping the ticket into his pocket. "Maybe this'll be more interesting than I thought."

"Wells…" Simon said as the doors closed and they began their descent.

"Just makin' lemonade, Cross. Makin' lemonade."

THE ELEVATOR DEPOSITED THEM on a level with multiple doorways and corridors. Each doorway had a set of complex gears embedded in the middle. They followed Travers to the right where he entered a code on a keypad. A small panel opened and he stepped forward for a retinal scan.

Simon and Elizabeth exchanged impressed looks. The Council certainly took security seriously, which was a darn good thing when you were dealing with something as powerful and potentially dangerous as time travel.

Once the scan was over, Travers stood back and the complex series of gears in the middle of their door began to spin and grind against each other. Like layers of an onion, they peeled away, each disappearing inside the wall creating a hole about two feet in diameter. Finally, the gears stopped and the doors slid open. The only thing that was missing, Elizabeth thought, was the Star Trek whoosh.

"This is our highest security area," Travers said as he stepped through the opening. "You're the only civilians to set foot inside."

"As impressive as all this is," Simon said as they walked down a long corridor, "you said you'd take us to Katherine Vale."

"And so I have." Travers knocked on an unmarked door. "Travers."

The door opened and another bulky man in a suit answered.

"You can wait outside," Travers said to him.

The man nodded once and then stepped aside.

Travers held out his arm, gesturing for them to go in.

"After you," Simon said pointedly. He was not about to go anywhere without Travers in grabbing distance. Travers went in and they followed.

The room was nondescript. It had a few chairs, a desk scattered with papers and filing cabinets covered most of the far wall except for another doorway. The other wall, Elizabeth realized once she was inside, was all glass, but it was dark and smoky, a deep midnight blue.

"Well?" Simon did little to hide his impatience.

Travers pressed a button and the smoky glass cleared, revealing an adjacent room with nothing but a table, a chair and Katherine Vale.

SIMON TOOK AN INVOLUNTARY step forward; his heart raced at the sight of her. He heard Elizabeth let out a breath next to him and he glanced over at her and they shared an uneasy smile.

This woman, this evil woman who'd haunted his nightmares for the last two weeks was here, and judging from the manacles around her wrists, their prisoner. She seemed wholly unaware of their presence on the other side of the glass. She hadn't given any indication she'd seen them, confirming his suspicion that this was some sort of one-way mirror.

Simon stepped a bit closer to study her. She looked a far cry from the woman he'd last seen in the catacombs of Egypt. Her wild expression was neutral now, almost bored. The blood-red ceremonial robes she'd worn were replaced with sky blue surgical scrubs. The manic energy she'd exuded was completely gone.

To all the world, she looked well captured. They should be safe from her, but Simon didn't feel the relief he'd expected. Seeing her again sent a chill through him he could not shake nor explain.

"How?" he asked, never taking his eyes off her.

"We traced her watch," Travers said.

Simon turned to face him and took a threatening step forward. "You what? You turned on the tracking device again?"

Good God, Simon thought as he looked back at Vale, she could have found them so easily.

"Yes," Travers said apologetically. "After we learned what happened in Egypt, and the incident here—"

"What *incident*?"

"She killed two men in the records office," a voice behind him said in a mild French accent.

Simon spun around to see a tall man, at least his own height, with broad sloping shoulders, leaning against the wall near the door along the back of the room. When had he come in?

"Who the hell are you?" Simon demanded.

"This is Victor Renaud," Travers said. "Victor, this is—"

The man waved his hand in dismissal. "I know who they are."

And, judging from the sour look on his hawk-nosed face, he was unimpressed.

Travers ignored the slight. "He's the one you can thank for capturing Katherine Vale."

"Thank you for that," Elizabeth said. "A lot."

Simon nodded his agreement. "We're in your debt."

Renaud grunted in acknowledgment with patented French smugness, as he pushed himself off the wall and walked toward the glass. Simon waited for something more, but nothing came.

Renaud cast an assessing glance at Simon and then Elizabeth, as he slowly walked to the glass divider. His expression remained dark and sullen, and never changing as his attention slid from them to Vale.

Simon bristled at the obvious show of disdain for their gratitude. Who the hell did he think he was?

"Did you get back all of the watches she had?" Elizabeth asked.

"Just one," Travers said. "The others…"

Simon grunted. Perfect, their entire mission had been for nothing.

"It's worse than that, I'm afraid. After her return, she broke into the records office," Travers said, his embarrassment clear, "and killed the men on duty before escaping."

"What did she take?" Jack asked.

Travers sighed. "Nothing."

"She must have been after something," Simon said, turning back to look at her.

"Oh, yes," Travers said. "It was after her escape that we reactivated the tracking device and Victor found her."

Renaud continued to silently watch Vale through the glass.

Travers looked at her anxiously and then continued. "She'd been there less than a day by the time Victor found her."

"That's good," Elizabeth said.

"Not good enough," Renaud said softly.

That chill Simon felt began to grip his spine. "Where did she go?"

"1887, London."

"Why then?" Jack asked.

"Her first assignment," Elizabeth answered. "She told me about it in San Francisco. She'd been sent back to study Jack the Ripper. With Charles Graham."

Simon's heart began to race again, but he forced it to slow, forced himself to focus. "But the Jack the Ripper killings were in 1888, not 1887."

Travers nodded. "The failsafe. The watch failsafe was reactivated with the tracking device. It keeps anyone from traveling to a time they've already lived through."

"But I went back to 1933 and I'd already lived through it," Jack said.

"The tracker was off then, so the failsafe didn't stop you."

Simon's mind whirled as he started to put the pieces together. "She couldn't go to 1888, but she could go to 1887 and wait."

"Exactly," Travers said, looking again at the woman behind the glass. "We're assuming she was planning to kill Charles Graham."

That was a logical conclusion, considering she'd gone to great lengths so far to do just the same.

"But Victor got to her before she could?" Elizabeth said.

Travers sighed. "Yes."

Clearly, there was more to it. "But?"

Renaud stared at Vale. "Not before she did something else."

"What?" Elizabeth asked, turning away from Vale for a moment. "What did she do?"

"That's the trouble," Travers said anxiously. "We're not sure what."

"That doesn't make any sense," Jack said. "Then how do you know she did something?"

"Cause and effect." Travers turned to Simon and Elizabeth. "We can't see the cause, but we can see the effect. And it's…a problem."

Renaud snorted. "A problem."

Inside the cell, Vale stood up and turned to look at the glass. Her eyes scanned it and seemed to know just where to look. Her gaze fell on each of them in turn and finally landed on Elizabeth.

"A rather large problem," Travers said as they all watched Vale move slowly toward them.

She walked to the far end where Jack stood and put her index finger on the glass. She trailed it along the surface, her finger squeaking as it slid across it.

Simon frowned. That wasn't right. Not right at all. Ahmed had shot off her index finger. He could still remember seeing the bloody stump as she held the watch in her hand before she'd disappeared. But now it was as if that had never happened.

Vale stopped in front of Elizabeth. She lifted her hands and splayed out the fingers of both hands against the glass. Her pale violet eyes seemed to see right through the barrier, and she smiled.

Simon's voice was soft as he spoke, as he realized what had happened. "Dear God. She's changed time."

CHAPTER THREE

Elizabeth heard what Simon said, but it barely registered. Vale's eyes were locked onto hers as if she could see, not just through the glass, but right through Elizabeth's soul.

"That's the curious thing," Travers said. "Whatever she's done, it's happening and unhappening. Or," he added with a thoughtful squint, "has happened?"

With an effort, Elizabeth looked away. "What do you mean happening and unhappening?"

"Whatever she's done it's created a paradox where events are changing one minute and then reverting back the next. It's a constant state of flux and entirely unpredictable. It's very disconcerting."

"That's one way of putting it," Jack said with raised eyebrows.

Travers looked nervously toward Vale. "Let's discuss this elsewhere, shall we?"

Elizabeth didn't need to be asked twice. Leaving sounded like a very good idea. She glanced back at Vale, but she'd already left the window and returned to her seat. Leaning back in it, her placid exterior returned.

Travers opened the door to the hall and Elizabeth, Simon and Jack started toward it.

"Are you coming Victor?" Travers asked as the others exited into the hall.

Victor slowly shook his head and kept his gaze on Vale.

"Tomorrow, then?" Travers said.

Renaud did not respond and Travers laughed nervously as he gently closed the door behind him, leaving Renaud inside. He turned to Elizabeth and the others. "Coffee?"

Simon frowned. "Just answers, thank you."

Travers' smile faltered, but he nodded. "My office is this way."

They traveled down a few more levels and down another long hall to Travers' office. He opened an ordinary looking door and held it open for Elizabeth and the others to precede him.

The room was not what Elizabeth had expected. Not that she'd given where Travers worked much thought, but from his rumpled suit and nervous, nebbishy ways, she'd expected him to have a little cubicle-like office. This, however, was not the office of any worker bee.

The room was substantial and plush—very Big Cheesy. Four dark leather club chairs huddled together at one end of the room and a large mahogany desk at the other, with a pair of antique globes on either side. And despite being several stories underground, it was light and bright. False windows let in simulated sunshine and ever-changing views.

"This is your office?" Elizabeth said.

He looked around the room, a little embarrassed. "I've recently been…promoted. Please," he gestured to the club chairs.

Elizabeth and Jack took their seats

Travers lingered, waiting for Simon.

"I'll stand," Simon said.

Travers opened his mouth to say something, but decided against it and sat down.

"As I was saying before. Time—"

"Why are we here?" Simon asked abruptly.

Travers looked nervously from Simon to Elizabeth and then back. "I'm afraid we need your help again."

"The last time you said that we were ambushed by that…creature and nearly killed." Simon took a step closer to Travers' chair.

"I'm sorry about that—"

"Come to think of it," Elizabeth said. "The other time you asked us for help, she was there, too."

"It is a bit of a theme, isn't it?" Travers said softly.

"If you expect us to risk our lives trying to stop whatever madness that witch has—"

"I do." Travers said the words firmly, but his downward glance at his hands as he worried them in his lap gave away his nervousness. "You must."

Simon still towered over him, but he wasn't cowed. "However she's managed it, and she has, her actions in 1887 have led to a change in history. This *one* change is the lynchpin for an entire series of events, for an entire group of people."

"The Council?" Elizabeth asked.

"And others, but I'm sure you can see why changing the history of the Council might have far reaching consequences, ones that directly affect each of you."

Elizabeth looked up at Simon. She saw her own thoughts mirrored in his green eyes. They'd been through this before. One change in history could result in a ripple effect with devastating consequences. As much as they tried to avoid the Council, she and Simon were irrevocably linked to it. A change in the Council's history would mean a change to theirs.

Simon turned back to Travers. "You said there was one change. You know what changed then? Specifically?"

"Yes. We don't know how she managed it or, frankly why, but our people have been able to pinpoint one historical event that is creating a cascade effect. Unless it's reversed, set back to the way it is supposed to be, time will be altered. Permanently." Travers stood and walked over to his desk.

"The small changes we're experiencing now will grow and multiply, and eventually stop reversing themselves. A new history will be written, and everything we know will be cease to be."

He stopped walking and picked up a file from his desk.

"What's the event that changed?" Elizabeth asked.

"As I'm sure you know, Jack the Ripper was never caught. In the altered timeline, he was."

"You know who Jack the Ripper was?" Jack asked, sitting forward now.

"No."

"But you just—"

"His body was found, mutilated beyond recognition, not unlike his victims."

Simon frowned. "How do you know it was Jack the Ripper then?"

"He was found in a boarding house room with..." Travers faltered here and took a breath, "parts of his victims. His clothing, his build, they all fit the known description. And the fifth and final victim, the most brutal of all of the killings, was never harmed. She lived another thirty years. Moved to Liverpool, married a shoe salesman and had 2 daughters before dying of influenza in 1918."

Elizabeth tried to ignore the sinking feeling in the pit of her stomach as it grew. "So, Jack the Ripper was killed and that's what led to the altered timeline?"

"Exactly."

The sinking feeling sank a little further. "And what is it you want us to do about it?"

Travers sighed and looked apologetic. "I'm afraid I need you to go to 1888 London, find out who Jack the Ripper was, and save his life."

"MACALLAN 25. NEAT."

"The same," Jack said, as he handed the cocktail menu back to the waiter, wincing as he did. "Make mine a double."

Elizabeth was tempted to order a martini and slowly slide under the table, forgetting what Travers had just asked them to do, but there was no ignoring it.

"Just water for now, thank you."

The waiter nodded and disappeared, and the three of them sat in silence.

The Laurel Court at the Fairmont was elegant and controlled. It was bright and airy, the exact opposite of how each of them was feeling. Simon idly ran his fingers along the edge of the brown leather portfolio Travers had given them, while Jack focused on flexing the hand of his injured arm.

"Well," Elizabeth said finally, leaning back in her plush wing-back chair. "That was an interesting day."

Simon grunted in response.

"Saving Jack the Ripper," Elizabeth said, then, feeling self-conscious, lowered her voice. "I don't know. The idea of it, it…"

"Is repellent?" Simon suggested. "Abhorrent? Repulsive even to contemplate?"

"I was going to say makes me want to barf, but yeah." Not to mention the other bombshell he'd dropped. Not only was Jack the Ripper dead and gone, people were disappearing, fading in and out all over history.

Jack stopped fussing with his arm and let it relax onto the table. "If what Travers said is true, do we really have any choice?"

Neither Simon nor Elizabeth replied. Since their meeting with Travers, they'd all been lost in their own thoughts. They'd been on difficult missions before, but this was something else entirely.

"It's terrifying to think of people just disappearing," Elizabeth said, hoping to shift her thoughts away from Jack the Ripper. Travers had told them that because of the changing timeline, several Council members had already ceased to be, or be there then, or something.

Whatever Katherine Vale had done to alter time, the consequences were already being felt. Her newly regrown finger aside, Elizabeth thought with a shudder, people were changing. Their memories, their histories were being rewritten. In some cases, actual people disappeared, relocated to an alternate timeline, only to reappear, and some to disappear again. In other cases, it was simply the memories of events that were wiped out, or at least that's how it seemed. Sometimes, just a day, a specific moment in time was lost and for others entire years were cut out from their memories, like ice-cream scooped from a carton.

Elizabeth looked over at Simon. She didn't know what she'd do if she forgot him, or if he simply disappeared.

Simon, as he always seemed to do, appeared to follow her thoughts. He stopped toying with the base of his water glass, offered her a wan smile and took her hand.

"It's troubling," he said in the master of understatement way the British had when discussing disasters.

Jack's brow furrowed, clearly trying to make sense of this nonsensical mess. "Travers said that these fluxes in time, that they're specific to the person, right? You could forget something that I remember or vice versa."

"Yes. It puts a new spin on 'time is relative,' doesn't it?" Simon paused as the waiter returned with their drinks. He took a sip of his scotch before continuing.

"It seems as though these instabilities are individualized, at least for now. The Council postulates that the effects will cascade with growing frequency and duration until they're universal and irreversible."

"But until they're permanent, they come and go," Elizabeth said. She pictured them like fireflies blinking on and off in the darkness.

"Yes, until one timeline or the other…wins, for lack of a better way to put it."

Elizabeth rubbed a few brain cells together. "So, the original timeline and the new timeline are sort of co-existing. The change has occurred and yet it hasn't? So, it's flip-flopping between them?"

Simon took another sip of scotch and nodded. "Precisely, until the new timeline overwrites the old completely."

"Dollars to donuts," Jack said, "any changes that head case made are ones we're not gonna like."

"No doubt. Of course," Simon said, "we're only accepting Travers' rather dubious word that we will be affected at all."

"Not really," Elizabeth said quietly. "I didn't want to say anything in front of Travers, but…"

Both men shifted in their seats to face her with varying degrees of *oh no, you di'int.*

"I didn't think anything of it at the time," Elizabeth said with an apologetic shrug. "I thought it was just fatigue playing mind games, but…earlier, I had a sort of dizzy spell—"

"Elizabeth—"

"It was nothing," she said quickly to fend off Simon's Lecture Mode. "It was really fast, but I had this strange feeling, just for a second, that our house wasn't…our house."

The worry lines between Simon's eyes deepened.

"It was over in seconds, but I think maybe it was one of these flux thingies. It was weird, like I wasn't who I am," she said and then met Simon's gaze. "It didn't scare me then, but it does now."

Simon nodded slowly, his jaw clenched.

"Well, then that's that, isn't it?" Jack said. He raised his glass. "To London we go."

CHAPTER FOUR

"WHY COULDN'T SHE HAVE chosen some other time to mess around with?" Elizabeth pouted as she waited to have her measurements taken.

Simon raised his arm at the tailor's silent urging and the man efficiently stretched out his measuring tape along it and then jotted down the results in a small notebook.

"It's not as bad as all that," Simon said.

"You wouldn't say that with a straight face if you had to wear a corset."

Simon chuckled. "No, I suppose not."

"I think we should go to seventeenth century Scotland next. You'd kill it in a kilt."

Simon gave her eyebrow waggles a sour look in return as he stepped off the small platform and helped her to take his place.

She smiled wickedly back at him and he let himself laugh. It felt good. Damn good. The last few weeks had been a study in tension. And considering it seemed it was not about to relent anytime soon, he would take any joy where he could find it. He hadn't expected it to be in the bowels of the Council Clothiers though.

He had to give credit where credit was due; the Council's resources were impressive. In this department alone they had a tailor, seamstress, and historical advisor, not to mention a cavernous warehouse of clothing from every era imaginable.

"Do I have to wear a corset?" Elizabeth turned and asked the tailor hopefully. "My figure's not bad, is it?"

The tailor huffed out a frustrated breath. "Please stand still. Your figure is perfectly acceptable for a modern woman. But," he continued, "for a woman of substance in the 1880s, it will not do to go *au naturel*, as it were."

He measured her chest and eyed her thoughtfully. "We could, however, add a bust enhancer."

Simon snorted and coughed to cover it.

Elizabeth gave him a searing look, but there was only humor behind it. She knew perfectly well he was more than content with every part of her just as it was.

"No, thank you," she said through gritted teeth.

"Some ladies prefer them," the tailor said with a shrug. "They tend to help balance out the bustle."

"Bustle?" Elizabeth scrunched up her face in distaste, but he knew that when the time came, she would endure it all with a smile. If only that were all they would have to endure.

Once they were finished with their measurements, what came next was every man's nightmare shopping trip. They spent hours selecting clothes, smalls, jewelry, hats, gloves, shoes, canes, and any number of other things. By the end of it all, Simon would have worn whatever they'd suggested. Even a kilt. Jack had the right idea. Get in and get out. He'd fled as soon as he could for more interesting pursuits, planning to meet them later in the armory.

With the bulk of the preparations left to them, Simon and Elizabeth arranged for traveling money at the Council's financial department. That not only included a considerable sum of cash, but a letter of introduction that would give them access to an account with Bank of England with nearly unlimited funds. There were, it seemed, some perks after all in working with the Council.

They were sent to a pharmacy where they were given discreetly labeled powders, draughts and ointments that would provide them with the safety of having modern medicine at hand. Next was a trip to the documents office where they were given any traveling papers they might need. That left only the armory, where Jack was waiting for them.

Unlike the other departments they'd visited, which were all stylishly decorated offices where no expense was spared, the armory looked more like a deserted bank. The room itself was large, but virtually empty except for a barred cashier's cage that ran half the length of the far wall. Inside was a large man in a dark suit and another who stood at the small opening in the bars. Jack stood fondling a large elegant pistol.

"Good. You're here. Look at this," he said, brimming with excitement. He held up a handsome gun with an outrageously elongated grip and muzzle. "It's an Albanian Rat Tail."

"Lovely," Simon said.

"You just don't know guns," Jack said as he held it up and admired it. "I would marry this gun if I could."

"Perhaps we can arrange that," Simon said, "when we get back."

Jack smirked and put the gun back onto the velvet pad atop the counter.

"It's a little long, isn't it?" Elizabeth said.

Jack shook his head. "Oh, it's not for the trip, I'd just never seen one before. You won't believe the stuff they have back there."

"Let's focus on our mission, shall we?" Simon said.

Jack sighed, but waved for the man behind the counter to take the gun away. He set it aside and brought out a tray of smaller revolvers and pistols.

"Find anything you like?" Travers voice said from the doorway behind them.

"Impressive place you got here," Jack said as he hefted a gun and then frowned, apparently finding it lacking, and put it back to search for another.

"Yes, we're rather proud of it," Travers said. He held out a large brown leather portfolio. "A little light reading for tonight. It's a great deal to take in, I'm afraid, but we don't have much time with the eclipse tomorrow night. We can't afford to miss it."

Simon nodded in agreement. He and Elizabeth had decided not to tell Travers about the key that Teddy Fiske had given them, which allowed them to travel in time without the need of an eclipse. Its presence was one even the Council didn't know about. Although, it was likely they suspected something, considering Simon and Elizabeth had traveled without the benefit of an eclipse several times. The Council might have been untrustworthy, but they were not stupid. Either way, Simon and Elizabeth decided it was best to keep it under wraps for as long as they could.

Simon strode toward Travers, Elizabeth close behind, leaving Jack to pick out their weapons.

"We'll read it tonight," Elizabeth said as she reached out to take the notebook.

"And these are journals." Travers gestured to three small books stacked on top of the portfolio. "You'll want to write down any-thing—"

"Guys," Jack said behind them. The nervous tenor of his voice immediately captured everyone's attention and as one they turned to him.

His hand was at his temple and he looked dazed.

He took a staggering step forward, the gun in his hand clattering to the floor. He looked on the verge of collapse.

"I think it's happening," he said breathlessly.

Both Elizabeth and Simon started toward him, but he held up a hand to stop them. They paused and he looked at them. His expression was worried, confused and apologetic. He tried to say something, but there was no sound. He blurred for a moment, as though they were seeing him through heavy rain.

"Jack!"

Elizabeth reached toward him, but Simon grabbed her arm. They had no idea what touching someone in this state could mean. Elizabeth pulled against him, but he would not let go. They both watched with horror as Jack looked at them helplessly.

And then, with words they could not hear on his lips, he was gone.

"Oh, dear," Travers said softly.

Elizabeth pulled herself from Simon's grip and hurried toward Travers. "Is he dead? Where'd he go?"

"I'm not sure," Travers admitted. "It's possible he's safe and sound in 1942 London. As safe as someone can be there then."

Elizabeth looked to Simon for an explanation. His mind reeled with what he'd just seen, but he was starting to understand. "If time for him was changed in such a way that we never met him," Simon thought aloud, "or that we never brought him back to the future, he'd still be in London living the life he would have lived without us."

"Exactly," Travers said. "We can't know for sure, but that's the theory."

"The theory?" Elizabeth's eyes were filled with concern. "Will he come back? You said things come and go? Will he just…appear again?"

Travers looked at her sadly. "Possibly."

Simon could see Elizabeth fighting down her emotions. Jack was far more than just a friend; he was family.

"When we set things right, he'll be back," Simon assured her.

After letting out a shuddering breath to control herself, Elizabeth nodded.

He might not have shown it outwardly, but Simon felt the same way Elizabeth did. For Jack to vanish so quickly, without any warning, was horrifying. Worse yet, there was no telling who or what might be next. He took firm hold of Elizabeth's hand.

"We can hope," Travers said. He looked anxiously between them. "I'm afraid time is not on our side though."

Simon looked back at the spot where Jack had stood just moments before. "It never is."

ELIZABETH HAD INSISTED THAT they wait in the armory, just in case. But it was no use. An hour went by and then another, and Jack did not return. Elizabeth's stomach tightened as they finally left. If the cold, hard reality of what might happen, of what was happening, if they didn't go back and complete their mission wasn't clear before, it certainly was now. Reality had punched them both right in the gut.

Tomorrow they would travel back in time, hunt down Jack the Ripper and save him. If today's events were anything to go by, the alternative was unthinkable.

They retired early to their hotel room and although neither of them had mentioned it, it was clear they weren't about to leave each other's sides. Elizabeth knew they wouldn't be able to keep that up 24/7, but for now, neither went anywhere alone.

Finally, they settled into the bedroom to do their reading for the next day. The files Travers had given them were extensive. They would never be able to finish them, much less remember everything in them. As tempting as it was, they couldn't risk muddying the timeline by bringing the files. It was far too great a risk.

The first few files had turned Elizabeth's stomach. She hadn't been expecting crime scene photos from the 1800s, and yet there they were. Somehow, the grainy, black and white made them just that much more disturbing.

There was a file for each of the five canonical victims and another dozen for the various suspects who ranged from an escaped mental patient to Prince Albert Victor, the Queen's son, himself.

The murders took place over the course of just under two and a half months. The exact date of the murder of Jack the Ripper was difficult for the Council to pin down. Their best guess was that it occurred sometime between the fourth and fifth murders, probably closer to the fourth.

The plan was to arrive a few days before the first murder to give them the best chance of discovering the killer. That meant they'd be in London for just over a month. It was a harrowing prospect to chase a madman for weeks on end. Perhaps the only thing worse than searching for him, would be finding him.

Although she knew it sickened him to his core, Simon gave no indication of the depth of his disgust as he leaned back against the headboard of their bed and read through the files. He was doing one of the things he did best—compartmentalize. It was a skill she envied right now. He was able, in most things, to keep a cool head. Sure as shootin', they would need every ounce of his Vulcan blood this time.

Elizabeth took a break from reading to get back to her journal. Travers suggested they write down important events that would help them remember who they were, if their memories became compromised. He'd advised keeping things brief, highlighting the watershed events that led them to this place and time. Things that would help ground them. It was a little Nicholas Sparks, but it made sense. If they lost their memories of their lives together, which would be terrifying, they could read about them in their own hand and at least be a little reassured. More importantly, they could be reminded why they were there and just what was at stake.

It was hard to narrow down a life so that it fit onto small pieces of paper. She'd already spent an hour or so detailing her early years and how she'd come to meet Simon. Stretching out on top of the covers of their king-sized bed, she flopped onto her stomach and got back to it.

She finished telling herself the story of their wedding. For a stuffy Englishman, he was pretty darn romantic. She turned back to admire her husband and reassure herself that he was still there.

His nose was still buried in the files, the worry crease between his eyes the only sign of his distress. His journal sat next to him on the end table. She hadn't seen him even crack it open.

"You know," she said, "you should probably put *something* in there."

He looked up from his reading and followed her gaze. Laying the files aside, he reached over and picked up the notebook.

"I have," he said, and held it out to her.

Elizabeth clambered up onto her knees and took it. She opened the book and inside, written in his bold hand, were just three words: *She loves me.*

Her heart clenched and she looked up at him.

"That," he said, "is the only thing I need to know."

Chapter Five

Elizabeth made a final adjustment to the front of her bodice jacket and then stepped back to see her full reflection in the changing room mirror. A small, plump woman fussed about her, straightening this and smoothing that, trying in vain to wrangle a stray curl that was trying to make a break for it.

Elizabeth looked the part—the ideal lady of 1888. Apparently, the ideal lady had no internal organs and a butt the size of Quebec. The corset was doing its evil work and her waist had been squished to Barbie-like proportions. If that weren't bad enough, the bustle, which she had fought against, stuck out in a way only Sir Mix-A-Lot could appreciate. From the front she looked all right, she supposed. But when she turned to the side she looked like a scoliosis patient in a medical journal.

She sighed as deeply as the darn corset would let her and turned to look at Simon, who, of course, looked dashing and dapper, and worst of all, comfortable.

He brushed the brim of his top hat with the cuff of his jacket sleeve and turned to her with smile. Putting on his hat, he held out his arm for her. "Ready?"

She wasn't. She was worried about Jack, worried about all of them, but the only way to save the past was to dive into it and hope it wasn't the shallow end. "Ready as I'll ever be."

Elizabeth slipped her arm through his and he covered her hand and gave it a comforting squeeze. "We always find a way," he said.

Elizabeth ignored the ballet of butterflies in her stomach. "We do." And they would again, she thought. There was no alternative.

The escort that Travers had assigned to help them navigate the maze that was Council headquarters stood waiting patiently for them out in the hall. He gestured for them to follow him. They started down one of the long corridors that radiated out from the central hub and then turned left to walk down one of the long curved hallways. Something inside Elizabeth clicked.

"It's like a wheel," she said.

Simon gazed down at her, one eyebrow arched in silent question.

"The layout," she explained. "It's like a wheel with spokes."

"It's a gear actually," the man said over his shoulder. "Each floor is designed in the shape of a unique gear. We call it the Watch Works."

"Don't tell me they move because—" Simon began, but stopped when they heard voices, raised voices.

"They're amateurs," a man said in a hard voice with a soft French accent. Victor Renaud.

The other was unmistakably Travers. "Don't underestimate them, Victor."

"It is insane to trust them with this mission," Renaud said. "Let me go alone. I work better alone—"

"I'm sorry, Victor," Travers said. "You have your orders. You'll—"

He stopped in mid-sentence as Simon, Elizabeth and their escort came into view.

Renaud leaned down and whispered something to Travers, whose eyes went wide briefly, but he nodded curtly, quickly, before crossing to meet Simon and Elizabeth. "You two look wonderful. Every inch the part!"

Behind him Renaud grunted and pulled his woolen cap from his ratty jacket pocket and put it on. His clothes were worn and tattered and, as they got closer, Elizabeth noticed also a little stinky. From his shabby clothes to the sackcloth bag he had slung over his shoulder, it was clear he was dressed for a London that was the same and yet wholly different than the one they were going to.

Travers tried to usher them into a room, saying something about their trunks being inside and waiting for them, but Simon stopped walking.

He ignored Travers and fixed his eyes on Renaud, looking him up and down. "What's this?"

Renaud met his disapproving gaze with quiet defiance.

"Oh," Travers said, with a voice straining to be casual, "Victor is going as well. We thought—"

"I think," Simon said icily, "you should have told us that."

Travers nodded. "You're right. I-I should have. I apologize. Just so many things—I'm sorry."

Renaud and Simon stood like two bucks who were deciding if they were going to smash heads.

On the one hand, Elizabeth agreed with Simon. Surprises from the Council were never good and they knew nothing about Renaud. But on the other, they'd lost Jack and she had a feeling they'd need a lot of help before this mission was over.

Sensing an opening in the quiet, Travers bubbled on. "Victor is a very skilled operative. If I were going, I'd be thrilled to have him along."

"Then maybe you should go," Simon said, staring down at the little man.

Travers laughed nervously.

"This is what I am saying—" Renaud began impatiently, but Travers waved him off as he checked his watch.

"We really don't have time for this."

Simon glared at Renaud and then looked to Elizabeth.

Renaud was an unknown, but while she didn't exactly get warm and fuzzy from him, she didn't sense anything villainous either. Not that he'd exactly be wearing a "Team Evil" t-shirt, if he were. For now, with all they had to face, they'd have to trust him. Some.

She nodded and Simon sighed heavily. "Let's get on with it then."

"Excellent!" Travers said and approached the keypad.

After he entered his code and the scan was complete, the gears embedded within the door began to unlock and the door swooshed open. The four of them stepped into an enclosed antechamber of sorts. The main door shut behind them.

Elizabeth's heart began to race as the lights dimmed to near darkness.

"Don't worry," Travers said. "It's just a scan. Making sure there's nothing anachronistic."

A long, thin blue beam of light washed over them and within a few seconds, the main lights came back up and the interior door opened. Travers led the way.

The main room was round, large and windowless. The ceiling was high, perhaps twenty feet and twice that for the diameter. In the center of the room was an enormous glass cylinder, ten feet across, divided vertically into two pieces. Each piece was embedded in a track on the floor. Their trunks were waiting for them inside it.

Simon walked over to it, but Elizabeth's attention was on something else.

Three people were already inside the room waiting for them. Two were the ubiquitous, large, armed security types, but more unsettling was the third, a doctor with full paramedic gear.

"What're they doing here?" Elizabeth asked, nodding toward the doctor and guards.

"Just precautionary," Travers said.

Simon carefully touched the glass cylinder. "Another precaution?"

"Bullet-proof glass."

At first, Elizabeth had thought it was all there to keep the wrong people from going, but, she realized, it was the opposite. It was all there in case the wrong people came back.

Renaud walked over to stand in the middle of the glass cylinder. He took out his watch and then looked up over Travers' head.

"Time," Renaud said, nodding toward the area above the door.

An immense screen hung over it. An image of the moon filled the black space. A clock had already begun counting down the time remaining in the eclipse.

"Yes," Travers said. "Are you ready? Have everything you need?"

Simon looked back once at Elizabeth before nodding. He took her hand and they walked into the glass cylinder.

Once they were securely inside, Simon took out his watch.

Travers gave a signal and one of the guards pushed something on the wall behind him. The two pieces of the cylinder began to rotate toward each other.

Elizabeth's heart sped and she tried to push out a calming breath, but her corset wouldn't let her. She tightened her grip on Simon's arm and laid her free hand on the trunks.

"Godspeed," Travers said.

The glass pieces met and then shifted slightly, sealing themselves together with a *thwump*.

She looked up, suddenly hoping this wasn't some sort of Star Wars trash compactor when she saw the tell-tale blue sparks of light. Renaud had activated his watch and snakes of light had already bound him. It was horrifying to see, and before she could finish her next thought, the blue lightning from Simon's watch snaked up her arms and the world shook itself apart.

"Six bob for the week. Eight, if you be wantin' dinner."

Victor frowned at the heavy-set landlady and grumbled softly, complaining about the cost. He didn't really mind, it was a fair enough price for the room which was, for the most part, clean and well-kept, but he knew her type. Mrs. McNally would feel better about renting to a Frenchman if he resisted, at least a little.

He dug into his pocket and pulled out a few coins, making sure not to pull out too many. Across the small room, he could feel her keen eyes already counting them.

Grunting in displeasure, he palmed the right number of coins and slipped the rest back into his pocket. He paused, as if weighing the wisdom of paying such an extravagant sum, and then closed the space between them and held out his hand.

She took the coins, a small, triumphant smile lighting her ruddy face for a moment.

She'd probably upped the price for him—a foreigner's special—but as long as it wasn't outrageous, something that would flag him as an easy mark, he was content to let her earn more than the pittance that was her usual lot.

The landlady slipped the coins into the pocket of her dress and then wiped her hands on her filthy apron. "Right then. Dinner's at one, no later, mind you. I'm not your servant."

Victor nodded, although he had no intention of eating with the other lodgers. Even in the best of hotels, he preferred to keep to himself.

The landlady gave one last look around the room, probably taking inventory should something come up missing or broken, and then left him alone.

The room and its furnishings were simple. A thin mattress covered with a coarse woolen blanket sat on a creaking iron and wooden bedstead along the far wall. In the corner, there was a small table and one chair. A dresser that had been worth something once, was now scuffed and water stained, the brass pulls on the drawers long-since traded out for knotted bits of rope. A water pitcher and chipped basin rested on top of it.

The lodgings were a far cry from the luxury of Mayfair where the Crosses were staying, but also just about as far from the horrors of the common lodging-houses where one room was shared by a dozen or more and twice as many rats.

Victor walked over to the small window and pushed aside the thin curtain. Overcast skies gave everything a dull, gray cast. Coal soot stuck to the sides of the buildings, darkening everything its fingers touched. The street below teemed with people slopping through the filth of life in the slums. Even through the closed window the stench was overpowering.

The room in Bishopsgate was a half-step up from most of the East End, but the street was still coated with a poisonous cocktail of animal and human waste. The urge to gag would pass soon enough, he knew. The human capacity to adapt, even, perhaps especially, to the worst of conditions always amazed and disturbed him. Of course, he thought, he was no different than the hundreds who streamed by his window, caught up in a current they could not break free from. His life wasn't the one he'd thought he'd have, but then lives seldom were.

Letting his hand fall to his side, he turned away and the soot-stained curtain dropped back to cover the window. His path was a dark one, and this dark, dank city suited it well.

ELIZABETH LOOKED AT HERSELF in the vanity mirror in the bedroom of their hotel suite. Bits of soot colored her cheeks and she wiped them away with an embroidered handkerchief.

"It's going to be impossible to stay clean," she said.

Simon arched an eyebrow and nodded toward the hem of her dress.

Elizabeth twisted around as best she could and lifted the edge of her dress. It was already filthy. "Poop."

"Probably," Simon said.

Elizabeth made a sour face, wrinkled her nose and let her dress fall to the floor. This was going to take some getting used to.

They'd arrived in London at King's Cross station. It was a hub of activity and a likely place to find travelers from America via Liverpool. Sadly, there was no sign of platform 9 3/4.

At least something had gone right though. Their landing had gone blessedly unnoticed, but before Simon could even prepare for another clash with Victor Renaud, the man had said that he would contact them and then disappeared into the crowd. Simon was just as glad to be rid of him as Renaud was to be rid of them, but his departure left Elizabeth feeling uneasy.

She'd felt so much better when she knew Jack was coming along. At least he would have had their back. Renaud, she sensed, had no one's back but his own.

She sighed heavily and Simon came to stand behind her.

"The hotel laundry can take care of it, I'm sure," he said, misreading her worried expression.

Elizabeth smiled and stood. It wouldn't do any good to worry about what might have been, irony aside, she thought. They were here now, and they had each other. She turned around and slipped her arms about his waist. His arms looped loosely around her in return.

Pushing herself up onto her toes, she kissed him.

"What was that for?" he asked.

"Does there have to be a reason?"

He smiled. "I was going to ask what we should do first, but..." he said, as he pulled her closer and kissed her.

Elizabeth let herself forget everything else and disappeared into that one perfect moment. A sharp knocking on the door shattered it.

A deeply dissatisfied sound rumbled deep in Simon's chest and he pulled away as the knocking came again.

He let go of her and strode into the sitting room, Elizabeth following.

Two bellboys brought in their trunks, depositing them in the bedroom.

As soon as they left, Elizabeth opened one and began to unpack. The gowns would probably have to be pressed. They were exquisite, and between them and the beautiful room they'd gotten at Brown's, she started to feel a little guilty. Here they were, staying at one of the most upscale hotels in one of the most upscale neighborhoods of London while the people who were hunted by Jack the Ripper lived in squalor just a few miles away.

She laid a dress out on the bed. "Do you think we should stay here?"

Simon looked around the room in confusion. "Is something wrong with it?"

"No. I just mean we're here and he's there. Maybe we should be closer to it all?"

Simon took a breath and sat down in one of the reading chairs. "There's some evidence to suggest the Ripper was a doctor or another man of means. If we're going to get anywhere near the wealthier suspects we can't be living in Spitalfields."

"I suppose."

"It's far easier to live richly and pretend to be poor than the other way around," Simon said.

Having done both, Elizabeth had to agree.

"Besides, the upper class here is afforded resources the rest simply are not," he continued. "Before this is over, we may need access to power and influence, and those things will be found here amongst the idle rich and not the working poor."

"You're right," Elizabeth said. "And I'm guessing from the way Victor was dressed, he'll be staying in the poorer section of town. Although, I wish he'd just told us his plan, or anything at all for that matter."

Simon grunted.

"But," she continued. "At least he's here."

"Yes," Simon said, unimpressed. "Somewhere."

VICTOR STARTED BACK UP Old Broad Street and tugged his cap down as afternoon sank into evening and the damp air grew teeth.

As he always did when he arrived, he'd spent the first few hours walking the streets of his new neighborhood. He'd studied every alley, every corner, and every beggar he'd come across. Tomorrow, he'd go to Buck's Row where Mary Nichols would be killed and do the same there. He'd walk the streets until he could do it in the dark. He'd have to. They would all have to.

Just the thought of the Crosses soured his mood. What was Travers thinking?

Victor had heard about the Crosses. Few knew about them, but there were no secrets among those who did. Their record was good, he had to admit, but she was young, impulsive and headstrong. He was more calculating, but a fool where she was concerned. That was a dangerous combination. The Crosses were his cross to bear, for now at least. He'd help them, until they got in the way.

He walked another block and stopped at a coster's apple barrow. Finally finding one that didn't have worms in it, he paid and slipped it into his pocket.

Across the street, a boy cried out. A large man had cuffed him on the side of the head and then held him up above the sidewalk by his lapels.

"You do that again, boy, and you'll lose your hand, you will," the big man bellowed, and then glared down at another, smaller boy who stood huddled nearby. "And don't think I didn't see you there."

"We wasn't doin' nuffink," the boy protested. "We was just looking is all."

Victor had noticed them earlier. They'd been following the man and his donkey cart full of potatoes down the street, waiting for an opening.

The man shook the boy and then tossed him aside. "Stay away!"

Victor's jaw tightened as he observed it all silently. He watched the big man urge his donkey cart on. The boys scurried away, but Victor saw the little one show his friend their prize, a small potato, before slipping it back under his jacket.

The duo ran to the corner and around it, but their little faces peeked back around to watch the man disappear down the street. Gleefully, they ducked back into the alley.

With a plan in mind, Victor dodged the traffic as he crossed the street. The boys were huddled together, the little one furiously gnawing on the raw potato.

Victor stopped at the mouth of the alley, the other side a dead end.

"You're lucky he was as blind as he was fat," Victor said.

The boys bolted upright and looked ready to make a run for it.

Victor held up his hands. "It's all right. I'm not here to take it from you."

The older boy, who couldn't have been more than ten, didn't move, but the younger one couldn't keep his hunger at bay and dug into the potato again.

"How'd you like to earn enough to buy a whole sack of those?"

The older boy stared at him and then jutted out his chin. "Doin' what?"

"Running a few messages." Victor took a shilling out of his pocket. "Of course, I need someone who can run fast. You look a little slow."

The boy stepped forward eagerly. "I'm fast. I can beat anyone on the street."

"Is that so?"

"I can do it blindfolded."

Victor didn't laugh at the boy's bravado. "I need a man I can trust."

"You can trust me," the boy said, eyeing the money and then raising his hand, crossing his heart and spitting twice. "I swear."

"All right," Victor said. "Do you know where McNally's is?"

"Sure. It's right up—"

"Come by there in an hour and I'll give you this to take a message to Brown's Hotel. If you do all right, there'll be more."

The boy's eyes glittered as he nodded. A shilling would probably buy him food for a week.

"What's your name?" Victor asked.

"Freddie, sir."

Victor watched him for a moment, then stuffed his hands into his jacket pocket as he turned to leave. He felt the apple, took it out and tossed it to the boy.

"An hour," he said over his shoulder as he left. "Don't be late."

CHAPTER SIX

VICTORIAN MORALITY WAS STRICT, prudish and absurdly earnest. Repression was the name of the game, and history showed how well that always works out. The Victorians' obsession with controlling all things sexual led to a fascination with it and a rise in the very debauchery they were so frightened of. At the beginning of the era, the mere mention of the word "leg" in mixed company could be considered inappropriate. Thankfully, Elizabeth thought as she looked around, things seemed to have loosened up a bit. A woman walking alone during the day only garnered a few hairy eyeballs and not a trunkful. Ah, progress.

Elizabeth ignored the lingering looks that followed her as she made her way down Brook Street alone. A Victorian woman without any sort of escort, male or female, was a rarity. While everyone smiled and nodded politely in greeting as she passed, she could feel the askance in their glance. Their upbringing forced them to disapprove, but it also forced them to do it silently with only the narrowing of an eye or the quirk of lip. She could swear though, that not all of the lingering looks were judging her poorly. Aside from the occasional reserved, but appreciative expression, she also saw no small measure of envy in some.

She would happily endure worse if it meant she could get out and about. The idea of being cooped up in the hotel while Simon was off actually doing things was unthinkable.

Last night, they'd received a note from Victor with the address of his room and a request to meet Simon there the following day.

Elizabeth scrunched up her nose at the memory. Just Simon, no mention of her at all. If he thought she was going to sit demurely by while they did all the work, that Frenchman had *une autre* think coming! Simon tried to soothe her and pointed out that he needed to find them appropriate clothes for tonight. He would probably need to go to places where a wealthy couple might draw too much attention.

They both hated the idea of being apart, but would have to risk it if they wanted to succeed here. Reluctantly, she'd agreed not to go, but she wasn't going to sit on her duff either. Young Katherine Vale and Charles Graham were somewhere in the city and she intended to find them. Simon had, predictably, protested until she reminded him that Graham was purportedly an expert on Jack the Ripper and young Vale didn't hate them, at least not yet. They could be useful. That was, if she could find them.

She assumed they'd also choose to stay at an upscale hotel, and so she'd set out wandering the streets of Mayfair in search of them. There was no shortage of possibilities. She'd started with the hotels on Albemarle—the York, Pulteney's, Buckland's—and was making her way north toward Claridge's.

She'd ask discreetly at the desk for both of them and then linger for a cup of tea in the tearooms, hoping to catch a glimpse of them.

She'd seen photographs of Graham and knew she could recognize Vale, twenty years younger or not.

So far, she'd had three finger sandwiches, two scones and no luck. The tea was up to her eyeballs by the time she reached Claridge's and was seated in the elegant, high-ceilinged foyer. She ordered, and set about her usual routine of inconspicuously scanning the room. From her vantage point, she could see most of the tables, but sadly none of them had any familiar faces sitting at them.

One good thing was that she'd finally gotten used to perching herself on the very lip of her chair. Since her bustle took up most of the actual seat, she had little choice. As far as victories went though, it was of the pretty sad variety.

The waiter brought over a tray of cakes and éclairs. She turned them all away. It was a bad sign when an even an éclair couldn't cheer her up. Elizabeth knew it was going to take some time and more than a little luck to find Graham and Vale this way, but she was disappointed nonetheless.

Elizabeth glanced at the clock on the wall. She'd give it a few more minutes, then pack it up and head back to Brown's. She sipped her tea and tried to overhear conversations, hoping against hope for the mention of her quarry.

At the next table, a business deal was begin brokered, and at another a romance. Neither was going well. The third party was just breaking up. Two very well-dressed gentlemen stood and said their goodbyes.

The taller of the two, nice looking and a little sad about the eyes, said, "I'll see you in the park then, John. Sunday?"

The other man, presumably John, nodded and smiled affectionately at his friend. They shook hands, clasping both hands and lingering for just a moment longer than usual, before the taller man looked about nervously and pulled away.

"Your carriage is waiting, Mr. Druitt," a hotel staff member said.

Perhaps more than friends? Elizabeth wondered.

"Around two?" John said, as he put on his hat. "On the bridge?"

The other man nodded and then his gaze slid again across the room to a table with two older women and their frowns of haughty disapproval. Whoever those two were, they'd noticed the same interplay she had and Did Not Approve.

When Elizabeth turned her attention back to the man, she found him looking at her, a worried expression on his face. Perhaps he thought she was in league with the women or would gossip about what she'd seen. Eager to reassure him, she offered him an understanding and commiserating smile.

Tentatively, he returned it before looking again at the older women and then back to her, his smile blossoming into something mischievous.

"Well hello, my dear!" he said loudly, as he approached her, reaching out for her hand. "Please play along and I'll forever be in your debt," he whispered.

Elizabeth offered her hand. "Well, hello to you, too," she said hesitantly.

"It's so delightful to see you again," he said as he kissed her hand and then asked if he could sit, doing so before she could reply. He tugged his chair closer to hers.

"Thank you," he said, casting a quick glance in the direction of the old women. "I have a reputation to uphold."

Elizabeth wasn't sure what to do. The path of least resistance seemed to be the best choice for now.

"One that involves sitting with strange women?" she said.

His smile grew wider. "Whenever possible. My aunt, you see, she's the one that looks like an owl with a touch of the dyspepsia, thinks of me as something of scoundrel, a ladies' man. And, if at all possible, I'd like to keep it that way."

"You're very forward, aren't you?" Elizabeth said, unable to hide her amusement at his outlandish honesty.

He shook out a napkin and laid it on his lap as he reached for a finger sandwich. "Far better than being backward now, isn't it?"

Elizabeth laughed. She liked this loon.

He took a bite of the sandwich and then wiped his hands on the napkin.

"So," he said as he took out a cigarette case from his jacket pocket and offered her one. She declined with a shake of the head.

After lighting the cigarette and exhaling toward the ceiling, he continued, "Whom do I have the pleasure of disgracing with my company today?"

"Elizabeth Cross," she said, holding out her hand, "and the pleasure is mine."

He shook it with a smile. "George Roxbury. And what brings you to London, my dear, and into my very lucky path?"

Elizabeth knew their planned backstory well. "Traveling with my husband."

His eyes widened in false alarm. "Husband? Should I prepare to defend myself?"

"If he were here," she said, "you would know it by now, I assure you."

"Mmm. Good point," he said, taking another pull from his cigarette. "He's let you out to play on your own, has he?"

"He doesn't *let* me do anything," she said pointedly.

George smiled approvingly. "We are a pair then, aren't we? Dangerous characters threatening the very fabric of society."

"Viva la revolución!" Elizabeth said raising her tea cup.

George laughed. "I do love you Americans. You're so wonderfully raw and unfinished." He caught her slight frown and continued, "I mean that in only the very best way. You forge yourselves. You can be born a pauper and build an empire. Here, you see, we're all born as we ever shall be. It's all rather dull."

"I find that hard to believe."

He sighed dramatically. "I'm the third son of a baronet. You can't go a mile in London without tripping over one of us. I'm hardly unique and unlikely ever to amount to anything more than I am at this moment."

"Poor butterfly," she said not unkindly.

He tried to force an affronted frown onto his face, but couldn't quite manage it. "Now you've ruined my lament. Feeling sorry for myself is the one area in which I truly excel."

"I'm sure there are others."

He laughed out loud. "Ah, Mrs. Cross. How glad I am that we've met."

IT WAS AFTER ONE in the morning when Simon had the night man at Brown's summon a cab for them. As they waited, Simon rolled his shoulders to try to dispel some of the pent up anxiety that had taken residence there over the past few hours. It had been nearly unbearable. Hours dragged by, each slower than the last, until, finally, the time had come to begin.

Simon felt a wave of relief and prickles of adrenaline as the hack pulled up to the curb in front of the hotel. He helped Elizabeth inside and gave the cabbie the address a few blocks away from Victor's boarding house. There was no reason to think anyone was watching them, tracking their movements, and yet, he felt he'd be a fool if he didn't assume the worst. Repeatedly.

Elizabeth leaned back in the seat as far as her ridiculous clothing would allow. She offered him a weak smile and then looked out of the carriage window as the dark streets of London rolled past. She'd been quiet all evening. He had as well, but quiet in Elizabeth was something altogether rare. Not that he blamed her. His thoughts had been filled with images of the night's horrors yet to come. None of them were things either wanted to give life to by speaking about them, but they would come to be whether they kept silent or not.

Tonight, Ripper would find his first victim. Tonight, Mary Ann Nichols would die.

The streets grew darker and dirtier, and Simon could smell the East End before they reached it. A few gas lamps, yellow and faint, lit their path toward Victor's. There were still plenty of people about and Simon felt acutely aware of the attention they drew as they passed through the lower-middle class streets. His already heightened sense of alarm ratcheted up a notch higher.

He put his hand over Elizabeth's as it rested on his arm and she looked up at him, supportive, nervous, reluctantly resigned to what they had to do.

Finally, they reached Victor's. The building was quiet except for one loud fight on the third floor.

Simon rapped sharply on Victor's door. It opened almost immediately, the Frenchman as pleased to see them as Simon was to see him.

"You're late," Victor said with a frown.

Simon glared at him. They were not late, and even if they were, it was a matter of minutes.

"We had to wait for a cab," Elizabeth explained and it galled him that she felt she owed this man an explanation.

Victor grunted and stepped aside, gesturing for them to come in.

The little room was as pitiful as Simon remembered, but the clothes he'd purchased earlier were laid out and waiting for them.

"We should leave here soon," Victor said.

Simon gave him a cursory nod and re-examined the clothes. They were rough, shabby and filthy. An unfortunate, but necessary, guise.

Simon shed his jacket and unbuttoned his shirt. Elizabeth began work on the absurd row of buttons that ran up the front her blouse when she looked up and cast a nervous glance toward the door. Victor casually leaned against it, as he pushed a plug of tobacco down into a rough-hewn clay pipe.

Simon cleared his throat.

Victor looked at him and then at Elizabeth. He arched an eyebrow. "I have seen people naked before."

Simon stood a little straighter. "Not my wife."

Victor puffed out a bit of air in that infuriating way the French did and looked at Elizabeth once more before shaking his head. Dropping his pipe into his pocket, he offered a mock bow before leaving. Simon heard his footsteps as he took the creaking back stair-case.

Elizabeth laughed lightly. "That was very 'grrr.'"

"What sort of man stands there while—"

"It's all right," she said with a patient smile. "He didn't mean anything by it."

Simon let out a breath, knowing he needed to calm his already jangled nerves. Victor would undoubtedly be the least of their problems tonight.

The clothes were an awkward fit, each piece a little too large, but the effect was as he'd hoped. They both looked like they could use a good filling out and that would help them fit in with a group of people for whom a good, solid meal was a rarity.

Elizabeth set about rearranging her hair and finally turned to him in triumph. "What do you think?"

It had been transformed from an elegant bun to something that might secretly house a nest of some sort. He nodded in approval, but couldn't keep a worried frown from his face.

"What?" she asked as she stepped closer.

He hadn't wanted to bring this up, but as the time grew closer, he had no choice. "Are you sure you want to do this?"

She started to argue, but he continued. "I know you want to and I'm not questioning your abilities, it's just that…"

"It's dangerous?"

"Well, yes, but that's never stopped you before. I have no reason think it would now."

Elizabeth tilted her head to the side. "So what is it?"

Simon pushed out a breath. "Are you truly prepared to do what we must do tonight?"

She nodded, and waited, knowing he had more to say.

"That what we must do is…watch," he said, and the images of the files he'd read just days ago flashed across his mind.

He walked to the window, but couldn't see through the dirty glass. "We will have to stand by, quietly, while an innocent woman is savagely murdered."

He turned back to her. "Can you do that? I'm not even sure I can."

She swallowed and then nodded. "Yes. We have to."

He crossed back to her. "You, who risks her neck to save every innocent creature that crosses our path? Can you stand in the shadows, *stay* in the shadows, while this man…" his voice trailed off and he cleared his throat of the bile that started to rise. "While this man brutally murders someone not twenty feet away?"

Elizabeth's breath caught and he could see the emotion play across her face. Her eyes searched his face for the answer.

He reached out and took hold of her arms. "We're here only to observe," he reminded her. "To find out his identity, and keep our own a secret, if possible. At least until there's no other choice."

Elizabeth chewed her lower lip for a moment before looking up at him, chin out. "I can do it," she said, but he heard the unease in her voice.

He had to believe her. It wasn't as if he could just leave her behind. She'd follow, and God only knew what horrors that would lead to.

"All right," he said, ignoring his own doubts as he tucked a finger beneath her chin, tilted her head up and kissed her.

She patted his chest. "It will be all right."

Simon hmm'd and held out his hand. She took it and he held hers tightly, quite sure he would never let go again.

CHAPTER SEVEN

E LIZABETH BREATHED THROUGH HER mouth, but it wasn't helping. The cool night air did help a little, but she could only shudder to think what it must be like in the heat of summer here. It wasn't so much the sewage in the open streets that made her feel sick, it was that people lived this way, had to live this way. That so many hovered on the razor's edge between life and death every day.

She really had no idea what to expect. She knew this wasn't going to be like seeing a road production of *Oliver!* But nothing could have prepared her for the squalor and hopelessness of Whitechapel.

Dilapidated tenements crammed with people lucky enough to find a bed for the night loomed darkly over the streets below where only a few gas lamps lit their way. The sky above was black, not a star to be seen. It was probably just clouds, Elizabeth told herself, but it felt like they were in some sort of netherworld where the stars never shined.

Somewhere in the distance, toward the river, she could barely make out the red glow of a fire and the faint smell of wood burning.

They passed a few prostitutes who were walking arm in arm toward them. Elizabeth strained to see their faces. Was one of them Mary Nichols, she wondered? One of the other victims? But she couldn't see them clearly, and even if she had she wasn't sure she'd recognize them. The autopsy photos were grainy and a little surreal. Wax works instead of people.

Elizabeth shivered and Simon tucked her arm more tightly to his side. "All right?" he whispered.

She nodded, but the feeling of dread that lodged in the pit of her stomach grew with each step they took, each second that passed and drew them closer to the murder.

Simon, his face smeared with soot, jaw set and eyes keenly scanning ahead, was as on edge as she'd ever seen him. Not that she blamed him. They were in an unfamiliar place and following an unfamiliar man.

Victor was an enigma. She wanted to trust him, but it was hard to trust someone who offered so little of himself. For now, though, they had no choice. God, she missed Jack Wells. The thought of him brought a pang of sadness and she pushed it away. She couldn't think about that now. She had to stay focused.

She and Simon had studied maps of the area, but the reality was far from the neat grids and clearly labeled intersections the Council had provided. Whitechapel was a warren of dark streets and darker allies. Victor claimed he knew the streets well and with a Thomas Guide out of the question, they followed silently behind as he maneuvered them through the maze.

There were a surprising number of people still out and about, stumbling from one pub to another, leaning against doorways, lingering by an open brazier. She'd been to slums before; she'd lived on the outskirts of a few, but the poverty she'd seen there was nothing compared to this—where people owned nothing but the clothes on their backs, and each day's earnings, if they could find work, disappeared with the cost of a sparse meal, and a shared bed.

Women like Mary Ann Nichols had only one thing of value—their bodies. At her age, in her mid-forties, and an alcoholic—she'd be lucky to get two or three pence for a trick. Enough for a stale loaf of bread or a glass of gin. As Elizabeth looked around, she understood why so many opted for the latter.

As they walked along, it seemed that nearly every other building was a bar. After another ten minutes, they arrived at a popular local pub—The Frying Pan—where, rumor had it, Mary Ann Nichols had been seen the night of her murder.

Situated on the corner of Brick Lane and Thrawl Street, it was in the heart of some of the worst parts of Whitechapel. Men so steeped with alcohol that it came off them in waves lingered by the front door. She wasn't sure if they were going back in or had recently left; either way, the stoop was as far as they could make it.

Victor stepped inside and made his way to the bar. He nodded for Simon and Elizabeth to take a small table at the far end of the room. Simon grumbled to himself, but he did as Victor suggested and ushered her toward it.

With a sweep of his hand, he brushed away the crumbs that littered the rough wooden table. A woman with a stained apron and a tired, worn expression came to take their order.

"Two pints, love," Simon said as he pushed two pennies across the table. All traces of his aristocratic accent gone, replaced by one that made him sound a bit like Michael Caine.

The waitress scooped up the coins and disappeared into the thickly packed bar.

"What time is it?" Elizabeth asked.

Surreptitiously, Simon took out the watch and checked. "2:30," he said as he closed it and tucked it back into his pocket.

They had less than hour. She'd wanted to get to the crime scene early, but Victor had advised against it. Two constables would be passing by the entrance to Buck's Row, where Mary Ann's body was found, at about 3:15 a.m. They wanted to avoid them at all cost. The last thing they needed was to get hauled in by the police.

However, knowing that the police had passed by the spot on their rounds and seen nothing, and that Mary Ann's body was found at 3:40, gave them a pretty good idea of the time of the attack. The plan was to leave the pub at three, allowing ten minutes to walk there. They would stay close, but not too close, and move into position just after the police and before the murder. That was, if everything went off without a hitch.

The waitress came back and put down two large beers on the table, some slopping over the rim as she did. Without thinking, Elizabeth picked hers up and took a sip. Warm and mostly disgusting. She made a face and Simon pushed his aside, choosing instead to focus his attention on the crowd.

She knew what he was thinking. Was one of these men Jack the Ripper? It sent a chill down her spine. Somewhere, maybe not here, but not far away, was one of the most notorious serial killers in history. And they were going to follow him.

Despite herself, she took another sip of beer. It wasn't so bad that time. At least it helped her wash down her fear.

Before she knew it, she saw Victor leave his spot at the bar and head for the door. They waited a minute and then followed.

When they got outside the pub, Victor was gone. Even though it was part of the plan, it made Elizabeth uncomfortable to lose the one other person she could trust. The few men looming outside the pub, leering at her despite Simon's presence, reinforced just how out of their element they were. But it was the plan.

Victor would leave first and find a spot on the east side of Buck's Row. She and Simon would follow a few minutes later and come up the opposite end of Buck's Row. Between them, they'd see something.

It was a good plan, but that didn't comfort Elizabeth and a chill ran through her.

Simon looked down at her. "All right?"

She shrugged and Simon nodded in understanding before winding her arm through his and setting them off back down Brick Lane.

In the half hour they'd spent in the pub, the streets had all but emptied. A few men slept in doorways. The only other signs of life were muted voices that could be heard behind the painted glass of the pubs they passed.

The path to Buck's Row was a simple one with few turns. As they made the first, Elizabeth heard footsteps behind them. It was probably just another pair of men searching for the next pub, but the echoing footfalls in the quiet darkness were unnerving. She felt Simon tense and he hurried their steps.

They'd just passed through the halo of one gas lamp and into the next stretch of darkness when two men stepped out of the shadows of a doorway and into the empty street.

"Just keep walking," Simon said softly.

She kept her head down, but her eyes up as they drew closer to the pair. They'd almost passed them when the men stepped in their way. Elizabeth's heart stuttered.

"What's your hurry?" one said.

Simon tried to guide her off the curb, but the other stepped that way to block them.

"You ain't even sayin' hello?" the skinnier of the two said with a broad smile that revealed two missing teeth.

"We don't want any trouble," Simon said, managing to keep his upper class accent under wraps.

The skinny one laughed and elbowed his friend. "He don't want no trouble?"

The other one laughed and then abruptly added, "I'm afraid you've found it, mate."

The sneer on his face made Elizabeth's blood run cold. These were men who enjoyed the sport of terrorizing people and didn't have anything to lose.

Simon led Elizabeth across the street and up another, but she could hear the two following behind. They'd barely gone half a block when two more men appeared in silhouette ahead of them. She could see the dark outlines of clubs in their hands.

She and Simon stopped abruptly. Her heart raced. They were trapped between the two pairs now.

Simon pulled her close to him, and she could feel his heart beating against his chest. She gripped his right arm more tightly. She saw his left hand dip into his pocket. He had a gun, but with four of them....

"You know where you are?" one of the first two men said from close behind them.

She and Simon spun around. The first two were nearly on top of them and she could hear the others drawing nearer.

Elizabeth looked around quickly. The buildings on either side of them were dark. She thought about calling for help, but it would surely set the men off, and she had a sinking feeling no one would come to their aid anyway.

One of the men waved his arms expansively. "All this belongs to me, see?" he said. "And you ain't got my permission to be here."

"Doubles the price, ya see," one of the new men said, as he took out a large knife from his waistband. The long blade glinted in the gaslight.

Simon held up one hand. "This is all I've got," he said as he dug into his pants pocket and pulled out a small handful of coins.

One of the men, he seemed to be the leader, took a step forward. He looked at the coins and then toward Elizabeth and back to Simon. His smile was thin.

"That's not all you have."

A jolt of fear rushed through her, knowing where this was probably headed, but she kept still.

"Take the money," Simon said with surprising calm.

The leader's eyebrows shot up in amusement. "Oh, I will. And your lady."

He nodded toward Elizabeth and one of the men grabbed her from behind.

He spun her around, but out of the corner of her eye, Elizabeth saw Simon start to pull out his gun. The moment he turned, one of the men brought down his club against Simon's arm. He cried out as it crashed into his hand, knocking the gun to the ground.

The other man scrambled to pick it up.

Simon clutched at his hand and one of the men twisted him around and punched him square on the jaw. Elizabeth winced as the she heard his knuckles connect with bone.

"Simon!"

The blow left him wobbly and the man wasted no time. He delivered two swift, powerful blows to Simon's midsection making him crumple to his knees.

Elizabeth struggled against the man that held her and called out to him.

Simon hunched forward, gasping for breath. One of the men rifled through his pockets and pulled out the watch. He whistled, impressed, and held it up to show the boss.

He stood and gave it to the leader, who practically purred. "Now what do we have here?"

"And this," the one with the gun said, as he gave it to the leader.

The leader admired them both and walked casually over to Simon who was still bent forward, his head hanging down.

"Hmm?" the man said.

Simon didn't respond and the man lifted his foot to shove him to the ground with it. It was an unfortunate miscalculation on his part as Simon quickly reached out and grabbed the man's leg and twisted. The man flipped up in the air and to the ground with a thud. Simon was on top of him before he or the others knew what had happened.

One quick punch to man's jaw and then Simon struggled to find the gun. By some miracle, he did. He cocked it and pushed it against the leader's throat just before his men could react.

The leader lifted up one hand to stop his men.

"Let my wife go," Simon said, as he knelt on the man's chest, holding the gun, pushing even further into his skin.

The leader, his lip split and blood trickling out from the cut, smiled. "Maybe I'll just have Len gut her first."

Elizabeth felt the tip of a knife press against her ribs. Worse yet, she felt the momentary panic of knowing their one chance had just gone up in smoke.

Simon turned and his face, wild with anger, fell. His eyes caught hers and the pain and apology in them was almost too much.

He looked down, defeated, and moved the gun away from the man's throat. One of the thugs grabbed it from him and another lifted him off the leader, who stood and brushed off his pant's legs and straightened his jacket. He looked at Simon once then back to Elizabeth.

"Do it."

Elizabeth struggled in the man's grip, desperate to twist out of it.

"No!" Simon lunged forward, but one of the men hit him hard in the stomach again with one of the clubs. He doubled over and the man lifted his club to bring it down against Simon's skull when Elizabeth heard a dull thud.

The man stopped in mid-swing, seemingly frozen, until his eyes rolled back in his head and he fell to the ground unconscious. Behind him stood Victor, a scarf covering his face and a lead pipe in his hand.

Another of the men charged him, but it was a man against boys. Victor dodged the man's awkward attack and swung his pipe against the man's back. He grunted in pain. Victor spun around and swept the pipe at knee level. The sound of bones cracking rang out in the small street. The man cried out in agony and fell to the ground.

The leader took out his knife and started toward Victor.

Elizabeth called out to warn him.

Victor spun around and in the same movement, reached into his jacket and pulled out a knife. It flew across the alley and embedded itself in the leader's chest.

The man looked down at it, stunned. Victor strode over to him. He pulled the knife out and the man gasped. He finished him off with one, sharp punch.

The man who held Elizabeth didn't dare let go to help his friends, and pressed the knife harder against her ribs. "Hey!" he called out. "I'll gut her."

Victor turned slowly and wiped his knife off on his leg. Slowly, he shook his head.

Elizabeth could hear the man's breath coming hard and fast. "I will."

"No," Simon said, from behind them both. "You won't."

She heard the man holding her swallow hard and then his grip loosened. Elizabeth slipped out of it and turned back to see Simon holding a knife to her captor's throat.

Carefully, Simon eased around so he was in front of the man and shifted the knife to his off-hand.

"Are you all right?" he asked her, but kept his eyes on the man.

Elizabeth let out a shaky breath. "I'm fine."

"Then it's your lucky day," Simon said to the thug.

The man narrowed his eyes in confusion. Simon lunged forward and punched him hard in the gut and then delivered a jaw-breaking uppercut as the man doubled over. Simon grabbed him by the collar to keep him from falling and hit him once more. The man was unconscious before he hit the ground.

Panting, Simon turned back to Elizabeth and Victor. He closed the gap between him and Elizabeth, and looked her over for injuries before turning to Victor.

"How did you know?" he asked.

Elizabeth knelt down and grabbed Simon's watch from the leader's pocket.

Victor picked up the gun and handed it back to him and then nodded toward the far street. They started toward it leaving the pile of injured men behind in the muck.

"I passed those two up on Montague, looking for trouble," Victor said quietly as he tugged down his scarf so that it now rested around his neck. "I was nearly there when I doubled back. I had a feeling you two would be trouble tonight."

And thank goodness for that, Elizabeth thought, ignoring the slight. "Thank you."

"Yes," Simon said. Elizabeth heard the pain in his voice. He probably had broken ribs, but she could see from the look on his face he wasn't going to relent now.

Victor grunted in reply and took out his watch. "3:25."

He snapped it shut and the three of them hurried down the street toward Buck's Row, hoping they weren't too late.

CHAPTER EIGHT

THEY TURNED UP A LITTLE street called Whites Row and Elizabeth could see the street widening ahead into a V-shape with a wedge of tenement buildings dividing it in two. On the right was the narrow little Winthrop Street and on the left was Buck's Row.

They hurried along until Victor held up a hand to stop them and motioned for them to move into a side street to the left. With her heart in her throat, Elizabeth pressed her body up against one of the buildings and hid in the shadows. In the darkness next to her, Simon groaned softly, his breath shallow and labored.

Elizabeth was about to reach out a comforting hand when she heard footfalls echoing not too far away and froze.

At the mouth of the side street she watched the faint glow of a lantern as it moved up and down with the natural gate of a man walking. Her heart beat a little faster. Whoever he was, he was getting closer.

Victor held out his arm, waving it urgently back toward the building. The three of them melted back into a brick arched doorway.

Elizabeth could just see the silhouette of the man as he reached the intersection—a police constable, his bulls-eye lantern casting a broad beam of light in the night. She pressed herself as far back into the cold bricks as she could and held her breath.

The beam of the PC's lantern swept past within inches of their hiding place. Thankfully, he didn't turn up their street and he didn't linger. He kept walking up Buck's Row.

The footsteps got farther and farther away. Finally, Victor, who was closest to the corner, inched forward toward the edge of the building. He peered out for a moment and then leaned back against the wall, tilting his head back and shaking it.

"Damn," he said so softly she almost didn't hear him.

Having to see for herself, Elizabeth edged forward and peered around the building. She could see the officer in the dim light as he veered to the left and Buck's Row. Then he stopped, the beam of his light frozen in place for a moment, and then he ran across the street toward something, his footsteps loud against the cobblestones.

In the street ahead, Elizabeth watched as he shined his light down on what looked to be a pile of rags. Her stomach fell with the realization. It was Mary Ann Nichols.

Elizabeth stifled a gasp and looked up at Simon. Even in the darkness she could see his anger and disgust, and more than a little sadness.

She scanned the streets near them, searching for someone lurking in the shadows, some hint of something, anything, but the streets were empty.

Jack the Ripper was gone.

VICTOR SILENTLY FUMED AS they walked the streets around Buck's Row looking for something that might lead them to Jack the Ripper.

If it hadn't been for the Crosses, he would have been there on time. He would have seen him and this folly wouldn't be necessary.

He sighed and took off his scarf, tossing it into an alley. He would probably have to get rid of his jacket as well. The gang members would be out of commission for some time, but they had friends, and friends talked. The last thing he needed was a group of idiot thieves mucking up his mission.

He glared over at the Crosses. Their inexperience had nearly cost them their lives. But he had to admit, Cross had acquitted himself fairly well, considering, and Elizabeth showed more mettle than he had expected. That, however, didn't change the fact that they were liabilities. Especially, he chided himself, if he kept letting his emotions get the better of him.

Victor grunted.

"Are you okay?" Elizabeth asked him.

He frowned at her, but a memory of another woman who once looked at him in the same sincere and guileless way pushed itself into his mind. With another grunt, he shoved the image back down into the past where it belonged.

He nodded curtly and looked away.

They fell in with the crowd that gathered at the crime scene. Victor could see the victim and hear the doctor who'd been summoned noting her injuries, but he knew them by heart. He knew each cut, each horrible wound and so his focus was elsewhere. He looked carefully at each man who stood among the onlookers. Was he here? Was he here to watch the drama unfold, to relish in his creation?

Was it the tall man who stood at the back and watched the crowd? The pock-faced one who smelled of butcher's offal? Or the one who looked like nothing at all? Victor crossed his arms over his chest and turned to scan the less likely hiding places. Where was that *fils de salope?*

Finally, the doctor ordered the body to be taken to the mortuary shed at the Workhouse Infirmary. Two policemen loaded her onto a stretcher and the doctor followed them down the street as a man began to wash away the blood.

"What is he doing?" Elizabeth whispered, sounding incredulous.

Simon made a sound of disapproval. "So much for CSI."

They watched as both citizens and police trampled over the crime scene, obliterating any potential evidence. Not that they would have had any idea what to do with most of it, but it was frustrating to see nonetheless.

As dawn broke over the city, Victor decided nothing more could be gleaned from the crime scene and they returned to his boarding house rooms. As soon as they entered, Elizabeth began tending to her husband.

He winced as she ran her hands over his ribs.

"I don't think anything's broken," she said.

He took a deep breath to test out her theory and winced. "They'll be all right."

Simon grimaced again as he arched his back to remove his shirt, but his ever dutiful wife was there to help him. It was nauseating. Victor stalked over to the window. The sun was nearly up now.

He heard Elizabeth's soft footsteps as she walked up behind him. He turned around just as she was about to touch his shoulder.

Yanking her hand back in surprise and a little embarrassment, she looked up at him. There was that look again. Familiar and painful. Whatever it was she had to say, he did not want to hear it.

He stepped around her. "You should go to Paris."

She frowned and tilted her head to the side as if she hadn't heard him correctly. "I'm sorry?"

"Until this is over." Victor walked over to his little dresser and eyed the small bottle of whisky he'd bought yesterday. "You are in the way."

"We were..." Simon started and searched for a word his ego could handle, "surprised tonight. It won't happen again."

"If it does, I will not be there to see it," Victor said. "Do you understand? I will not risk the mission—"

Simon stood and faced him. "Unless you've forgotten, finding Jack the Ripper is *our* mission."

Victor arched an eyebrow. "You are doing a fine job of it."

Simon took a step forward, but Elizabeth moved between them. "Same team, guys."

Victor snorted. "We are not a *team*."

She turned to him, her blue eyes sparking fiercely before she subdued them. "We're on the same side. And we're going to need each other before this over. Katherine Vale, who by the way, is ten kinds of crazy, did something to change time. To. Change. Time."

She looked over at her husband and then back to Victor. "Even if we weren't chasing one of the most notorious serial killers in history, shouldn't that be enough for you two to stop this bickering and at least try to work together?"

Simon said nothing and just continued to eye him warily.

Victor ignored him and scowled at Elizabeth. She was, however, not the least bit cowed. It was disconcerting.

He did not work with others. His job was something he was uniquely qualified to do. It required someone with nothing left to lose, except perhaps, his soul. For him, it may have been too late even for that.

Regardless, he thought with growing bitterness, his part of the mission would not come to pass if they failed in theirs. And judging from tonight, they would not be put off.

"You were in over your head tonight. A rich man among ruffians," he said, getting the desired blustery reaction from Cross.

He smiled and continued. "While I am better suited to these sorts of people," he said, hating to admit it, "you will be welcome in places I will not."

Simon glared at him, trying to fathom just what he meant. Victor saw the exact moment the light bulb switched on.

Simon nodded, forgoing more sparring for the moment. "Quite a few of the suspects were…upper class?"

Victor smirked and nodded. He was from a small village. He had no interest in the finer things in life and they no interest in him.

"Without witnessing the crime," Simon continued, his wheels finally spinning in the right direction, "we'll have to rely on old fashioned detective work, I suppose."

"We should divide the suspects," Victor suggested.

"You take the East End and we'll take the West?" Elizabeth asked.

Victor grunted in agreement. It might not be the best solution, but it would keep them occupied and, perhaps, they would even stumble upon something helpful.

"I suppose that's logical," Simon conceded. "Agreed"

"Voilà," Victor said to Elizabeth, spreading his arms. "Détente."

CHAPTER NINE

SIMON EASED HIMSELF UP out of the cool bath, his ribs aching with the effort. He probed his side. Sore, but not life threatening. Somehow, that did little to ease his mind.

"Pathetic," he muttered and snatched a towel off the rack.

He toweled himself off roughly, clenching his jaw and ignoring the discomfort as he did. Tossing the towel aside, he grabbed a pair of drawers, pulled them on, and loosely tied the drawstring as he headed for the bedroom.

Elizabeth sat on the bed, a tray of food in front of her. "I liberated some things from the kitchen."

Simon forced a smile and moved to join her.

She held up a scone. "Cranberry or original recipe?"

Despite his best efforts to conceal his discomfort as he climbed onto the bed, Elizabeth noticed. "Maybe you should see a doctor?"

She reached out to touch the bruises that discolored his side. He stopped her and shook his head.

"Simon?"

It wasn't the ribs that were bothering him, although they were sore. He sighed. "I'm sorry about last night," he said finally.

Elizabeth frowned. "For what?"

"For not realizing those thugs were waiting for marks like us. For being marks like us."

"Simon," she said, reaching out and taking his hand. "There were four of them—"

He pulled away and paced across the room "I should have been better prepared. If it hadn't been for..."

He could barely finish the thought.

"If you're going to be mad at anybody," she said, "be mad at me."

He turned to face her. "You?"

She shrugged and moved to the edge of the bed. "At least you did something. I just stood there."

"With a knife held to you," he reminded her.

"And he was pretty strong," she said.

"Very."

She smiled at him. "And yet you should be able to defeat four men single-handedly?"

He hated it when she did that, maneuvered him so deftly. He offered her a defeated smile. "I should have done better."

She slipped off the bed. "Is that you or Victor talking?"

Simon grunted. A little of both, if he were being honest. Victor was grating and superior, but damned if the man wasn't right. They were unprepared. Simon knew he'd been unfair with Victor this morning, that he'd misdirected his own frustrations onto the man. Of course, his being a complete pompous ass helped.

Simon sighed again. "He's right about one thing. Many of the suspects are wealthy. And we do stand a better chance of learning about them than he does."

"Right. So," she said, moving back to the bed and the food. The woman's appetite was legend. She grabbed a scone. "Who have we got?"

Simon rifled through the files in his mind. "There are a few doctors. Blackwood, Gull and Tumblety, although he's hardly upper class. Druitt—"

Elizabeth stopped mid-chew and swallowed. "Wait. Druitt?"

Simon furrowed his brow as he tried to remember the details. "Montague John Druitt. Why?"

Elizabeth sat up straighter. "John. It's got to be him."

"Who does?"

"George's friend."

Simon frowned. Ah, yes, George, the man who makes advances to married women. "Your *lunch* date?"

Elizabeth laughed. "Oh, you're going to feel silly when you meet him."

"I doubt that."

Elizabeth smiled and then frowned in thought as she considered their options. "We can't just show up on Druitt's doorstep."

Simon nodded and walked back over to the bed. He took half of the scone she offered and wondered what she was cooking up in that twisty brain of hers. "We need an invitation."

"And we need to know somebody in order—" she started and then smiled broadly. "And we do. George."

Simon frowned, although he knew she was right. "And how do you propose we find him? Lunch around until he accosts you again?

He hadn't liked the man's forwardness with Elizabeth at all. No gentleman would have done such a thing.

Elizabeth's grin grew even wider. "In the park. George said he was going to meet his friend John in Hyde Park at the bridge on Sunday. We'll find our Montague John Druitt," she said as she popped a small bit of scone into her mouth triumphantly. "Sunday in the park with George."

THE CROWD WAS ALREADY three deep at the Working Lad's Institute and the inquest into Mary Ann Nichols' death hadn't even started yet. Victor shouldered his way along the edge of the gallery to find a spot near the front where he had a good view of the crowd.

As they typically did, his broad shoulders and generally unpleasant attitude served him well, and he found a space in a corner of the room. He took off his cap and shoved it into his pocket. Leaning against the wall, he scanned the crowd.

The group of men on the far side of the room were clearly reporters. Even if their pads and pencils hadn't given them away, they had the hungry look of men about to feast on another's misery. A quick survey told him nearly half the crowd fit that bill.

It wasn't surprising. Nothing sold papers like murder.

The rest of the crowd was a mixture of East End locals and a smattering of upper class men and women, no doubt slumming for sport.

Mr. Baxter, the coroner for South-East Middlesex, opened the proceedings with an interview of Nichols' father and their estranged relationship. Even though Victor had read the files, it was a far different experience to be in the chamber as the testimony was given. Edward Walker was not a name on a page, but a man, flesh and blood, who had lost a daughter.

Polly, as her friends called her, was a mother of five children. She'd been in and out of the workhouse, drank too often and too much, but had no enemies to speak of.

Next to testify was PC John Neil. Victor listened for any inconsistencies in his testimony, but found none. Things had happened as the PC said they had. That left Dr. Llewellyn, who had been called to the scene and later examined the body.

As the doctor testified, Victor turned his attention again to the crowd. He didn't need to hear the testimony anyway. He had read the autopsy file, seen the drawings. In his mind's eye, he could recreate each wound in perfect detail.

The sort of man who had committed that horror would be here to relish in it. To relive each cut as it was described with vivid precision. Gasps went through the crowd as Llewellyn testified about the two slashes across her neck.

"This incision completely severs all the tissues down to the vertebrae. The large vessels of the neck on both sides were severed. The incision is about eight inches long. These cuts must have been caused with a long-bladed knife, moderately sharp, and used with great violence."

One man, short and thick-necked, wearing a boot maker's leather apron caught Victor's eye. There was something off about him.

The man turned to look at the people on either side of him before turning his full attention back to the doctor as he described the multiple cuts and jagged wounds that had been carved into Nichols' abdomen.

News of those wounds caused a murmur of surprise to filter through the crowd. But the man Victor watched remained stoic, focused. And then, as though he felt Victor's eyes upon him, he fidgeted and glanced nervously about again.

Victor looked away and by the time he looked back, the little man was gone.

Chapter Ten

Elizabeth took Simon's offered hand and climbed into the hackney coach. He smiled at her, his color and his mood noticeably better.

After the night of the murder, they'd slept through what was left of Friday. That night, he'd put on a British upper lip so stiff it was positively starched. She knew he needed a little time to heal and there was nothing that made him happier than taking care of her. Sometimes the best cure for what ailed a person was found in helping someone else.

And so she'd faked a small stomach ache. Nothing too worrisome, just enough for them to stay in for a day and rest. Next time, though, she was going to fake a headache. By nightfall she was hungry enough to eat her pillow.

She should have felt guilty over her little deception, about not searching for the Ripper for a day, but she couldn't manage it. They were going to be in London for over a month. The next murder was still a full week away. Pacing themselves would be important.

And, after their inauspicious beginning, maybe even more so than she'd thought.

Luckily, the day of physical and emotional rest had done the trick. By Sunday morning, Simon was back to his old self and growing irritated with their lack of progress. They set off early to Hyde Park in hopes of finding George and John Druitt, and their first honest to goodness lead.

After a short carriage ride, they pulled up at Hyde Park corner and Simon paid the driver. Other carriages trundled past and into the park.

"Why are we getting out here?" she asked.

Simon looked after a fancy barouche coach that passed by. Even the horse was well-dressed. "Private carriages only. I'm afraid we'll have to walk from here."

He held out his hand and helped her down. She didn't mind walking at all. The park was a welcome and enormous expanse of greenery. Finally, they could leave the dark grays and the soot behind. She wound her arm through Simon's and let him guide her. They'd barely walked a hundred feet in and she could already feel the difference in the air. No wonder the park was called one of the lungs of London.

As they entered the park proper, the few carriages she'd seen turned into dozens and dozens. There were probably even more people on horseback. The carriages all broke off to the left and rode down one of two broad straight tracks, with horses to the right.

"Rotten Row," Simon explained. "Where the fashionable come to see and be seen."

He wasn't kidding. While some of the carriages were unadorned, some were absolutely pimped out. From elaborate crests to ridiculous frilly frills, they were apparently a way to show off your status and wealth and, she realized, judging from the amazing outfits of the people inside, your wardrobe.

"We're this way," he said, leading her carefully through the traffic. Even so, they barely made it across.

"It'll be far worse this afternoon," he said. "These are just the opening act."

They walked into what appeared to be a grove of trees. As they grew closer, Elizabeth saw water ahead.

"The Serpentine," Simon said. "The bridge your…friend's friend referred to is undoubtedly the bridge that borders Kensington. It's about a mile away."

He pulled out his watch. "We have an hour yet, so no need to rush."

Elizabeth leaned into him and enjoyed the walk. For the first time since they'd been here, they both felt solid on their feet. The whole mission had happened so quickly, so abruptly, it wasn't until now that she started feel the reins in her grasp.

They walked along a path on the edge of the lake under a canopy of large shade trees. It was an incredibly beautiful and peaceful place. There was a lot of hat tipping and polite nodding as they went. Victorian manners demanded no less.

A few people in boats rowed lazily across the lake, basking in an oddly sunny London day. Elizabeth was about to ask if they could rent a boat when Simon stumbled slightly and came to an abrupt halt. He put a hand to his forehead, paused for a moment, and then stood almost frozen in place.

"Are you all right?" she asked.

He turned and looked down at her, the corners of his eyes tight with confusion.

"Miss West?"

Elizabeth nearly laughed. That was a blast from the past. He was being silly. But she stopped herself before it bubbled up. It was clear from the look in his eyes that he wasn't joking at all.

WHAT WAS SHE DOING here? What was *he* doing here? In…London? Simon put a hand to his temple and shut his eyes tightly. Hoping whatever dream he was having would end when he opened them again.

It didn't.

"I think," he said slowly, "I'm unwell."

Was he having a stroke? Had he gone mad?

Elizabeth squeezed his arm and smiled up at him. "It's all right, Simon."

When had she started calling him that? And when had he flown to London?

He glanced around, the surroundings were familiar, but it still took him a moment to place them.

"Hyde Park," he whispered.

"Yes," she said at his elbow. "Why don't we sit down?"

He looked down at her again, poised to remind her he could think for himself, but there was something else off about her as well. Why in God's name was she in costume? And not just her. Simon turned to make sure. Everyone, including himself, was in some sort of ridiculous period attire. What the hell was going on here?

Set to demand an explanation, Simon turned back to her, but she smiled so kindly that he felt the knot in his chest ease just enough for him to breathe.

"Over here," she said and led him to a bench.

He sat down, his head still swimming. He'd been in his office at the university, she....He glanced over at her and she laid a comforting hand on his forearm.

"It'll pass soon," she said.

He looked at her uncertainly.

"Your memory," she continued. "It's kind of mixed up, right?"

He nodded slowly. His memory was, indeed, mixed up. Images were missing and broken. He could feel the gap in them. He had the uncomfortable sense that something had been carved out of him.

"What's happened to me?"

His hands gripped his thighs tightly. He would hold himself together by sheer will.

She paused a moment, a small, curiously sad smile quirking the corner of her mouth. "I don't know where to start."

"Miss West," he said impatiently. "Either this is a dream or I have gone insane. Either way, I'd appreciate it if you'd start *somewhere*."

She smiled again, her eyes growing oddly moist. She nodded quickly and Simon reached out take her hand. It was forward and inappropriate, and felt right.

"I'm sorry," he said. "I didn't mean..."

He stared down at their hands. Her small kid gloves in his and he remembered. He remembered taking her hand a thousand times before. The feel of it in his. The strength it gave him.

In an instant, his memories flooded back to him. He closed his eyes as the empty parts of him filled again.

He remembered.

He let out a quick short burst of relieved breath.

"Simon?" she asked, her eyes filled with worry and the start of tears.

"Yes," he said, swallowing down his own emotion. "It's passed."

"You're you again?"

He nodded and Elizabeth blew out a quick, bracing breath of her own. "That was terrifying."

He couldn't have agreed more. Without warning, he'd suddenly lost the last year of his life. He squeezed her hand more tightly. He'd nearly lost the most important thing to him.

"Well," she said finally, "we knew it could happen. At least it didn't last long."

Simon clenched his jaw and nodded. And when one did? When the changes in time caused memory gaps that lasted for hours, days? Or worse. What would they do then?

THEY SAT ON THE bench for another few minutes gathering themselves before continuing on. When she'd experienced her own mini-episode before they'd left, it had been strange and disconcerting, but it was much worse being on this end of it. Although, having seen the fear in Simon's eyes, she wasn't so sure.

And Jack's, she thought. She could still see his expression—confused and worried—as he disappeared in Council headquarters.

They walked in silence for a few minutes before she glanced up at Simon and he turned his head to face her.

"Still here," he assured her.

She laughed. "It's like waiting for an earthquake, isn't it?"

He arched an eyebrow in question.

"One's bound to come, but you never know when it's going to hit or how bad it's going to be."

He nodded. "It won't do us any good worrying about it either."

She knew he was talking to himself as much as he was to her.

"Right," she said. "And I think we're here."

Just ahead was the Serpentine Bridge with its long stone balustrade and large sloping brick arches.

Forcing herself not to dwell on what ifs, she and Simon made their way to start of the bridge. She scanned it as far as she could see and shook her head.

Simon nodded and they started across. By the time they'd reached the other side, Elizabeth's heart began to sink.

"It's just now two," Simon said. "Give them a chance."

They walked back to the middle where they had a fairly good view of each entrance and waited. Elizabeth started to lean back against the railing, but her forgotten bustle got in the way. She couldn't quite feel when she was touching it and leaned a bit too far. She felt herself losing her balance when Simon grabbed her arm.

His eyes flared at her and she started to explain when she saw George.

"There," she said, nodding toward him.

Simon gave her one last admonishing look before following her gaze. "And Druitt?"

She scanned the people around George, but didn't see Druitt and shook her head. "I don't see him."

George checked his watch and looked around expectantly. A moment later, a young boy ran up to him and tugged on his sleeve. George nodded and the boy handed him a note.

He gave the boy a coin and read the note, his face falling as he did. With a sigh, he tucked the paper into his pocket and turned to stare out at the water.

"Come on," Elizabeth said, pulling Simon along.

He caught up with her and she wove her arm into his, and they strolled past the spot where George was.

"George?" she said casually.

He turned around, his morose mood lifting immediately. "Elizabeth!"

He took her hand and kissed it. "My fellow revolutionary."

Simon arched an eyebrow, whether it was at the hand kissing or the epithet, she wasn't sure.

"Simon, this is the man I was telling you about, George Roxbury. George, this is my husband, Simon."

George's mouth quirked into an appreciative smile. "Is he?"

Elizabeth stifled her laugh.

"He is," Simon said coolly, completely unaware of the subtext.

"Oh," George said, holding up his hands in mock surrender. "He's not going to challenge me to a duel, is he?"

His face sobered slightly and he leaned toward Elizabeth. "Is he?"

"No," she assured him, although looking at Simon, he seemed to be considering the idea. She slipped her arm back through her husband's. "He's just a little protective."

George nodded sagely. "As he should be. You, my dear, are trouble," he added with a smile.

Simon grunted in agreement.

Elizabeth sighed dramatically. "I'm interesting."

"You are," George agreed. "Most people here are as dull as ditch-water."

"Somehow, I doubt that."

George hmm'd in reply. "You'd be unpleasantly surprised."

"Then come out with us tonight," Elizabeth said quickly. "I know it's short notice," she added looking up at Simon, trying to silently urge him to participate.

He cleared his throat. "Yes," Simon said. "We'd love to have you."

His deadpan delivery almost made Elizabeth giggle, and would have if they hadn't needed George to say yes.

George sighed. "I can't tonight, I'm afraid. I've got plans, theater and a party that's likely to be as exciting as the Queen's bath, but…" He frowned for a moment and then a broad smile took over his face. "Why don't you come with me?"

Jackpot. Elizabeth tried to look hesitant. "Are you sure?"

He waved his hand. "Of course. I've got a box for the theater and you can be my guests at the party."

"We were going to try Monico's in Piccadilly," she said, casting a quick glance at Simon, hoping she sounded sufficiently reticent, but not too much so.

"It'll be beastly there tonight," George said. "No, you must come with me. At least, with you along, the night won't be a total waste."

Elizabeth smiled at the compliment.

Even Simon smiled agreeably. "Very kind of you."

George clapped his hands together. "Excellent. Shall we meet at the theater at eight, then?"

"Perfect," Elizabeth said. "What's the show?"

"A new spectacle at the Lyceum. A bit macabre given the recent news and the most popular ticket in town because of it—*Dr. Jekyll & Mr. Hyde.*"

Chapter Eleven

Victor took a sip of warm beer to help wash down the lump of chalk and gypsum plaster someone had sold him, billed as bread. It looked like bread and there was probably was some grain in it, somewhere, but the process of bread-making had become so adulterated that additives of all sorts, some more poisonous than others, had been incorporated to save costs. By the time the flour made it to a bakery, and the bread to a pub like this, it was barely edible. No wonder the people here were so sickly. What little they did get to eat had no nutritional value at all. With little to choose from, as bad as it was, it was better than nothing.

He put the slice of bread aside and returned to his fried fish. They called them dabs although there was no telling what sort of fish was used. It was greasy and cold, but it was dinner.

He wiped his fingers on the legs of his pants and tipped back his chair against the wall. The pub was busy; they were always busy. The noise from the crowd was boisterous and bawdy, with prostitutes clinging sanguinely to customers and everyone drinking away the day.

He scanned the crowd looking for a murderer.

No doubt many of them were, or would be. Life here was harder than even he anticipated. Thousands hovered on the brink of death in this slum every day. That sort of existence, living like animals, brought out the darkness in the human soul. Ripper could be any one of these men, he thought. Pushed beyond their own mind's endurance and into madness.

The sounds of the bar faded as he studied each face, reading their lives in the lines that scarred them. Red, angry burns on the side of a face from working near the hellish heat of a furnace day in and day out. Red, raw fingertips from separating bits of rope for hours on end in the workhouse. Or the so-called gin blossoms, red splotches on the nose and face caused by broken capillaries beneath the skin from too much drink.

Red and raw. All of them.

A man shouldered his way past a duo that had just arrived at the bar. The three exchanged unpleasantries and Victor let his chair rest on the floor again. One of the men was the one he'd seen at the inquest.

Ignoring the other two, he made his way to the door. Victor waited a moment and then followed him out into the cool night.

"I DON'T KNOW HOW I'm going to keep this clean," Elizabeth said as she looked at herself in the mirror.

The dress was gorgeous—silver silk with an elaborately embroidered chiffon overlay and pale blue lace trim. It had small poofs at the shoulders, and was beautifully tailored, but unlike her other dresses, had an actual neckline. Most of her décolletage was obscured by floofs of lace, but it was oddly thrilling to be wearing anything that didn't go up to her neck in some sort of fabric prison. She twisted around to try to see herself from the back.

She looked great coming and like she was smuggling a small circus going. If only she didn't have to wear the darn bustle. Simon made an appreciative sound and she turned to give him the better of the two views.

He, of course, looked perfect. With his black tailcoat and straight cut black wool pants, crisp white shirt, and white silk waistcoat and tie, he looked as though he'd walked off the fashion plate of some Victorian magazine.

"You look beautiful," he said, coming to her side.

Elizabeth smiled and Simon turned to observe himself in the mirror, critically looking for anything out of place.

"You don't have to be so hard on George, you know," she said. "He's harmless."

Simon continued his inspection. "You said he had a reputation to uphold. A ladies' man?"

He turned to her and she nodded.

"Well then," he said, tugging needlessly on his perfect cuffs. "What serves him better? A husband who doesn't mind his overly friendly nature with you or one who does?"

He arched a knowing eyebrow.

And here she thought he'd been actually jealous. "You sneak."

He laughed and then pulled her into his embrace. "I will say though, it is a part that comes very naturally to me. I don't like to share."

Elizabeth felt the thrill that went with hearing those words. Unfortunately, they had places to go and people to meet. "We have the theater and a party and you have sore ribs."

He pulled her more tightly against him. "Which are much improved."

She sighed and put her hand to his chest. "Simon…"

He sighed, picked up his gloves and guided her toward the door. As he opened it for her he said with a smile, "No party lasts forever."

THE LYCEUM THEATRE THRUMMED with excitement after the play. The two women who had passed out due to momentary hysteria were still being tended to as Simon helped Elizabeth on with her coat.

The story was an age-old tale of outward honor and respectability, and inward evil and lust. It was the very dichotomy that defined the Victorian era. But it was more than mere social commentary. It was a study in man's dual nature, the evil inside every man.

The staging had been simple, straight-forward, and Richard Mansfield's performance as Dr. Jekyll had been so flat, it was on the verge of concave, Simon thought, but his Mr. Hyde was an altogether different story. His on-stage transformation—talent aided merely with cleverly hued make-up and lighting—was impressive. He was repulsive, animalistic, and disturbing.

The frightening duality of his personality and its parallels to Jack the Ripper were painfully obvious. Was the Ripper a man suffering from a split personality like the good Dr. Jekyll? It seemed far more likely to be the case than a man who could not hide his demon. It was not a comforting thought.

Mansfield was on the suspect list Travers had given him. Although, like so many others, there was very little credible evidence to link him to the crimes. In some cases, merely being in London at the time seemed sufficient reason for suspicion. However, having seen him as Hyde now, Simon had to wonder.

"I'd take you backstage to see Richard," George said as they left their box. "But it's nearly impossible to wend your way through the crowds down there. He'll be at the party, I think. I'll introduce you then, if he can pry himself away from his admirers. Which I cannot guarantee," he added with a smile.

He lifted the velvet curtain at the back of the box and held it for them to pass through. "My carriage should be out front. Why don't you ride with me? We can send for a cab when you're ready to escape."

Elizabeth looked to Simon for confirmation before agreeing.

"Excellent," George said, taking Elizabeth's arm and winding it through his own. "And you can tell me all of the gossip from America. Do you know the Vanderbilts?"

Elizabeth looked to Simon in panic. He merely smiled and lingered behind.

She turned back to George. "Not exactly," she said, trying to buy time. "But I did meet Buffalo Bill once."

"The cowboy?" George said excitedly.

And with that Simon knew he'd lost them.

VICTOR FOLLOWED THE MAN until he knocked on a nondescript doorway on Commercial Road. He waited there and a minute later a big, bull of a man opened the door. From his vantage point across the street, Victor could just see inside. He knew the look, the smoke, the bad piano playing, and the women walking back and forth through it all in a daze.

A whorehouse.

The big man hesitated and then finally stepped aside letting the other man inside. Victor took out his pipe and pushed a finger in the bowl to re-secure the plug of tobacco. If it had been elsewhere, he might have followed the man inside. But not here. A woman's touch was always welcome, but the prostitutes of Whitechapel brought sadness, not comfort. Not to mention, crabs.

Victor contented himself with his pipe, sure the man would not last long. He was right although not for the reasons he'd suspected. Twenty minutes later, the little man was bodily escorted from the premises and tossed, quite literally, out of the door and onto his ear.

Pushing himself up, he stood on wobbly legs and rubbed his jaw.

"You stay outta 'ere, Pizer!" the big man threatened. "Next time I'll knock your block off."

And with that he slammed the door.

So it *was* Pizer, Victor thought. He'd suspected the man might be John Pizer, a boot maker who was better known for his nickname, Leather Apron, and a very viable suspect.

Pizer picked up his hat from a puddle it had fallen into and shook it off. Still sopping wet, he pulled it down onto his head and started to stumble down the street.

Victor followed him to another bar, the Ten Bells. There, Pizer argued with another man briefly.

"They say it's a Jew," he said, his voice thick with drink.

"They say everyfink bad that 'appens 'ere is a cause of a Jew!" the other man agreed loudly.

Pizer nodded before telling his friend what he thought of the local police in colorful and barely understandable English.

"Shaddup!" a man at a nearby table said.

Pizer started to stand, but the other man reached out and shoved him. He was already so far gone, he probably passed out before he hit the floor.

"All right, all right," his friend said as he surrendered to the angry customer. He helped Pizer back up into a chair and left him to sleep it off at the table.

"They'll pin it on somebody," a woman at another table said. "You can bet on that."

"They won't be spendin' time tryin' to solve no murder of the likes of us," her friend said with a sneer.

Then she affected a middle class accent. "Scotland Yard is looking into it, love." Then she laughed. "My arse, they are!"

Her friend cackled. "Lookin' into your arse. That wouldn't be the first now would it, Annie?"

Another woman at the table joined in. As she spoke, Victor noticed that she was missing all of the teeth in her lower left jaw. "No one cares what becomes of us. Least of all the rousers. They's just in someone's pocket, that's all. It's thems that you got to look out for."

Annie, a tough looking little woman with a fresh black eye said, "You should know, Lizzy."

Lizzy. Annie. Victor had to wonder. Were these two of Ripper's victims? They fit the descriptions he'd read, but then so did hundreds of other women here.

Lizzy grinned and pushed back in her chair. "Oh, I do, my dearie. I do. But we've got a plan for them, ain't we?"

Annie and the other woman laughed. "A pretty little plan."

CHAPTER TWELVE

THE PARTY WAS A sort of social bumper cars—aimlessly circling, randomly bumping into people only to veer off and collide with someone else. Having mastered the aristocratic air of indifference so well, Simon glided through it all effortlessly.

It took Elizabeth a little longer to get into the flow. While she and Simon had spent a fair share of time on their missions with the upper crust, it always started out the same way for her. A little unsure. After all, pre-Simon she had no crust at all.

And this wasn't just a fancy dress party; it was one step from Buckingham Palace. But, she told herself, she could do this. She took a cleansing breath.

Simon, always attuned to her, leaned down and whispered. "They're just people, Elizabeth. With sticks up their arses, but just people."

Elizabeth laughed, relaxing.

The house was owned by the Marquess of Kildare: Gerald FitzGerald, 5th Duke of Leinster, which, she realized belatedly, was one person. According to George, the land had initially been part of the grounds of St. James' Palace and later, when the first house was built, the town residence of the Prince Regent. Eventually, it was sold, demolished and turned into the two enormous white stucco terraced-buildings they were now.

Enormous hardly did them justice. They were four stories high with grand terraces on each side, one with a perfect view of the park. The outside was nearly as opulent as the inside.

The party spilled from the main downstairs salon through the elegant domed entry hall, up the grand double-staircase, complete with statues in alcoves and into the main ballroom. So far, she'd met a duke, a viscount, a baron, a couple of earls and fistful of knights, and they'd only just arrived.

Now this was a party.

The dresses ranged from the sublime to the ridiculous and beyond. It seemed that the more fabric and layers you displayed, the higher up the food chain you were. It was a wonder some of the women could move at all.

George led them around, introducing them to all and sundry, as a small orchestra played in the corner. Most of the guests were gracious, although there were a few who found an American among them, an American woman reporter at that, discomfiting. Lord Salisbury had been most put off. It was all Elizabeth could do not to say how much she loved his steaks just to see the look on his face.

An artist named Sickert was busy doing sketches in the corner— capturing his subject's dual nature by drawing two separate faces for them, their Jekyll and Hyde, much to everyone's amusement. Both Simon and Elizabeth passed on that, but there was quite a crowd gathering.

They had almost reached the end of their first circuit when George smiled and waved them toward two men talking in the corner. She recognized one as Montague John Druitt. The other was more whiskers than man, with a large belly that strained his pearl grey waistcoat.

As they approached, Elizabeth overheard the tail end of their conversation.

"You should regularly," the whiskered man said with a slightly scolding tone. "...an appointment tomorrow afternoon."

Druitt nodded. "Yes, especially after mother, I—"

Both of them stopped talking as they realized they weren't alone and their serious countenances instantly changed to the same *isn't it a delight?* expression everyone seemed to assume when they came across a new person.

"John," George said, shaking hands with his friend.

The other man seemed glad to see him, but perhaps a little embarrassed as well.

"Doctor," George said, extending his hand to the whiskered man who humphed and shook the offered hand quickly. The doctor then turned his attention to Simon and Elizabeth, and coughed in a not so gentle reproof of George's lack of manners.

"Oh, forgive me," George said. "Dr. Blackwood, may I present Mr. and Mrs. Simon Cross?"

Dr. Blackwood. He was another one of the names on the suspect list. Between the doctor and Druitt, they'd hit the perfecta.

The doctor eyed them warily for a split-second before extending his hand.

"It's Sir Simon, actually," Simon said, not unkindly, and earning a warmer reception from the doctor.

"Oh," George said. "Are you?"

Simon arched an eyebrow in an English shrug.

George looked questioningly at Elizabeth.

"Never came up," she said.

George smiled, amused. "We usually lead with that sort of thing here," he said before getting back to the introductions at the end of which, he asked permission to pull Druitt away, leaving them alone with the doctor and his whiskers.

Elizabeth couldn't endure the awkward silence. "So, what sort of doctor are you?"

The man frowned. "I beg your pardon?"

"She means, what do you specialize in?" Simon clarified.

"Diseases of the mind. It is the most misunderstood and mysterious part of the human anatomy. Delirium, derangement, melancholia. What some would simply call madness. I suppose that's in keeping with tonight's theme of madness," he said looking rather pleased with himself. Elizabeth smiled politely, encouraging him. He didn't need much.

"The study of the mind with my methods is a rather new branch of medicine. We've made incredible strides in the last decade, but the established medical community, is, well, not prepared to embrace them fully just yet."

"Could I interview you for my paper back home?" Elizabeth asked seeing an opening. "I'm a part-time reporter and I'd love to bring them back a story like this."

Worried she'd made her move too soon, she did the only logical thing and plunged ahead full-speed. She raised her hands in the air and moved them across in front of her as though highlighting an invisible marquee. "A Great Man of Science Makes Great Strides Across the Ocean."

The doctor seemed surprised and definitely flattered, but hesitant. "I'm not certain it's—"

"I'll write it," she said. "And if you don't like it, we won't use it. I'll tear it up in front of you."

He looked to be considering it.

Elizabeth dipped into what she could remember about newspapers of the day. When she'd decided to use that as a cover story, she'd done a bit of quick research. Don't fail me, Google.

"I think Mr. Pulitzer would like it very much," she said.

The name drop had the desired effect.

"Pulitzer? You work for *The World*?"

Was that Pulitzer's paper? For a moment, she couldn't remember. "In a way, don't we all?" she said lightly, casting a quick, nervous glance at Simon.

"It's really much easier simply to acquiesce, Doctor," Simon said.

He still looked undecided.

"Once she gets an idea for a story, there's no stopping it," Simon continued. "It will either be about you or one of your colleagues, I'm afraid."

That kicked the old buzzard over the fence.

"Very well," Blackwood agreed. "Perhaps you can come by the hospital this week? I can probably spare a few minutes."

"Very gracious of you, Doctor." Elizabeth grinned. "I'd like that very much."

"Tell me, Doctor, as a man who studies madness," Simon said. "What do you think of this recent business in the East End? Work of a madman?"

Blackwood tugged on one end of his mustache. "Oh, that?" he said, disinterested. "Well—"

Before he could respond further, his attention was pulled away by a servant, possibly a footman, standing nearby expectantly.

"Yes?" Blackwood said a little irritably.

The man bowed quickly. "I'm sorry to interrupt your evening, Dr. Blackwood, but someone delivered this."

He held out a white gloved hand and a folded piece of paper. The doctor harrumphed and took it.

"They said it was urgent, sir," the man explained.

"You'll excuse me," Blackwood said as he turned to read the note. After a moment, he looked back at the man who'd brought the note. He seemed almost angry. "Send for my carriage."

With another quick bow the man was gone. The doctor's face pinched as he re-read the note.

"Is everything all right?" Elizabeth asked.

The doctor looked up at her, distracted for a moment, and then nodded and tucked the note into his pocket. "Fine," he said. "Duty calls, I'm afraid."

He was lying. Elizabeth was sure of it.

He turned to face them properly and held out his hand. "A pleasure meeting you. If you'll come by the hospital, I'll be glad to discuss my work with you. I'm at London Hospital. Whitechapel."

She and Simon watched him go.

"Whitechapel," Elizabeth whispered and looked up at Simon.

"Curiouser and curiouser."

Just as Elizabeth was about to suggest they shove off and find George, and hopefully Druitt, she spotted George coming toward them through the crowd, alone.

"I'm sorry about that," he said. "I hope the doctor didn't bore you to death with his research."

"No, it was actually quite interesting," she said.

George looked at her blankly, as if he couldn't imagine such a thing, before shaking his head. "Well, I'm glad you thought so."

He craned his neck, searching the crowd. "There are some people I'd like you to meet. Americans actually," he said.

"Adding to your collection," Elizabeth said with a smile.

George laughed. "I think you'll like them. Interesting sorts. Ah, there."

He gestured for them to walk with him. The center of the ball-room was filled with couples dancing and so they skirted along the perimeter. It was beautiful. The light from the massive chandeliers, which had actual candles in them, was soft and inviting. There was even a fire burning in a large oversized hearth. The walls on the perimeters of the room were covered with huge portraits.

Eventually, they approached a couple who were admiring a painting of the Duke of Wellington, who looked positively resplendent in his snazzy red uniform.

When they reached them, George cleared his throat. "I'm sorry to interrupt, but these are the Crosses I mentioned."

He looked back toward Simon and Elizabeth as the couple turned around. "May I introduce you to Charles Graham and Katherine Vale?"

"Hello?"

Victor shifted in his chair and pulled his attention away from the conversation at the next table.

"I am not—" he started to say, expecting to see another of the usual prostitutes, tired and toothless, but was surprised to find a younger woman, tall, not exactly pretty, but attractive with blonde hair and sad blue eyes.

"Can I set with ye?" she asked with the classic singsong tones of Cornish accent.

He looked around the pub and it was packed by now. The chair at his table was one of the few left. Reluctantly, he nodded.

She smiled broadly. "Cheers," she said and sat down before he could change his mind. "Are ye new here?"

"Yes," he said and turned his attention to the rest of the bar. The last thing he wanted was to get involved in…anything.

"You're French!"

He glanced back at her and nodded again.

"I lived in Paris fer a bit. Beautiful," she said, her face dreamy with the memory. "I took to Paris, but it didn't take to me."

She laughed, and it wasn't bitter, but resigned.

"What's yer name?" she asked. "I'm…Marie. Marie Jeannette."

"Victor," he said, barely meeting her eyes, hoping she would get the hint.

"That's a nice name." She scooted her chair a little closer and finger walked her hand across the table until it landed on his. "Buy a girl a drink?"

Reluctantly, Victor followed the line of her arm up to her face. She was still young enough, still fresh enough to escape this life. She almost looked like a younger girl pretending to be grown up.

"How old are you?" he asked.

"Twenty-five."

He wasn't sure he believed her, but in the end, it didn't matter. Victor sighed and slid a penny across the table. "Buy yourself some food."

She looked down at the coin. "I'm cheap, but I'm not that—"

"I don't want anything."

She looked at him oddly, and before he could change his mind, swept the penny off the table and into her hand. For a moment, some sort of emotion filled her eyes, but she forced a cocky smile to her face.

She turned toward the door. "Billy," she said brightly, and with one last look at him, regret or confusion, Victor could not say, and she stood and hurried toward the young man who'd just come in.

He grabbed her about the waist and stole a kiss that she tried to half-heartedly squirm out of. Victor watched her for a moment and then put her out of his mind. He refocused on the task at hand.

Pizer snored loudly, still asleep at his table and probably wouldn't wake until morning. The rest of the crowd was winding up for a long night.

Another woman, this one with bright red hair, sidled up to his table, bumping into it as she did and laughing as his drink sloshed in its glass.

"Is this seat taken?" she slurred with a half-toothless grin.

"No," he said.

She pulled out the wooden chair and flopped down into it.

Victor stood. "They are both free," he said as he downed what was left of his beer. "Goodnight," he said to her shocked expression.

He left Ten Bells, almost managing not to look back at Marie as she sat on Billy's lap and laughed at something he said.

The streets were wet and a cold drizzle rolled down the back of his neck. He put on his cap and flipped up the collar of his coat. He looked down the dark street. Small gas flames struggled in the rain. Stepping off the curb, he started toward the next pub in line.

CHAPTER THIRTEEN

Elizabeth was sure she stopped breathing or all of the air had left the room, or both, as Katherine Vale stood in front them. Like a dolly zoom in a Hitchcock movie, the room around her seemed to blur and distort, moving past her while Vale stood highlighted and unmoving, unnatural.

She'd experienced this exact moment before. In an instant, Elizabeth was back in the salon of the Winter Palace in Cairo. She gripped Simon's arm.

"Hello," Vale said with a genuine smile and no hint of the crazy, maniacal murderer she would become in her violet eyes. Her eyes had always struck Elizabeth, not because of they were unusual or beautiful, but because they always seemed cold and soulless, like a serpent's.

But the woman looking at her with growing concern in them was anything but that. It took Elizabeth a moment to realize she was talking to her.

"I'm sorry," Elizabeth managed. "Hello."

This is not the same Katherine Vale, she reminded herself. Well, technically, it was the same one, but this one seemed almost... normal. The Vale Elizabeth knew had aged considerably from the twenty-something beauty in front her. Of course, twelve years in Bedlam and a lifetime of crazy did that to a person, but it was still a surprise. Like seeing a picture of Stalin as a boy in short pants.

This Vale was twenty years younger, and seemed bright and pleasant. And best of all, not trying to kill them. In fact, this Katherine Vale didn't even know who they were.

The realization let Elizabeth unclench a little and gather her senses. She smiled back. "Nice to meet you."

Simon shook hands with Charles Graham, the man Vale had spent years hunting. It felt odd to be face to face with them both, knowing what would come to pass. Katherine took Graham's arm and looked at him, not with the fiery vengeful hatred older Vale would have, but with love and adoration.

For his part, Graham looked strikingly like the photograph she'd seen. She'd somehow expected him to be much younger, like Vale. He looked to be nearly forty. All and all, he was nice looking, average height with brown hair and matching mustache. He smiled amiably as he shook Simon's hand.

George sighed and apologized as he was pulled away again.

"What did you think of the play?" Vale asked her.

Was that a loaded question, Elizabeth thought. "I enjoyed it," she said. "You?"

"I thought it was very good. I felt a little guilty going after what had happened, you know..."

Elizabeth stared at her, still processing that this was Katherine Vale.

"The murder," Vale said discreetly.

"Yes," Elizabeth said. "Of course."

"Curious business," Simon said.

"It is, isn't it?" Graham said, a head of excitement laced through his tone. "I'm sure you'll think me morbid, but I do think it's fascinating. What drives a man to do such things?"

Elizabeth knew that Graham's fascination for Jack the Ripper went far beyond polite conversation, if one could have polite conversation about a brutal murderer. He was the Council's foremost expert on the crimes.

She glanced over at Simon, who was politely listening to Graham, and wondered if he was thinking the same thing. They'd both been conflicted, for obvious reasons, about finding Graham and Vale. Elizabeth had looked for them, albeit somewhat half-heartedly. Secretly, she'd hoped they would never run into each other, that she and Simon could solve the mystery, stop the murder and never see Katherine Vale again. But the universe had something else in mind. And now that Graham was standing in front of them, a virtual encyclopedia of Ripperology, they'd be fools not to try enlist his help.

"I'm a bit of an amateur criminologist," Graham said modestly.

Vale leaned into his side. "He's brilliant."

"My wife's a reporter," Simon said, testing the waters.

She and Simon had discussed it before, and agreed that they would keep their true identities a secret, at least at first. The less *any* Katherine Vale knew about them the better.

Graham's eyes brightened. "Are you? That's unusual, isn't it? A woman as a reporter, I mean."

"I think it's wonderful," Vale said, giving Elizabeth that shared smile women do. It was all Elizabeth could do not to laugh.

"Oh, I agree," Graham said. "Good for you."

"I think there's a good story in it all," Elizabeth said.

Graham's eyes grew even brighter. "Oh, a very good story indeed."

A waiter appeared with a tray of champagne. They each took a glass and Elizabeth noticed that Vale winced as she took a step away with her drink.

"Are you all right?" she asked.

"I'm afraid, I'm a little clumsy," Vale explained. "Twisted my ankle a few days ago. So silly. You don't mind if I sit down for a few moments, do you?"

Elizabeth shook her head and Graham handed her the cane he'd been holding. Elizabeth had thought it was his, just an affectation, but Vale used it to hobble to a nearby settee.

"I thought I could do it," Vale apologized to Graham as he helped her into her seat.

"It's all right, dear. Too much, too soon."

Vale blushed, embarrassed, an emotion Elizabeth hadn't thought her even capable of. She smiled up at Elizabeth, obliged to offer an explanation now that she'd given them a show.

"I thought I could carry on, but I seem to have reached my limit." Her smile faltered and she reached a hand up to her temple.

"The headache again?" Graham asked, concerned, as he sat down next to her.

"It's nothing," she said, smiling bravely and holding out her hand for the glass of champagne he was holding for her. "I'm sure that will help."

As Graham gave it to her, Elizabeth noticed the small bandage on his palm.

"Did you have an accident, too?" she asked nodding toward his injury.

"Oh, no," he said. "Broken glass. We're quite the pair though, aren't we?"

Elizabeth looked to Simon who seemed to be weighing what, if anything, to do.

"There are doctors here," he said finally. "If you'd like me to—"

Vale shook her head slightly. "It's all right, really. It's going away already."

Was it a time travel headache? Heavens knew she'd had lulus the first few times she'd used the watch. This could even be Vale's first trip. As Elizabeth looked at her, she did have that slightly glassy-eyed look about her.

"When did you arrive?" Elizabeth asked. "In London, I mean."

Graham gave Vale one last concerned look and stood. "Just a few days ago. Took the *Augusta Victoria* from New York."

Elizabeth had to smile. It was fun being on the other side of a "time traveler's lie."

"And you?" he asked.

"The *Umbria*," Simon said without hesitation. "Cunard," he added as though that explained everything.

Apparently, to Graham, it did. He smiled and dipped his head once in deference and then glanced back at Vale.

"I think, perhaps I should take you back to the hotel, Katherine."

She looked like she was going to protest, but then nodded. "If you think that's best, Charles."

"No reason to overdo," he said, helping her up. "We're here for several months, after all."

He held out his hand to Simon. "Perhaps we'll run into each other again."

Simon nodded. "I'd like that," he managed with a straight face.

"I hope so," Vale said and then looked to Elizabeth. "I feel like such an outsider here."

Elizabeth knew the feeling, and her sudden empathy for Vale surprised her. She put it aside, but noticed she didn't feel the hatred she felt for older Vale for the woman standing in front of her.

"Where are you staying?" Simon said.

Graham smiled. "Hyde Park Hotel. Perhaps you're free for lunch this week?"

Simon looked at Elizabeth and then back to him. "I'm sure we can find time in our schedule for that."

"Very good," Graham said.

Vale wound her arm through his and gripped the cane with her other. "I'll see you soon then," she said to Elizabeth.

They said their goodbyes and watched Vale and Graham disappear into the crowd.

"I don't know about you," Elizabeth said, "but I could use some air."

Simon grunted in agreement. Once they'd made sure Vale and Graham had left for the evening, they found the French doors leading to one of the terraces on the second floor. The stones were wet, but the rain seemed to have moved on. The air was cool and heavy.

They walked over to the balustrade and Elizabeth took a deep breath. "That was…strange. She was so different," she said, thinking aloud. "It's hard to believe she becomes that…thing we left in San Francisco."

"Yes," he said, although he sounded distracted.

"Do you think it's a good idea, buddying up with them?" she asked.

Simon looked out into the park. "I don't trust her," he said finally, and cast a wan smile down at Elizabeth before continuing. "But I think considering Graham's expertise and the challenge before us, it would be foolish not to use every tool at our disposal."

Elizabeth looked out the same way Simon was, but all she could see the black of night. "Should we tell him who we are?"

Simon tugged on his ear. "I've been thinking about that. I doubt he'd share much in the way of, well, spoilers, if he thought we were merely curiosity seekers from 1888. Fellow Council members, however...."

Elizabeth frowned. "Even though this Katherine Vale doesn't know who we are or what sort of history we'll have together, it's unnerving to think we'd be working *with* her."

"Very," Simon agreed. "But they seem to come as a pair. I'm not sure we can tell Graham something and not expect him to tell her."

"Poor guy." Elizabeth put her hand down on the railing and then realized it was wet. "He has no idea what sort of woman he's really with."

Simon slipped his arm around her waist and pulled her toward him. "Love is blind."

Elizabeth looked nervously over at the doorway. Victorian etiquette didn't allow for much, or anything, in the way of PDAs. "Simon. The world is watching."

He sighed. "Then let's go back to the hotel. I think I've had enough of the world today."

ELIZABETH HATED BEING A prisoner—a prisoner to convention, to expectation, to her darn clothes. A lady of substance didn't venture out alone, but this lady was going to go nutso if she had to stay in the hotel for another minute.

Earlier that morning Simon had received an invitation from George Roxbury to join him at his club for lunch. At first, Simon had wanted to turn it down; the idea of being separated if—when—she corrected herself, when another of the time shifts occurred was terrifying. But in the end, they'd agreed that they wouldn't be able to remain together every minute of every day and do the investigating they needed to. Simon had reluctantly accepted George's invitation, but only after securing a promise from Elizabeth that she wouldn't wander off.

That had been two hours and ten cucumber sandwiches ago. Elizabeth just couldn't sit there waiting for him to come back if there was something, anything, she could be doing to help. If the only thing she could manage that wouldn't draw too much attention was a quiet walk that happened to pass near Vale and Graham's hotel where she might be able to spy on Vale a little, then so be it. She left her small corner table at the hotel's cafe and started for the front desk.

Ever since the party, Elizabeth couldn't get Vale out of her mind. They might be there to find Jack the Ripper, but older Vale had chosen this point in time for a reason—presumably to alter not just the course of history, but her own history. And that meant all of this had something to do with her younger self, that some action or lack of action would change what happened to her. And whatever that was, she wouldn't learn spit about it just sitting in her hotel room.

She asked the hotel clerk for pen and paper and started to write a note to Simon letting him know where she'd gone. She'd probably strike out and be back before he even knew she was gone, but—

"Hello," a familiar voice said.

Elizabeth kept herself from jumping at the sound and felt the same chill she always did at the sound of that woman's voice. Quickly composing herself, she turned to find a smiling Katherine Vale.

"I was hoping I'd catch you," Vale continued.

Elizabeth managed a confused, but amiable smile. "Oh?"

Vale smiled back and touched her arm in a casual, friendly gesture. "I'm sorry," she said. "George told me where you were staying. I hope you don't mind."

Elizabeth shook her head and put down the pen. "No, of course not."

"Good, I didn't want you to think I was stalking you or…"

Elizabeth laughed and hoped it didn't sound as strained as it felt. "I'm glad to see you. Your ankle's feeling better?"

"Oh, much. Thank you."

They stood in awkward silence for a moment.

"I'm not keeping you from anything, am I?" Vale asked, clearly hoping the answer was no.

It was strange to see her so unsure, so needy.

"Not at all," Elizabeth said. "Is something wrong?"

Vale shook her head. Then she took a step closer and lowered her eyes in mild embarrassment. "It's just that Charles is off doing things today and I, well, I have two tickets."

She pulled two cardboard tickets out of her small handbag. "I don't suppose…?"

Elizabeth tried to read the tickets, but the print was too small. "Another show?"

"Not quite," Vale said with a slight blush. "It's a sort of a talk really. Have you heard of the Theosophical Society?"

Boy, had she. The Theosophical Society and its members were part of every occult studies student's first class. The founders had taken eastern and western religions and combined them with mysticism and metaphysics to create an occult-based philosophy that was firmly located on the edge of crazy town.

"No," Elizabeth said. "It sounds interesting though."

Katherine Vale's eyes lit up with excitement. "It's fascinating. Charles thinks it's nonsense, of course, but when I heard that Madame Blavatsky herself was here in London and giving a lecture…"

Madame Blavatsky was a renowned psychic or charlatan, or both, depending on who you asked. And that was an all-too familiar persona, Elizabeth thought with a sinking feeling.

"It's a bit like spiritualism," Vale explained.

Slowly, pieces were falling into place—disturbing bit by disturbing bit. She had spent the better part of the day wondering how this seemingly charming and open young woman had become the monstrosity they'd last seen in Council headquarters. Was this the start of it? Was Blavatsky the genesis for Madame Petrovka, the identity Vale would assume when she escaped Bedlam?

The thought horrified her, but she kept her face placid.

"I know it's not for everyone," Vale said, misreading Elizabeth's expression. "I'm not sure I believe any of it honestly, but it is intriguing, isn't it? The idea that there are answers, something beyond all of this?"

She laughed at herself, embarrassed, and put the tickets back in her bag. "It's all right if you don't want to go. I just thought—"

Know your enemy, Elizabeth thought and rushed to accept the invite before it disappeared. "I'd like to," she said, "very much."

Vale grinned broadly, surprised and pleased, and pushed out a relieved sigh. "Wonderful."

Sun Tzu would be proud. Simon, however…

Elizabeth held up a finger. "I just need to write my husband a note," she said as she picked up the pen she'd left on the clerk's counter. And, she added silently, hope his head doesn't explode when he reads it.

Chapter Fourteen

"**A**BSURD."

Simon gritted his teeth. Again. Lord Stansbury was the exact sort of pompous ass he usually relished in dismantling, but under the circumstances, Simon had to keep his mouth shut. He couldn't burn any social bridges just yet. The result meant he had to sit and listen to idiots like Stansbury.

He'd endured inane celebrations of feats like Lord Walsingham's shooting of over one thousand grouse in a single day. Nearly all of the men at the club had found that particularly impressive. For his part, the allure of hunting for sport always eluded Simon, and in particular events like Walsingham's, which meant only to impress. But then that was part and parcel of life amongst the gentry—a perpetual pissing contest.

To make matters worse, the smell of curry powder in the dining room was nearly overwhelming. Simon had eaten some terrible curry at school, but the fare at today's Savile Club special "oriental" luncheon was truly ghastly. England had taken a great many things from India during its reign there, but Simon was certain the chef was not one of them.

Couple that with a shockingly ignorant screed against Indians, their history and religion, and Simon was very much ready to hit someone.

"These inferiors need their honorable masters," Lord Stansbury intoned. It was an all too familiar rationale. "I cannot imagine the state of the subcontinent without the British Raj. Absolute chaos. The Empire does what it can though."

Several of the men at the table agreed with requisite humphs, the lone exception being Charles Graham. Simon hadn't expected to see him at the club, but his appearance was a welcome one. Not only might it provide an opportunity for Simon to reveal himself and see what Graham knew about the killer, but he seemed to have even less tolerance for nonsense than Simon did.

"The empire might consider giving them back their sovereignty," Graham said as he took a sip of wine. "We're rather enjoying it in America."

Stansbury grunted dismissively and turned to Blackwood. Simon hid his smile. Graham caught his eye and gave him a mildly, amused shrug.

"So, Doctor," Simon said, hoping to turn the conversation to a more profitable subject. "I do hope you'll be available this week. My wife is very much looking forward to it."

"Is she mad?" Stansbury said bluntly.

Simon coughed. "I beg your pardon?"

Stansbury shrugged. "The doctor's expertise…"

"No," Blackwood said quickly. "An interview. Mrs. Cross works for an American newspaper. Wants to do a feature on my work."

"You shouldn't encourage that sort of…behavior, Robert," Stansbury said.

Simon felt his blood pressure rise again. "And what behavior is that?"

Stansbury fixed him with his most disapproving glare. "Moving beyond her place."

"Her place?" Simon said. He knew that misogyny was typical of the time, but this was just too much.

"It's quite well-known that women are inferior both physically and mentally," Stansbury said. He turned to Dr. Blackwell. "Surely, you've found that to be the case in your studies."

The doctor nodded, but hedged. "Women are more fragile, yes."

Graham shook his head and frowned. "Maybe it's because I'm an American and a little more progressive—"

Stansbury snorted.

Graham continued, "But I couldn't disagree more."

"I would expect no less from you," Stansbury said in a dismissive tone. "Your women are practically as wild as those savages you pretend to tame."

He dabbed the corners of his mouth with a napkin. "No, women are best kept in the background of politics and industry."

"They are not well-suited to those tasks," Blackwood agreed. "Motherhood and companionship—"

Graham caught Simon's eye and cleared his throat. "Just so I'm clear," he said turning to Stansbury. "You think women are inferior and should stay out of messy things like politics."

Stansbury inclined his head.

"Forgive me," Graham continued, "but that seems an odd position for a man whose country is led by a woman. Or do you think the Queen is inferior and frail of mind as well?"

Stansbury spluttered. "That's entirely different."

"Is it?" Graham said, clearly enjoying Stansbury's discomfiture. He turned to Simon and added, "Perhaps your wife can add that to the story."

Simon smiled, impressed with the deft way Graham had maneuvered Stansbury.

The older man glared at them both and then pushed back his chair. With a final indignant humph he left the table. Blackwood looked almost apologetic as he stood and followed, leaving Graham and Simon alone at the table.

Graham smiled and raised his glass. "Like shooting grouse."

Simon chuckled and raised his glass of Claret. He was beginning to like Graham very much.

Finally, the luncheon part of the lunch was over and the men retired to one of the smoking rooms.

Like so many others, the club was a relatively small, intimate affair in what was once a private residence in the heart of Mayfair. Several hundred members paid several hundred pounds to escape their wives and their lives. Two of the three stories had been converted for gaming, socializing, reading, eating, drinking, smoking and generally being anywhere other than home or office.

The smoking room was decorated much as the rest, dark woods and lighter ceilings, leather chairs and crystal chandeliers. Decadent, but not gaudy. It was the epitome of the wealthy bachelor's home without a trace of a woman's touch.

The notion turned Simon's thoughts to Elizabeth. He wondered how she was faring back the hotel. God knew what trouble she'd manage to get into left to her own devices, he thought with a smile. Given their circumstances, he hated to be away from her, even for these few hours, but they would have to do that and more if they were to solve this mystery.

Simon carefully lingered on the periphery of the smoking room as everyone found their place, making sure he could float freely to the area George and Druitt occupied. He'd spent a little time with Druitt before lunch, but not nearly enough to get a feel for the man.

Finally, Simon settled into a large leather chair opposite them and listened, letting them carry the conversation. Druitt seemed an unlikely suspect. He was well-spoken, amiable, if a little melancholic. Apparently, he was quite the cricket player and enjoyed lively political debate. Although, when he was alone with George, Simon realized, the topics shifted to more subdued things, literature and the arts. The two spoke at length about the Romantics, Keats and Shelly. Hardly the stuff Simon imagined to be coursing through Jack the Ripper's mind.

It was difficult to imagine Druitt committing such heinous acts. But then it was difficult to imagine any man doing the things that had been and would be done. Although, he thought as he shifted his attention to Dr. Blackwood, who sat nearby, some seemed more likely than others.

"Virginia's condition is unchanged," he said as he took a sip of brandy and then sat back in his chair, lacing his hands across his belly.

A tall thin man named Morgan, who'd been sitting at the far end of the table during lunch, looked at the doctor sympathetically. "I'm sorry to hear that, Robert."

Blackwood grunted. "I had hoped for improvement with the last treatment, but…"

"Well, if anyone can find a cure," Morgan said, raising his glass in salute. "I'd be dashed if Claire suffered so."

The doctor grunted again, his hands bouncing slightly on his belly

"Are you married?" Morgan said, politely folding Simon into the conversation. "Cross, isn't it?"

"Yes," Simon. "On both counts."

"She's a reporter," Blackwood said in with the arch of an amused and slightly disapproving brow.

Morgan, if he felt the same way, didn't show it. "A lady reporter? The times are changing, aren't they?"

Simon dipped his head in agreement.

"Too quickly for me, I'm afraid," Morgan said and then held up a hand to ward off any misconception. "Not that I'm against progress, mind you. It's just that I feel as though the world is a raging river and I'm stuck on the shore, unable to swim."

He gave a small self-deprecating laugh. "That's never been a problem for you though, has it, Robert? Always at the forefront."

Blackwood smiled modestly, or at least what he seemed to consider modestly. Simon wasn't sure the man was capable of it in any sincere form. "Science, by its very nature, must advance or it ceases to be relevant."

"Quite so," Morgan agreed.

"The treatments you mentioned," Simon said. "Are those part of your work?"

Blackwood shook his head and thoughtfully twisted the end of his mustache. "No, no. For my wife. She is an invalid."

Simon was surprised at the offhand way the doctor said it. The thought of Elizabeth suffering from such a fate made his stomach tense.

"I'm sorry."

Blackwood sighed and Simon could see the frustration in his eyes.

"Has she been ill long?" Simon asked.

"Several years."

Morgan leaned forward. "It must be terribly difficult. On both of you."

Blackwood nodded. "It is for her, of course."

"She was a lovely girl," Morgan said to Simon and then added hastily, "still is, of course. I didn't mean—"

Blackwood waved the apology away. Abruptly, he seemed to have had his fill of the subject and checked his watch. He closed it with a snap before sliding it back into his vest pocket.

"I'm afraid I must return to hospital," he said as he stood.

"Surely you can have—" Morgan began.

"No," Blackwood said abruptly. The shift in his demeanor was abrupt and disconcerting.

He turned to Simon. "Cross."

Simon nodded. "Doctor."

With that Blackwood bowed and took his leave.

"You'll have to forgive him," Morgan said as Blackwood left. "It's terrible what they've been through. She was so vibrant and now…" He trailed off and shook his head.

Simon nodded. "What happened to her?"

"Dashed if I know. She just took ill one day. And I'm afraid, she's been in declining health ever since. In and out of hospital, traveling looking for all sorts of cures. Man worships her. Must be terribly lonely for him."

Simon nodded and tucked that bit of information away. Lonely enough to drive him to visit other women, he wondered. The man did work in Whitechapel as well.

Issues with women, both at home and in general. Druitt might be less appealing as a suspect, but the doctor was looking more and more interesting. Although, it was a rather large leap to assume he was serial killer.

Simon sighed and took a sip of his port. At least the wine was good.

Graham, who had been sitting with a man Simon hadn't spoken to, rose and walked over to the window. He stood there looking out at the city and Simon excused himself to join him.

Graham turned to him and smiled in greeting before turning back to the view. "It's a wonderful city. So…alive."

Simon had to agree. Although London was filled with personal ghosts and ambivalent memories, he did love the city. Today, miraculously, the sun was shining. But it would set and the darkness would come again and in just a few days, Ripper would strike again.

As loath as Simon was to ask for help, after the debacle of their last foray into Whitechapel, he knew he'd be a fool to ignore the help Graham could provide. Not to mention that they'd inevitably run into each other during their investigations and their fascination with Ripper would be hard to explain away. Even with Elizabeth cast as a nosy reporter, there was a limit to what they could learn if they didn't tell Graham the truth.

Victor would no doubt not approve of his choice to involve Graham. It was a risk, but one Simon deemed worth the taking. And now, it seemed, was as good a time as any to broach the subject.

Simon lowered his voice. "Do you think we could we talk privately?"

Graham seemed surprised, but agreed.

Simon turned back to the main room. Everyone was deeply involved in discussion. He doubted they'd even be missed. Having remembered passing a small reading salon adjacent to the smoking room, Simon gestured for Graham to follow him.

Once he and Graham were in the salon, he closed the doors behind them.

Graham stood in the middle of the room and looked at him with concern. "Is something wrong?"

"You could say that," Simon said.

Graham watched him expectantly. Simon reached into his pocket and held out the watch in the palm of his hand.

Graham arched an eyebrow. "The Council?"

"Yes," Simon said as he put the watch back in his pocket.

Graham laughed and ran a hand through his hair. "I'll admit, I didn't see that one coming. Why did they send you? Has something gone wrong?"

Simon knew he had to tread carefully here. "I need your help. There has been an incident."

Graham laughed again. "You're definitely with the Council. Why speak when double-speak will do? You sound like Travers."

"There's no need to be insulting," Simon said with a small smile. "I am sorry though. I can tell you some of it, but…"

Graham frowned, but then sighed and waved a hand. "It's all right. I understand. They have their reasons, I suppose."

"It's complicated."

Graham chuckled to himself. "Isn't it always?"

His attention fell on a nearby drink cart. "Sherry?" he asked as he moved to pour himself one.

"No, thank you."

Graham poured himself a glass. He turned back to Simon and took a sip. "Sweet. A small vice," he said with a smile and gestured toward two chairs.

Simon sat down in one of the leather wingbacks and waited for Graham to do the same.

"So, what can you tell me?" Graham asked as he put his glass aside.

Simon leaned back in his chair. "Not much, I'm afraid. Our mission is…related to the Jack the Ripper case."

Graham nodded. "I assumed as much."

"I can't go into any specifics, but it's very important that we find him," Simon said. "Do you know who he is?"

Graham opened his mouth and then paused. His brow furrowed. "No, I'm ashamed to say. The foremost expert and I don't know the one thing that really matters."

Simon's heart sank. He'd hoped it would be simple, but he should have known nothing related to the Council was ever simple. "You didn't go to the crime scene?"

Graham put a hand to his neck and rubbed the skin beneath his chin. "I did. Kat had turned her ankle and so she stayed behind. I was even there quite early, hid in alleyway. But, I'm afraid, from my vantage point, I couldn't get a good look at him, couldn't see his face."

He shook his head and smiled apologetically. "I wanted to. I'd dreamt of that moment so many times, but when it happened, when I had the opportunity….I was…afraid. I'm not ashamed to admit. When I recovered myself enough, it was too late."

He looked down at his hands and rubbed hard at his palm with his thumb. "I'd read about it so many times, I thought I was prepared." He looked up helplessly. "It was horrific."

Simon could imagine, and he felt for the man, but there wasn't time to dwell on any of that. "You couldn't make out anything about him?"

"He was a good thirty feet away and with his back turned."

Simon nodded, disappointed.

Graham looked at him curiously. "You didn't go yourself?"

Simon grunted. "We tried. Fate had other ideas."

Graham picked up his sherry glass and looked into it. "You must have some theories though as to who it might be. You don't strike me as the sort to come unprepared."

"A few suspects," Simon conceded.

Graham took a sip. "Any in particular?"

"It's early days, but I have to admit, Dr. Blackwood is near the top."

Graham pointed a finger in the air and set his glass down. "Blackwood. Now, that is interesting. And," he said, as if seeing something for the first time, "the man I saw was roughly his height. Difficult to say from that distance, but I do think the man's clothes were far finer than the so-called eye witness accounts would have us believe. I'm assuming you've read them."

"I have, although," he admitted, "I did not have long to study them."

Graham smiled. "That's all right. I've got it all up here," he said, tapping his temple. "The only person who knows as much as I do about the case is the murderer himself."

"Good," Simon said.

"I'm not sure it's related, of course," Graham said, "but I did notice a coach that night. I thought it a bit odd to see one so late at night there, but it was several blocks from the scene."

"Can you describe it?"

Graham laughed. "It was a coach. Black." He frowned and squinted as if trying to see a memory more clearly. "I think it had yellow wheels. I wasn't very close to it, but..."

"Something to consider," Simon said.

Simon was disappointed he hadn't learned more about the Ripper's identity, but at least it was a comfort to know that he could work with Graham moving forward. Between them, surely they'd be able to discover the identity. But there was still one problem.

He had to tread carefully here. "It might," Simon continued, "be better if no one else knew about Elizabeth's and my involvement."

"Who would I tell?" Graham said. It was only after Simon's pointed look that he connected the dots. "Oh, *no one?*"

He pursed his lips in thought and at least seemed to be considering it.

"Katherine," Simon said. "I have to ask—is this her first mission? She seems rather young."

Graham cleared his throat. "Yes, it is. I recruited her actually. Found her at a university."

Simon smiled, but didn't mention the parallel to his finding Elizabeth. That was, after all, where the similarities between them ceased.

"She's a bit green," Graham said, "I'll grant you that. And hasn't taken to it quite as I'd expected, but I don't like the idea of keeping something from her. We're...involved."

Simon practically bit his tongue to keep from saying what he wanted to. *Dear Lord, man, the woman is a psychotic; run as far and as fast as you can.* Knowing how he would react to something like that if their roles were reversed, Simon kept on a more subtle tack.

"Obviously, I can't keep you from telling her, but the nature of our mission is delicate. It requires a steady hand. Her inexperience... She could put us all at risk without even realizing it."

Graham's frown deepened. He started to speak when a knock on the door interrupted him.

The door opened and the house steward, a tall, thin hawk-nosed man, appeared there and bowed. "I'm sorry to interrupt, Sir Simon, but there is a...boy here to see you."

The way he said boy made it clear he considered it a generous appellation.

"Says he has a message for you," the steward continued. "I tried to take it from him, but he insists on giving it you personally."

Simon nodded and stood. "Thank you."

"Trouble?" Graham asked.

It was either from Elizabeth or Victor; neither bode well. "Probably."

The steward escorted them downstairs to the servants' entrance at the back of the club. Freddie stood at the bottom of the steps, staring up admiringly at the house.

When he saw Simon, he took off his cap and dug a note out of his pocket. Wiping his running nose with one hand, he held out the note to Simon with the other. "From the missus."

"Do not touch anything," the steward said from the top of the stairs.

Freddie looked at him unflinchingly and rubbed his gooey hand up and down the wrought iron railing.

Graham chuckled and interceded as the steward strode forward to discipline the boy.

"It's all right," Graham said, putting himself between them. "We can handle it from here."

The steward narrowed his eyes in warning at the boy and then went back inside.

Simon took the note and read it. Damn that woman. He should have known she wouldn't just sit still. He was sure she hadn't passed a day in her life waiting for anything.

With a sigh, he dipped into his pocket, took out a coin, and gave it to Freddie. "No reply."

Freddie put his cap back on. "Right, sir."

With one more defiant lift of his chin at the grand house, he hurried off down the street back to his post at the hotel.

"Trouble?" Graham asked again.

Simon sighed and refolded the note. "It's from my wife."

"I take that as a yes."

Simon looked at him questioningly.

"You're not the first married man to have that look on his face."

Simon nodded. "It seems my wife and your Katherine have gone to see a presentation."

"Blavatsky," Graham said with a snort. "I told her that was nonsense."

Simon tucked the note into his pocket and looked around for a cab before turning back to Graham. "Not a believer?"

"I prefer my fiction in fiction," Graham said.

Simon had to agree with that assessment, at least where Blavatsky was concerned. But Madame Blavatsky and her worship of Lucifer, among other things, were the least of his worries. Right now, Elizabeth was out there alone with something far worse—Katherine Vale.

CHAPTER FIFTEEN

Victor's stomach rumbled, but for once, not because he was hungry. Just the opposite. He was too full. He'd had enough of nearly rotten fish and very stale bread and had walked to Cheapside to get a real meal. It hadn't exactly been the stuff of kings, but it would do him well. He would live among the poor, but if he were to keep his wits and his strength, he would need more than the pubs and the carts of Bishopsgate and Whitechapel could provide.

On the way back, he passed people scraping out a living in any way they could. Board men wore large sandwich boards advertising everything from cigars and soaps to bawdy entertainments. They were taunted by street urchins as they walked back and forth. Men painted cards and placards for stores and carts. Women sold flowers and fruit and shoelaces. A man caned chairs and another sold blood purifiers and healing ointments. If they were lucky, they would make just enough to survive.

They came in droves from the country in search of jobs and found only desolation. London was overflowing with people, like too many fish in a barrel. It was too loud, too noisy, too crowded.

How he yearned to finish this and go back home where there was air to breathe and no one to bother him.

It would not last though, he knew. Eventually, he would find the quiet as unbearable as this. Everywhere was the same in the end. No matter how the world outside changed, the man he was did not. Travers would call and he would go. Until the day he could not, and then he would finally find peace.

Victor stepped off the curb and into the street without looking, jumping back out of the wagon's way just in time. He laughed to himself. Apparently, today was not that day. Although, he thought with his customary cheer, the day was still young.

He turned up Shepherd Street toward the Ten Bells when he noticed a disturbance across the street. Two young men, one barely a man at all, were having what they thought was fun at the expense of an older couple. Picking on the weak and vulnerable was an amusement that never seemed to go out of style. Two of the men stood on either side of a wobbly old man, who could barely stand without his cane. They pushed him back and forth between them like a toy. The woman was too weak and too afraid to help, her basket of small wares—cotton, ribbon and bits of tape spilled onto the pavement at her feet.

And no one cared.

People passed by because it was not their problem. They had more than enough problems of their own without finding new ones that offered them nothing but risk. And so the weak and the vulnerable were preyed upon. So it was and so it would always be.

It was not his problem either and yet he felt himself crossing the street and calling out to them.

"That is enough," he said.

Only one of the men even bothered to notice him. The other kept on playing with his toy, like a spoiled child. Spoiled children needed to be taught manners.

"I said that was enough," Victor repeated, this time reaching out and pushing one of the men aside.

He stumbled back in surprise. His comrade looked at Victor, not in fear, as it would have been wise to do, but in petulant anger. So very spoiled.

"What's it to you?" he demanded.

Victor ignored him and turned to the poor old man who was struggling to stand without the aid of his cane. "Are you all right?"

The old man started to answer, but the other interrupted.

"I said—"

Victor's hand struck out like a coiled snake. His fingers bit into the sides of the man's throat, cutting off the rest of whatever idiocy he had to offer and whatever air he needed to breath.

The man gasped and clawed helplessly against Victor's hand.

"You have said enough," Victor said, tightening his grip for emphasis.

He looked over his shoulder at the other man. He was in a state of shock over the sudden change in their fortune and stood dumbly watching.

Victor turned back to the man in his grip. "You will not bother these people again. Do you understand?"

He waited, and finally the man managed a small nod. Victor released him and he stumbled backwards, gasping for breath. His friend, freed from his stupor, moved to his side.

They both glared at him, but the fear was there now. A good healthy dose of fear.

Victor feinted a step forward and they both flinched and then turned and ran off down the street. When Victor turned around the old woman was helping the man pick up his cane.

"Thank you," she said in a thick Polish accent. "They have been bothering me for days. My husband came to help, but..."

The old man stood as straight and tall as his bent body would allow.

Victor nodded at him with respect. "A man must stand by his wife."

The older man looked up at him with a hint of pride, even though embarrassment and anger still colored his cheeks.

"I don't have much," the woman said, as she gathered her bits and pieces and put them back into her basket. She held out a piece of blue ribbon, the sort that you might put into a little girl's hair.

The memory came unbidden and unwanted. Juliette.

Victor closed his eyes briefly and then shook his head. The woman held it out further, her expression entreating him to accept it.

It was like a knife in his heart, but he took it. He felt the smooth fabric between his thumb and forefinger.

"Thank you," he said and then cleared his throat and put the small piece of ribbon in his pocket.

The old woman smiled at him, and for a moment he wondered if she knew. It was ridiculous, of course, and he pushed the thought away.

The woman turned back to her husband and together they walked down the street. Victor watched them for a moment and then, feeling suddenly foolish, he turned away and started back toward home.

ELIZABETH'S EYES GLAZED OVER. She wasn't sure what she'd been expecting, but this wasn't it.

Blavatsky was just as she'd imagined her—small, stout, forceful. But she hadn't realized the program was not for beginners, but devotees. Half of what the woman said, and that was being generous, made no sense to Elizabeth at all.

"The Secret Doctrine is the accumulated Wisdom of the Ages, and its cosmogony alone is the most stupendous and elaborate system. Even in the exotericism of the Puranas."

What on earth did that mean? Elizabeth had no idea. She was sure most of the people in the audience had no idea either, but none of them would dare show it.

Spiritualism had taken some lumps recently. Too many frauds caught out, but Blavatsky was more than just a mere psychic; she was the center of a movement, a philosophy that, judging from the crowd, was growing every day. And why not? Who didn't want to know the secrets of the universe? It had been a compelling selling point for millennia.

The little Russian woman, complete with babushka and hard weathered face, stood center stage in the small auditorium and commanded every eye in the house. The thrust of the presentation was to announce the near completion of her second magnum opus, *The Secret Doctrine*, dictated to her by Mahatmas, a sort of ascended master or spiritual being that had chosen her to bring forth the wisdom of the age. Soon to be available by Random House for $14.95.

As near as Elizabeth could tell, her version of theosophy was a mashup of just about every known religion, some good old-fashioned occultism and a hefty dose of esotericism. She professed knowledge of the seven races of man which included not only Atlantians, but Aryans. All and all the entire experience was giving Elizabeth a headache.

Katherine Vale, on the other hand, was enraptured. It was an odd and disturbing thing to see. The woman sitting next to her was, for all intents and purposes, fairly normal. Sane. Kind. But whether it was a moment that changed her or a seed that grew in the manure they were both listening to, something changed her. Elizabeth hadn't thought she was capable of feeling compassion for Katherine Vale. But in that auditorium, as she saw the woman who was and knew the woman who she would be, Elizabeth felt pity for her.

Suddenly, the room erupted into applause and Elizabeth realized Blavatsky was finished. Vale clapped loudly and turned to Elizabeth, her eyes full of wonder.

"Amazing, wasn't it?"

"It was a lot to take in," Elizabeth managed.

Katherine's smile broadened. "Yes. There's some literature at the door that might help."

Elizabeth smiled politely and then followed Katherine toward the exit. A man at a small table handed out pamphlets. Katherine took two and handed Elizabeth one.

"I think this—"

"Elizabeth."

Elizabeth flinched. She knew that particular "Elizabeth" and it was one that was relieved, but not happy. Slowly, she turned to see Simon and, to her surprise, Charles Graham.

"Hi," she said.

Simon started to say something, but thought better of it. Whatever it had been, his frown changed into the sort of smile that melted her heart. The one that said, his world was set right again just because she was in it and nothing else mattered.

She took a step toward him and laid her hand on his chest. "I didn't mean to worry you, but…" she said casting a glance at Vale who was already enmeshed in conversation with Graham.

Simon nodded his understanding and took her hand in his.

"I've told you how I feel about this," Graham said.

Vale ducked her head and then cast Elizabeth an embarrassed glance. "I don't see the harm in it. And I have my own mind."

Graham was clearly frustrated, but forced a smile on his face. "Of course, you do. As it should be. I just," he added as he took hold of her elbow, "worry about you."

The gesture and words had the desired effect and Vale's pique dropped away. "I know," she said softly, intimately, before seeming to remember they were not alone.

She smiled a bit shyly and then started to pull on her gloves. "So, how was the club?"

Graham gently tapped the thumb side of his fist against his chest twice and grimaced. "Curry."

Vale laughed lightly. "Anything exciting happen?"

Graham cast a look at Simon before responding with a shake of his head. "No, nothing out of the ordinary."

Elizabeth looked up at Simon, trying to suss out what that little exchange meant. Simon kept his eyes on Graham, caught his gaze once more and gave a quick, almost imperceptible nod of acknowledgement.

Graham turned and stuck out his hand. "Been a pleasure, Cross. I'll keep you updated if I should learn anything that might be helpful with your business venture."

Simon shook his hand and thanked him.

Vale came over to Elizabeth. "I hope we can do this again soon."

"I'm sure we will," Elizabeth said.

Graham tipped his hat, and he and Vale wound their way out of the auditorium.

"What was that all about?" Elizabeth asked as she watched them go.

"Progress, I hope. Progress."

CHAPTER SIXTEEN

VICTOR ROLLED ONTO HIS side and his arm fell against the empty bed. He groaned as he came awake. Was she up again checking on Juliette? The fever was low. She was such a worrier.

He opened his eyes and his breath caught.

The room was dark and foreign. He sat up in bed, his heart beating faster now, his mind fully awake. Where was she?

Where was *he*?

"Emilie?"

There was no answer.

He pushed aside the covers, and they felt wrong in his hand. Rough and damp.

"Emelie!" he said again, his voice rising with the fear that started to clutch his heart.

He bumped into a small chair and it fell to the floor. Where *was* he? This was not their home. He strode over to the doorway, his eyes now adjusted to the dark and he pulled it open—a dimly lit hallway and stairs. What was going on here?

He turned back into the room and heard a noise outside his window. He hurried to it and saw two men driving a horse-drawn cart down a cobblestone street. His hands gripped the frame and he tried to think. He'd been home. Juliette was…

Juliette.

He squeezed his eyes shut as she slipped away and became only memory.

Clenching his jaw against the emotion that made him tremble, he took in a deep breath. He was in London. 1888 London, for the Council. Emilie and Juliette were gone.

Victor straightened and opened his eyes to see the dull, dingy window and the world outside. It was another event, but this one had cut straight to his heart. It was like losing them again.

He walked back over to the bed and sat down heavily, the mattress giving under his weight. For the others, losing themselves into the past was horrible, frightening, but for him, it was the opposite. The cruelty lay in coming back.

It had been all at once foreign and familiar. The feeling of being whole, of being happy. He'd wasted so much time with them. If only he'd known what was to come.

He laughed at his own foolishness. His past, although it lingered in him, was gone. They were gone. And he was just a shadow.

He pulled a hand down over his face and scrubbed his chin and then looked around the sad little room. Run down, dirty, dark. It suited him now. This was his life. It took darkness to fight darkness, and he would do so until he had no breath. Maybe that would be today.

He looked toward the soot-stained window and saw the faintest hint of light. He sat there until dawn, but the sun did not come up. Rain came instead and the dull gray night became a dull gray day.

Victor walked among the crowd that lined Old Montague Street early Thursday morning. Rain showers had come and gone and come again, leaving the streets thick with sludge. It was just before eight in the morning and despite their hangovers and their jobs, nearly everyone in the neighborhood showed for the spectacle of Mary Ann Nichols' funeral procession.

Most funerals in Whitechapel were simple affairs. Death was a common occurrence and no money was wasted that could be spent on the living. Word had gotten out that Nichols' father and estranged husband were footing the bill for a not-quite lavish, but respectable, funeral. And so the people who knew her, ignored her, and had never heard of her all lined the streets for a glimpse of something out of the ordinary, something to talk about that night in the pub while they wondered when or if the murderer would strike again.

The costermongers and peddlers were out, working the crowd, selling apples, roasted nuts, ham sandwiches, coffee and ginger beer. It wasn't quite the Queen's Jubilee, but where there was a crowd, there was a penny to be made.

The people milled about waiting and Victor scanned the crowd. He'd already come to know dozens of the faces. He saw several of the women from the pubs he'd frequented, including several of Ripper's next victims who stood huddled together in the rain, oblivious to what awaited them. The only thing worse than knowing he could do nothing to stop it, was knowing what he would have to do when the time came.

Elizabeth Stride and Annie Chapman shared some secret between them and laughed. Marie appeared and ducked under the cover of a tarp that partially sheltered a store front. He felt the urge well inside him to act, but he was just an observer, he reminded himself. Stand and watch.

A man dashed across the street and slipped in muck, falling face first into the mire. The crowd laughed, delighted, as he slipped again and wiped the mud from his face.

Near the corner, leaning against a lamppost, was John Pizer. He'd left his leather apron at home this time, and he struggled to light a pipe in the drizzle.

Victor recognized a few other men from the pubs, and one he'd only seen old photos of, George Lusk. He took off his black bowler hat and shook the rain off while he patiently waited with the others. Victor knew that Lusk would soon form the Whitechapel Vigilance Committee when the police efforts fell flat. He'd also be the unlucky recipient of a piece of bloody kidney in the mail courtesy of Jack the Ripper. With it would be a note explaining that he only sent half because he'd fried and eaten the other. Although many believed it to be a poor joke, a taunt sent by someone else, it was another part of the Ripper case that added to the legend. But Victor was not here to find a legend. He was here to find a man. And that man was somewhere near.

Under the sanctuary of a large black umbrella stood Vale and Graham. Well dressed and out of place among the rest who'd come to watch. It was the first time he'd seen them here. He studied her face, but there was little resemblance to the she-devil he'd captured. She was, he supposed, a beautiful woman, but hard, even in youth.

Next to her, Charles Graham looked exactly like the photograph Travers had shown him. Average looking, average height, average in every way except intellectually—the perfect person to blend into a crowd in any time. Graham keenly studied the people around him, probably doing exactly what Victor was, wondering who among them was their man.

A murmur from the east end of the street pulled Victor's attention away. It grew louder and he could just make out a driver and wagon coming near. A hush fell over the crowd.

Black horses with black plumes led the way. The ostrich feathers were wet and stuck up like matted sticks from the horses' bridles. The driver, dressed in fine black clothes, soaked to the bone, kept his eyes forward and his pace measured as he drove the cart-like hearse past. On the sled behind it, rested a polished elm casket, glistening in the rain. It was followed by two black mourning coaches. Inside them, Victor could just make out the silhouettes of three men in black top hats, undoubtedly her family—father, husband and son.

The small procession passed by in silence; the only sound the horses' hooves, the wooden wheels against the cobblestone street and the tapping sound of the rain as it beat down on the brim of his cap.

Once the carriages were past, the crowd livened again, and began to chatter and disperse. Victor waited and watched. Ignorant of what was to come, the people of Whitechapel went on with their lives, not knowing how much would change in just two days at the sharp end of a knife.

LONDON HOSPITAL ALWAYS MADE Elizabeth think of Joseph Merrick, the Elephant Man. He'd been paraded as a spectacle in penny gaff entertainment, a low-brow theater show, in a shop across the street before eventually being rescued from a life of humiliation by a kind doctor. After that, he lived the rest of his days in one of the rooms of London Hospital. He was in there somewhere, right now. She frowned and scanned the windows of the grand stone and brick facade as their cab slowed to a stop.

"I'm sure a visit can be arranged," Simon said, clearly knowing where her thoughts were.

She shook her head. "I feel silly. I know he'd probably welcome a visitor, but I feel like I'd be intruding."

Simon didn't argue with her, but merely helped her down from the carriage to the street. She pulled her up her skirt to avoid a puddle of sludge.

"If you change your mind," was all he said. He would help her if she wanted it and leave it alone if she preferred that. She loved him for that.

She smiled up at him and wound her arm through his. "I'll think about it."

But she didn't, her mind shifted to Dr. Blackwood. She'd spent some time last night preparing what she thought would be the sort of questions a reporter would ask, although she had the feeling she wouldn't have to do much talking when the time came. If she could get the doctor started, talking about himself wouldn't be a problem. Stopping him might.

The hospital was massive and impressive. They got directions to the doctor's office and made their way to the right wing. They'd just turned the last corner when they heard Dr. Blackwood's voice, raised in anger.

"I told you not to come here," the doctor said. "Roderick!"

A woman's voice came next, her East End accent clear. "You fink you can do what you like, don't ye? Doctor?" The last word was layered with contempt.

"Get out!"

There was a short scuffle of feet and an indignant cry of, "Get your 'ands off me!" and then the woman was bodily escorted from the doctor's office and out into the hall by a short, muscular man.

He twisted her arm behind her back as she struggled. "That's enough, Lizzy."

Elizabeth started to protest when Simon beat her to it.

"Is something wrong?" Simon asked.

Both of them turned in surprise.

"It's in hand," the man said, squeezing the woman's arms tightly as she tried to turn out of his grip.

Simon glared at the man and looked meaningfully at the way he was holding her. "Then perhaps you should let her go."

He ignored Simon's implied threat and looked back into the office. The woman turned her gray eyes to Simon, and Elizabeth could see she wanted to say something, but the doctor's appearance in the doorway shut her mouth.

"Nothing's wrong," the doctor said. "A misunderstanding. Roderick?" He nodded toward his man's tight grip.

Reluctantly, the other let go. Lizzy snorted and rubbed her arms, but held her tongue. The doctor took a step toward her and she flinched, backing up a step warily.

"I think we're clear on things now," he said.

She looked at him with venom and fear. "Crystal."

"See her out, Roderick," the doctor ordered and his man reached for Lizzy's arm again, but she snatched it away. She straightened the sleeves of her grubby dress and lifted her chin before walking away with as much pride as she could muster. Roderick followed a menacing pace behind her.

"What was that all about?" Simon asked once she and Roderick were out of earshot.

"Nothing."

"That was rather forceful for nothing," Simon said.

The doctor sighed. "You have to be firm with people like that. They're used to behaving like animals; sometimes you must treat them as such." He smiled then as though none of it had happened, and gestured for them to precede him into his office.

"Is she a patient of yours?" Elizabeth asked as she walked into a large office with more books than air in it. It was all she could do to pretend two men manhandling a poor woman was perfectly normal and acceptable.

"No," he said with a gasping laugh. "Perhaps she's seen me at the clinic or Bethlem."

"Bethlam?" Elizabeth asked. "Bethlam Royal Hospital?"

He arched an eyebrow. "I don't think there are any others. Several of my test subjects are there. Patients that are beyond healing, but can still give us answers to the questions we seek."

Elizabeth nodded and tried not to look surprised. Bethlam Royal Hospital, better known as Bedlam, played an important part in Vale's future. It had to be more than coincidence that Dr. Blackwood worked there as well.

"Of course," she said, casting a quick glance at Simon.

The doctor moved around to sit behind his desk. "In addition to my heavy schedule, I volunteer once a week at a local clinic. Some of the patients think that means I'm available to them for everything, including skinned knees or the mumps."

"So you do hands on medicine in addition to your research?" Elizabeth asked taking a chair opposite him.

"There is a shortage of capable physicians. I do what I can to pitch in," he added with a modest smile. "But you're not here to hear about that, are you? We have far greater things on the horizon. Our work is at the vanguard of discovering the clues to the Pathology of the Mind. The very essence of man."

He leaned back in his chair, pleased with himself. "Far more interesting than the mumps, don't you think?"

VICTOR LEANED AGAINST THE cold stone of the building and waited. Pizer was at work and with little else to go on, he decided that following the victim instead of the suspect might bear more fruit. Or any fruit at all.

He'd found Annie Chapman leaving the Ten Bells at about ten o'clock that morning with Elizabeth Stride. They'd talked briefly and then walked over to Whitechapel Road. He wasn't sure where he'd expected them to go, but the hospital wasn't it.

While Stride went inside, Chapman lingered out front. She flitted about, obviously a little nervous until she saw someone she recognized. A thick-necked cab driver smiled as she walked over to him. From Victor's position, he couldn't make out what they were saying to each other.

He was surprised to see the Crosses go into the hospital, but he supposed they were following up one of their leads. Such as they were.

About twenty minutes after she'd gone inside, Stride came down out of the hospital. It didn't look as though she'd been treated for anything, there were no obvious signs anyway, but she was agitated. When she reached the bottom of the front steps, she turned back angrily. A stout man in a nice suit seemed to be the target of her temper. He was unmoved by it and turned to go back inside.

Stride marched over to Chapman and the driver. The two women said their goodbyes to the man and walked off talking, each glancing back at the hospital before leaning in to whisper to the other.

He trailed after them, wishing now he'd followed Stride inside the hospital instead of waiting out front with Chapman. Whomever Stride had spoken to and whatever they'd spoken about, both women had something to do with it. And when both women were soon-to-be victims of the Ripper that connection loomed all the more important. There was nothing he could do about it but stay with Chapman now and be there when the moment, however horrible, came.

Chapter Seventeen

Elizabeth was glad she didn't have a mirror to look in. If she looked half as bad as Simon, well then, she looked perfect. That didn't do anything to calm the butterflies in her stomach though.

"Let me see," Simon said as he took her by the shoulders and turned her toward him in the faint lamplight of Victor's room. He studied her face for a moment, making sure each soap and vinegar bubble looked like a blister or flaking skin.

Inspired by their visit to the theater and Dr. Jekyll and Mr. Hyde, they'd found a small theater shop and bought make-up and false teeth to enhance their East End looks. It had done the trick. Their healthy complexions were sallow now, their skin diseased, even the shapes of their faces were changed by the false teeth.

Simon finished examining her and nodded, his eyes catching hers and lingering. In them she could see all of her fears and worries reflected, and enhanced. Last time they'd done this, they'd both nearly gotten killed. And tonight, Victor would not be there to save their bacon. He was on his own path, as was Charles Graham. It seemed the best idea to separate, increasing their chances of seeing what needed to be seen. But now, alone together, about to head out again into the miasma of Whitechapel, Elizabeth felt a chill that had nothing to do with the weather.

Simon squeezed her shoulders gently in comfort.

"It will be all right," he said, and then let her go to recheck the pistol in his pocket that he'd already checked and rechecked half a dozen times.

"We've been in worse situations," Elizabeth said, leaving off that this one felt different somehow.

It felt like the night itself was a physical presence all around them, pressing against them, fighting them. They'd gone into dangerous situations before and she'd always been frightened, it was foolish not to be, but there was something about this entire mission that left her feeling off balance. Maybe it was the way time could alter, like an earthquake, without warning and the earth beneath their feet suddenly shifting. Or maybe it was that the whole thing was tainted. They'd saved people before, people who deserved a second chance. She shuddered to think what Jack the Ripper would do with his.

"All right?" Simon asked.

She nodded and Simon slipped in his false teeth.

"Stay close," he said and she couldn't help but laugh.

The teeth changed his voice and gave him a marble-mouthed sound and whistling "s".

"Elizabeth," he said and she laughed again.

It was nerves and she shook her head in apology.

He took out the teeth. "Elizabeth."

"I'm sorry."

He fought down a smile and started to put the teeth back in, but instead took a step toward her. His hand gently cupped her cheek. His eyes darted back and forth across her face, taking her all in.

There was a slight smile at the corners of his mouth. "You're…hideous," he said. She would have laughed if it wasn't for the way his eyes darkened into something emotional.

His voice grew low and rough. "And I love you so very much."

An instant lump formed in the back of her throat and she tried to swallow it. She nodded and took a small hiccuping breath.

He leaned down and kissed her. As his lips touched hers, she wanted to stop time. She wanted to stay right there in that moment and forget everything that came before and everything that would come after. But time wasn't on her payroll and ignored her.

Simon gently pulled away and looked at her fiercely. "Stay close."

"If I could get in your pocket, I would."

He smiled and nodded.

She put in her false teeth, and with one last look at each other, they started for Whitechapel and the murder of Annie Chapman.

THE STREET OUTSIDE OF Crossingham's lodging house was nearly empty. A few people staggered past, but none gave Victor a second thought. He saw a few carts and carriages drive past as he waited. One was the same cab from the hospital with the driver Chapman had talked to, but the carriage didn't stop here; it drove past and disappeared into the night.

Victor leaned against a wall across the street, and packed a new pipe as he continued to wait. It was his third. He was smoking far too much. Not that it mattered. Something else would surely kill him first.

He lit the pipe and settled in. He'd been following Annie Chapman all day. She'd made the usual rounds, pub after pub, until finally stumbling back to her lodging house.

From reading Travers' files Victor knew what was happening inside. She'd run out of money, having spent her last penny at the pub. Right now, she was probably promising the deputy that she'd go out and earn enough, and to please save her a bed for the night. Without it, she would be out on the street.

Victor took a pull from his pipe and blew the smoke up into the cooling night air. Modern people thought they knew what a hand to mouth existence was, what surviving day to day really meant, but most had no idea how literal it was in Whitechapel.

A few minutes later, right on cue, the night watchman escorted Chapman from the lodging house. She would come back with the four pence for a bed or not come back at all, he told her.

She would not come back at all.

The line between life and death was always thin—turning left instead of right, being five minutes early or five minutes late—made all the difference. For Annie Chapman, the difference between life and death was four pence.

Still quite drunk, Chapman teetered on her feet before aiming herself in the direction of Bushfield Street. Victor waited until she was far enough ahead and then followed quietly behind.

He was nothing more than a shadow in her shadow. Even if she were sober, he was sure she would take no notice of him. This was what he excelled at—following, watching, waiting.

As they made their way through the rabbit warren of streets that made up the East End, he was glad he was on his own and didn't have to babysit the Crosses. They would no doubt get into trouble here again, but it would not be his problem this time. This time the mission would come first, as it should have before. He wasn't sure what had come over him then. He should have let those thugs cut their throats and be done with them, but he hadn't. Couldn't.

Perhaps some spark of humanity lived inside him after all. If it did, he thought with a tightening in his gut, it would die tonight.

Gently slapping his pipe against his palm, he knocked the last bit of smoldering tobacco out. It fell into a dank puddle, fizzled briefly, and then disappeared.

Chapman turned toward Spitalfields Market and her fate, and Victor followed. They'd only gone a few blocks when Victor noticed a man casually leaning against a lamppost, arms crossed over chest. The clothes were different, and it took Victor a moment to place the face under the bowler hat, but he recognized the man—Charles Graham. It wasn't surprising to see him here. After all, he was on the same hunt.

Even though he didn't know who Victor was, thank God Cross had at least enough sense to keep him out of his plan, Victor kept in the shadows. He didn't like to be seen—by anyone, if he could help it, and Graham was no exception.

Luckily, Victor could see Annie Chapman quite well now. She walked down the center of the street, meandering along some invisible line. When she saw Graham, she wove her way over to him.

Victor couldn't get close enough to hear their conversation without giving himself away, and so he stayed put and watched.

Graham tipped his hat and she set about trying to earn her four pence. She leaned against his arm in what was supposed to be a seductive way, and might have been if she hadn't nearly fallen in the process. Graham helped her stand back up and she laughed, trying to straighten her hat. She placed a "don't you want to?" hand on his arm and jerked her head toward a nearby alley.

They spoke for another moment before Chapman ran a finger along Graham's cheek and then started off down the street. Graham watched her and then started north, probably heading to the scene of the crime from the back way. If the Crosses managed to stay alive tonight, it would be like a damned train station there.

Victor waited long enough for Graham to be out of sight and then hurried along the sidewalk to catch up to Chapman. It was easy enough work; she was slow on her feet. He could hear her humming something to herself, but he didn't recognize the tune.

Spitalfields Market was just up ahead. The large open-air market was as quiet as a graveyard. This time tomorrow it would be filled with costermongers and carts readying for the early Sunday morning shoppers. But for now, it lay still and empty, a promise of something to come.

Chapman stopped for a moment and looked longingly through the gate. When she continued on, she didn't keep going east as Victor had assumed she would. She turned left and he had to cross the street to follow her. As he did, two men stepped out of doorway.

"What're ya doin'?" one of of them said, as they blocked his path.

He tried to ignore them and move around the big one, but he sidestepped in front him.

"We don't like strangers," he said, " 'specially strangers that follow girls."

Victor gave them both a quick study. They were no match for him, even with the blackjack the smaller one held in the palm of his hand. They were both out of shape. The big man wheezed just standing there.

"Mind your own business," Victor said and started forward.

The big man put a meaty hand on his chest and Victor grabbed his wrist and thumb, twisting it until the man cried out.

The other one lunged forward and Victor spun his friend into him, sending them both tumbling to the ground. They struggled to their feet and Victor stood ready.

"I don't have all night," Victor said. The last thing he could afford was to waste time with these two idiots.

"Oh, I think you do," one of them said with a wide gap-toothed smile.

Victor started forward, but he never finished the step. He felt something hard crack along the back of his head. He only had time to curse himself before darkness came and he fell unconscious to the street.

SIMON KEPT HIS HAND in his pocket, the metal of the gun barrel cool against his fingers. His eyes swept the area constantly, looking for anything, anyone that might be a threat. He would not be caught off guard tonight.

Elizabeth shuffled alongside him, doing a very good impression of a drunk. Her steps were uneven and she wobbled a bit as she walked, occasionally veering off course and bumping into his side.

They had arrived near the crime scene early, but knew they couldn't linger there. The backyard where Annie Chapman would be killed was surrounded by a fence. There were only two ways in—the front door of 29 Hanbury Street and a gate near the back. They'd circled the block several times, standing in the shadows of doorways while they took stock of the area. The streets were fairly narrow here, and the buildings rising three and four stories high. The gas lamps struggled to give off any appreciable light.

There weren't many people out. Simon made a quick check of his watch, nearly four in the morning. It could happen at any time now. From what he could remember, the eyewitness accounts had been debatable at best. Annie Chapman hadn't been seen since just after 1:30 a.m. Others had claimed to have passed through the yard and seen nothing until later. One woman said she thought she saw

Chapman as late as 5:30 a.m., but the coroner's report put the death at least an hour before that.

Simon and Elizabeth had no way of knowing what, if any, of that information had been right, and so they stood and waited. The policemen made their rounds like clockwork, but thankfully none of them walked up Hanbury Street.

Elizabeth rubbed her upper arms to warm them from the night's chill. Simon started to remove his jacket, intending to give it to her, but stopped when he heard a sound coming from inside the yard. He froze in place, his heart beating a bit faster in his chest.

He and Elizabeth exchanged glances and he eased them back further into the doorway. The side gate opened and a man stepped out. He scuffed his shoe on the ground and looked up into the night. Whoever he was, he was in no hurry.

Elizabeth gripped Simon's arm and looked at him in silent question. Simon looked back at the man, remembering that a resident of the apartments had walked through the yard, stopping to fix a boot on the way.

He turned back to Elizabeth and shook his head. Her face fell, both relieved and let down. Simon let out a breath and tried to let the adrenaline that had shot though his body fade. Rolling his shoulders he leaned back against the wall and they resumed their vigil.

It wasn't long before they heard footsteps—two pairs—growing nearer. Simon edged forward and peered around the corner of the building, sure to remain hidden from view. In the distance he saw a couple, a man and a woman. They were too far away to make out clearly, but the woman could have been Chapman.

Simon moved silently back to their hiding place in the arched doorway and began to raise a finger urging Elizabeth to keep quiet. But when he turned, she wasn't tucked into the doorway, she was standing in the middle of the street, looking at him with shock.

He reached out to her, to pull her back into the shadows, but she stepped away from him. Her eyes were wide with fear and confusion. She looked at him like he'd grown another head and, suddenly, he realized what had happened.

"Elizabeth," he whispered.

She seemed shocked that he knew her name and inched farther away. His heart clenched with the realization that she didn't even recognize him.

"Come here," he said, stepping slowly toward her.

"No," she said, edging even farther away, and then they both turned toward the sound of someone growing closer.

Simon's heart raced as he spun back to grab Elizabeth. But just as he did, a man stumbled out of a doorway and right into her. He grabbed her, to try to stop her from falling, but she shoved him away.

The man was falling down drunk and the force of her push sent him to tumbling into Simon. In that split second before she ran, he could see her face clearly, he could see the absolute confusion and terror. Simon struggled against the drunk man and before he could do anything, she turned and ran up the street.

"Dammit," he said softly, as he disentangled himself from the man and took off after her.

She wasn't far ahead, but when she turned right and disappeared around a corner, Simon's heart lurched. Seconds later, he rounded the same corner, expecting to see her running straight ahead, but there was no sign of her. The street was empty.

If he lost her and she didn't recover her memory…

He hurried forward and saw several alleyways branching off the street. With a force of will, he stopped moving and listened. Over the sound of his own thrumming heart, he heard footfalls to the left, and he raced after them.

He sprinted through the alley and emerged onto another, larger street. Elizabeth ran down the center of it, her dress billowing out, slowing her down. She grabbed fistfuls of the fabric and hiked it up to give her legs more room to run.

"Elizabeth!" he called after her.

She looked back at him over her shoulder, but kept on running.

Simon had nearly caught up to her when she made another sharp right and just as Simon was about to follow her, a man called out to him.

"Oi! You!"

It was a policeman. Simon thought about just running, but then the officer would blow his whistle and others would come and he'd lose Elizabeth completely. Simon slowed and let the policeman approach, cursing silently every moment that ticked by.

"Why such a hurry?" the constable asked, shining a light from his lantern into Simon's face.

Simon shielded his eyes. For a split second, he considered just clocking the man with the pistol in his pocket and making a run for it, but hoped he would just let him go quickly. If he didn't…

"Late for work," Simon said, breathlessly. "Please, gov," he added, "the boss'll sack me if I'm late again."

The constable looked him up and down for a few seconds that dragged painfully on. With each one that passed, Elizabeth was farther and farther away, and deeper and deeper in danger.

The constable studied him a moment further, but flicked his head down the street. "Right. Go on with ya."

Simon nodded quickly and ran in the direction Elizabeth had gone. He ran to another intersection and had to stop again. He paused, but didn't hear anything.

He shouldn't have stopped. He should have done whatever he had to do to keep going. If he lost her…

The thought made him physically ill and he clenched his jaw to control the churning in his stomach. He forced himself to take a deep calming breath. She couldn't be far. It had felt like hours, but it had been less than a minute.

He slowed his breathing, watching the cloud of condensed vapor billow out into the cold night air as he breathed, again and again. And listened.

Please, let me hear her.

His prayer was followed by a long, protracted silence, but finally he heard another sound—something being knocked to the ground and he raced toward it.

Skidding around a corner, he saw her kneeling down between two piles of crates. For a moment, he thought she'd been hurt, but she stood up to face him, terrified, but defiant.

The alley she'd taken this time was a dead end. A lone weak gas lamp danced over her head and she looked every bit the cornered animal she must have felt.

Simon's heart slid out of his throat. She was terrified, but unharmed.

"Elizabeth," he said, feeling his body sag with relief.

She looked around in a panic and picked up a wooden board from one of the discarded crates. She held it up like a club. "Stay away from me."

"Elizabeth," he said, taking a tentative step forward.

She readied her plank to swing. "How do you know my name?"

"It's me," he said, hoping somehow she'd remember. "Simon."

In the dim light, he could just make out a hint of recognition in her eyes.

"Simon Cross," he continued, hope flaring in his chest.

She shook her head. "You're not him."

He started to protest and realized—it was the disguise. To her, he wouldn't look like the man she knew. He tore off his cap and took out his false teeth, tossing them aside and held out his arms to the sides in supplication.

"It's me. Simon."

She looked at him warily and then her eyes filled with cautious remembrance. "Professor?"

Simon's heart leapt. "Yes. It's all right."

She didn't lower her weapon, but he could see she was almost ready to.

"What's happening?" she asked, fear and uncertainty making her voice tremble in a way that made him want to do nothing more than take her in his arms, but he resisted the urge.

"It's all right," he said. "It's confusing, I know, but you're all right."

She was still unconvinced.

He took another small step toward her and this time she didn't step back. He took another and another, until he was right in front of her. He held out his hand to her and she looked at it nervously.

"Trust me," he said.

She looked around the filthy alley, still afraid and confused, but when she looked back at him and met his eyes, he saw her defenses come down. She nodded, and took his hand.

The knowledge that he had her now, that she was safe and with him, was overwhelming. He couldn't stop himself and pulled her into his arms.

After a moment, she spoke softly, her voice muffled against his chest. "Professor?"

He eased her back and gave a short embarrassed laugh. "I'm sorry."

"Is this a dream?"

He shook his head. "Not a dream."

He squeezed her hand tightly in his. "I'm afraid it will take a little explaining."

She looked around the alley uncertainly and then back to him. "And a lot of booze."

Simon gave a short laugh. It was good to see a bit of his Elizabeth again.

She looked up at him. "Why are we dressed like Little Dorrit?"

He smiled down at her and started them down the alley and back to the main street. "It's a long story."

Glancing to the left, back toward the crime scene, he knew that there was no going back now. Elizabeth was in no condition to try to do what needed to be done. He would take care of her and hope Victor or Graham had had better luck. Or any luck at all.

CHAPTER EIGHTEEN

THE FIRST THING HE heard was someone laughing. It was far away
at first, but as he rose to the surface of consciousness it grew
louder and more annoying. Victor knew from experience to remain
motionless, to listen and learn what he could while his captors still
thought him incapacitated.

He kept his eyes closed and tried not to move, although his arms
ached. They were tied behind his back, and from the numbness in
his hands, they had been for some time.

He heard men's voices mostly, a few women. Loud and boisterous.
They were talking about the latest murder, Annie Chapman's murder.
His heart sank. He'd failed again. This was becoming a bad habit.

Then he heard the tell-tale sound of glassware and smelled the
unmistakable odor of stale beer. He knew before he opened his eyes
that he was in a pub. Captured by a bunch of amateurs, he thought
with disgust.

The last thing he'd remembered was following Chapman and
then he'd been ambushed. He'd been foolish to underestimate them.

Not the men themselves, he could have easily dispatched them both, but their number. It was a beginner's mistake. One he would not make again.

He rolled his shoulders to bring some life back into his arms and groaned. They hadn't just knocked him out, he realized. They'd taken a little of their frustration out on him. His ribs ached and now that he opened his eyes, he realized one was swollen, not shut, but it was thick and blood had dried at the corners, making his eyelid stick.

He opened his good eye, pushed himself back against the wall and took stock of his surroundings. It was the Ten Bells. He was tied up and tossed in the far corner, a sad little makeshift jail like a children's fort made out of chairs surrounding him. And he was not alone.

Next to him, another man leaned into the corner of the wall, his head wedged uncomfortably there. His chest rose and fell slowly. Either asleep, passed out or unconscious, but alive.

"Finally got 'em to listen me. Stupid coppers."

That was Pizer's voice.

"I told 'em I was down at Shadwell's, watchin' the fire that night," he continued and then laughed. "They didn't believe me. Till one of their own said he saw me with his own two eyes. Berks."

So, Pizer had an alibi for the murder. Wonderful, Victor thought. His suspect list was non-existent again. He turned and looked around the bar. He started to speak, but his throat was dry and he coughed and tried to swallow.

"Look who's awake," a man said as he tapped a friend on the shoulder.

The friend, the larger man from last night, turned around and grinned down at Victor. "Sleep well?"

Victor tried to sit up straighter, but his ribs protested. He looked up at the big man evenly. "Like a baby."

Both men laughed.

Victor shifted his position to start working on the ropes that bound his hands. They were tied tightly, but the rope was thick and the job poorly done.

"Well," the taller one said. "You should. Old Frank here hit ya pretty hard. I thought you might not wake up again."

"Frank will have to try harder next time," Victor said casually.

The little man, apparently Frank, glared down at him. "We can take of that right now, if ya like."

Victor ignored him and looked up at the big man. "Would it be too much to ask what the hell is going on?"

The big man chuckled and pulled up a chair. He spun it around to sit backwards on it. "We don't like outsiders. And we don't like ones that follow our women around at night."

"Hmm," Victor said in agreement. "And did it help?"

Both men's faces colored with anger and embarrassment.

"No," the taller one said. "Another murder last night."

"I did not think so," Victor said with a sigh. "But I suppose I should thank you."

"Yeah?"

"You have proven my innocence."

"How'd we do that? Frank said.

"I could hardly commit the crime while I was tied up here all night under your ever watchful eye."

The little one looked surprised at the realization, but neither man was quite ready to give in.

"That don't mean—"

"Victor?"

All three men turned to see Marie.

"Never you mind—" the little one said, stepping in front of her.

But she would have none of it. "Ye two lump heads. If ye don't beat all."

"You just leave it to—" the little one tried again, but Marie interrupted again.

"'Cause you two is doin' such a fine job? Annie's dead. Did you stop it? No, ye were out there playin' copper and tyin' up the good ones."

"You know 'im?"

"Name's Victor, and he's twice the man the both of you are put together."

Victor appreciated the help, but she was gilding the lily a bit much. "I am no saint."

"I saw what you did the other day," Marie said, her eyes filling with admiration. "Helped that old woman."

Victor felt a wave of embarrassment. It was an unusual and unwelcome feeling.

The tall one stepped forward. "You'll vouch for him?"

Marie nodded and that seemed to turn the tide in Victor's favor. The big one nodded for the other to help Victor up.

After he did, Victor handed him the ropes, enjoying the look of shock on the man's face.

"Next time use a better rope," he said. "Or a better man," he added to the big one, who did little to hide his amusement.

Marie looped her arm through his and started to escort him to a table. "Are ye all right?"

"I am," he said.

"A pint here, Charlie," she said to the barkeep.

Victor shook his head. "I'm afraid I cannot stay."

"Oh," Marie said, self-conscious now.

The bar was abuzz with the night's events. One murder was something to talk about, but two…

"I'll be back later," Victor said. "And I will buy you that drink."

Marie smiled and Victor tried not to care. This was all part of the game, he told himself. She was an ally here now, that was all.

"All right," she said, needlessly smoothing her hair. "Later, then."

Victor grunted in acknowledgment and, with one final look back at the men who had ambushed him, left the Ten Bells.

He walked to the crime scene, but it was crowded with people. The police were finally doing a better job of keeping people away from the evidence. Of course, he noted, the policemen themselves still trampled over every inch anyway.

Through the open gate, Victor saw the blood smears on the fence above where Annie Chapman had been found. Her body had already been taken to the coroner's office. Judging from the sun, at least an hour ago. Not that it mattered. Even if he had been able to see her, it would have told him nothing he did not already know. She was butchered, and he had failed to be there. Jack the Ripper was as free and as unknown as he had always been.

Sick to his stomach, Victor studied the crowd. The usual faces looked on with fear and disgust. There was a strained edge to every voice, a pinched look of anxiety in every expression as they began to realize that this was just the beginning.

Victor scrubbed his face with his hand and winced as he felt the fresh bruise growing near his eye. He needed to sleep for a few hours, to clear his head, and so started back toward his room.

He stopped by a fish market and paid a farthing for a bag of ice. It stank of herring, but it would do.

Finally, back at his boarding house, he trudged up the stairs and as he reached for the doorknob, he heard a man's voice inside. His body tensed until he heard another sentence and recognized the accent and the entitlement—Cross.

ELIZABETH FOCUSED ON FINISHING the buttons of her blouse and shook her head. "I still feel guilty."

"It wasn't your fault," Simon said for what must have been the eleven hundredth time.

Somehow, that didn't matter, she still felt guilty. If she hadn't had her memory lapse, they would have been able to do what they needed to last night. But she'd up and gone all Memento on him and they'd missed their chance. Again.

"There's nothing either of us can do about those events, Elizabeth."

She was about to protest, when the door to the room opened. She gasped in surprise as she turned to see Victor looking like fresh hell.

He stood in the doorway for a moment and eyed them both tiredly. "You are still alive."

He didn't sound all that pleased, but then he never sounded pleased about anything.

As he walked further into the room, she could see that his right eye was swollen and dried blood streaked his face from the eyebrow above it.

"You're hurt," she said and started toward him.

He waved her away and put a sodden bag on the dresser. He took the cloth off of the pitcher and poured some water into the basin, before turning back to her. His eyes dipped to her unbuttoned blouse and then narrowed in disgust, his assumption clear.

Elizabeth blushed despite herself. What must he think of them to suspect they'd make love while a woman was being slaughtered?

Simon caught Victor's expression as well and started toward him, but she put her hand on his arm. "We weren't…doing that. We went to Whitechapel, but I screwed it up."

"Elizabeth."

"I had one of those time shifts," she said, fresh guilt stinking up the room like too much rosemary.

Victor looked at her and nodded. It was as close to an apology as they were likely to get.

"It was awful," she continued. "Have you had any?"

He looked at her, his face unchanged, except for something in his eyes. He cleared his throat and turned back to the basin, her question unanswered.

"Did you see him?" Simon asked. "Did you see Ripper?"

Victor splashed water onto his face and wiped away the dried blood. "No," he said, letting out a long breath. "I did not."

He took the towel and patted his face dry as he turned back to them. "I was accosted by friendly neighborhood vigilantes."

"Damn," Simon said softly.

He wiped his hands dry. "It seems the universe does not want us to know."

Simon snorted, but he'd said something similar himself just a few hours ago.

Victor prodded his eyebrow with a dirty finger and then winced as he felt along the back of his head.

"Let me," Elizabeth said, stepping forward. The gash on his head was ugly and matted with dried blood and hair. She motioned for Simon to bring the water basin over.

"I don't need your help."

She started to argue because clearly he did, but Simon shook his head and Elizabeth relented. Victor's pride had suffered enough.

"Did you see anything that might help?" Simon asked.

Victor shook his head.

Simon frowned. "Nothing?"

"Graham was there, only minutes before the murder. Perhaps he managed to see something useful."

Simon nodded and then sighed. "How can so many of us learn so little?"

Victor made a sound in his throat that earned him a glare from Simon, but neither one was in any position to throw stones.

"Did you learn anything yesterday?" Simon asked.

"I followed Chapman, but she did little else than drink, I'm afraid."

Victor grunted as he probed the back of his head with his fingers, wincing.

"She did go along with a friend to the hospital, but she didn't even go inside. I saw you—"

"Hospital? In Whitechapel?" Simon said. "What time was this?"

Victor shrugged. "Eleven, eleven thirty."

"And she went with a friend?"

"Elizabeth Stride."

The name sent a shot of adrenaline through Elizabeth. "Lizzy!"

Victor turned to her in question.

"We were there, inside, about to interview Dr. Blackwood when we heard the end of an argument he was having with a woman named Lizzy."

"About this tall?" he asked holding up his hand up to about shoulder height. "Grey eyes?"

"Yes," Simon said. "Elizabeth Stride, the fourth victim?"

Victor nodded.

"Do you know why they were there?" Simon asked.

Victor frowned. "I overheard them talking about some sort of plan. Some sort of revenge."

Simon started to pace. He liked to move as his mind moved. "It's got to be more than a coincidence that Stride and Chapman were both involved. But what's the doctor's connection?"

"She said something about how he thought he could get away with it," Elizabeth said, remembering the bit of the argument they'd heard.

"Maybe he did," Victor said.

Elizabeth turned to him in question.

"Maybe he got away with murder."

ELIZABETH WAS SURE SHE'D never get used to the first floor being the second floor, at least to an American. She and Simon were meeting Graham and Vale for dinner at the Wellington, an upscale restaurant on Piccadilly just a few blocks from their hotel. Apparently, the preferred and more private dining salon was too good for the ground floor and up the stairs they went.

Simon had tried to contact Graham earlier in the day, but hadn't heard back until the afternoon. Graham had invited them to dine that night and they'd accepted, hoping they could find an opportunity to talk with him alone.

The maitre d' escorted them through the small, but elegant dining room. While the downstairs crowd paid six shillings for a prix fixe menu cooked by the English kitchen, the upstairs crowd paid an extra two for French. Elizabeth was so hungry she would have eaten just about anything.

Across the room, Graham waved to them and stood as they approached.

He smiled broadly in greeting. "So glad you could make it."

"Thank you," Simon said as he waited for the maitre d' to help Elizabeth into her chair before taking his own.

For her part, Katherine Vale smiled tightly. Elizabeth knew that look—the slight squinting of the eyes, the firmness of the line of the mouth, the slightly off-color complexion. She was in pain, but trying to pretend she wasn't.

"Are you all right?" Elizabeth asked, before remembering that she shouldn't care. This was Katherine Vale, after all.

Vale let out a quick breath and smiled an almost genuine smile. "I'm fine. Just a bit of a lingering headache."

She touched her temple and laughed lightly shaking her head as she picked up her menu.

Elizabeth studied her for a moment, wondering if that's all it was, before picking up her own menu to study the offerings.

"Wow."

"It is quite a lineup, isn't it?" Graham said.

He wasn't kidding. The meal included soup, fish, an entree of meat, some sort of roast duck or goose, an appetizer thing she couldn't translate, potatoes and peas, rum cake, assorted fruits and nuts, and finally petit fours. It was gluttonous.

The waiter appeared and they made their selections of entrees, and Graham ordered a bottle of wine for the table.

"That second murder," Vale said when the waiter was gone. "Ghastly, isn't it?"

Simon and Elizabeth shared a quick uneasy glance. Had Graham told her who they were and why they were there?

"Surely, you've heard about it?" Vale continued. "Every news-paper in town is covering it."

"Oh, yes," Elizabeth said, relieved.

Vale picked up her wine and took a sip. "I'm surprised your editor hasn't wired you, begging for a scoop."

"I'm sure he will," Elizabeth said. "He never met a gruesome murder he didn't love."

Everyone laughed, but it died quickly.

"I'm sure Charles could help you with it. A story on the murders, I mean," Vale said and then looked as though she'd crossed some line and tried to retreat. "Of course, if he has time, he's terribly busy."

Charles smiled kindly at Elizabeth. "I would be happy to help."

Elizabeth caught Simon's eye again and thanked Graham for the offer.

"I read something about a psychic who'd been to the police, but they ignored him," Vale said, her excitement at the idea obvious.

Just as obvious was Graham's displeasure with it. He frowned and took a long drink of wine.

Katherine noticed and laughed a little nervously. "Charles thinks it's nonsense, but I think all sorts of things are possible."

"Like fairies and the Easter Bunny," Graham said with a quirking smile.

Not to be put off, Vale continued, "Supposedly, he went to the police before the crimes—described them perfectly."

"Perhaps he's the killer," Graham said.

"It would be silly of him to go to the police then, wouldn't it?"

Graham nodded. "Or it's a clever place to hide, in plain sight."

"Well," Vale said. "I just thought you might find it interesting. Apparently Robert Lees, that's the psychic, is a friend of your Dr. Blackwood's, or his wife anyway."

Simon arched an eyebrow. "Really?"

"That's what I've heard."

"When exactly did you hear this?" Graham asked, a bit of irritation showing in his voice.

Vale laid a placating hand on his arm. "It just came up at the meeting this morning, is all. I thought it was interesting. Lees and Madame Blavatsky are going to try to reach out to the poor deceased victims later this week."

"Ridiculous," Graham muttered.

Elizabeth leaned forward in her chair. "You mean a séance?"

"Yes," Vale said, a gleam in her eye. "I think it would be fascinating to see."

"Hocus pocus," Graham said. "That woman, and I'm sure this Lees as well, are delusional. At best. At worst they're preying on people's fears to make money."

The waiters came with the soup course and conversation waned until they'd left.

"I just thought it might be interesting," Vale said finally, as she dipped her spoon into her consommé.

"I think it would be," Elizabeth said, earning surprised looks from both Graham and Simon. "Stranger things have turned out to be true."

"And besides," she continued, tucking into her soup, "it'd make a great angle for the paper."

Vale smiled at her, both pleased and in solidarity. Both were unnerving. While it was probably nothing more than a show, there was always the chance they might learn something. Vale's future Madame Petrovka persona was a charlatan, most mediums they'd come across were. However, Elizabeth, as a time traveler who'd saved ghosts and had dinner with vampires, didn't write anything off.

The rest of the meal progressed without any more talk of Ripper or the murders. Finally the last course had been served and removed.

Vale's excitement from earlier had faded and her expression was once again the pinched and tired one they'd seen at the start. Her fingers idly massaged her temple and her eyes grew tighter around the edges.

"Port?" Graham suggested.

Simon and Elizabeth accepted, but Vale shook her head.

"None for me," she said.

Graham nodded. "Your head again?"

She smiled wanly in apology. "I'm sorry."

"I'll take you back to the hotel."

"I don't want to break up the party."

Graham thought for a moment. "How about this? I'll take you back, get you settled in, and I can rejoin the Crosses in the bar for a nightcap?"

He glanced at Simon. "What do you say? It's not far."

Simon nodded.

"Very good," Graham said, as he stood and helped Vale up.

Simon, always the gentleman, even to the evilly endowed, stood as well. "We'll see you shortly."

Vale offered Elizabeth another apologetic smile. "I'm sorry I'm such a wet blanket."

Elizabeth kindly waved off her apology. The sooner she went to her rooms the sooner she and Simon could get Graham alone.

Graham took out several bills and put them on the table. "I'll see you in the bar."

"Get some rest," Elizabeth said as Vale and Graham left the table. "And why am I being nice her?" she added quietly once they'd left.

Simon turned to her and covered her hand with his. "Because you pity her?"

She did. Despite everything, seeing her this way, it made Elizabeth wonder if not for the Grace of God…

Simon looked toward the door. "Just don't forget who she really is."

"She tried to kill me. And you. More than once," she said. "That's not the sort of thing one forgets."

"Or forgives."

"I just wonder if things had been different," Elizabeth said, "would she be? Different, I mean."

Simon's eyebrows went up and he let out a sigh. "We will never know, will we? It's our job to make sure things aren't different. For her or for us."

Elizabeth squeezed his hand. "We're lucky."

Simon nodded. "Let's make sure we stay that way."

About ten minutes after they'd found a table in the corner of the Hyde Park Hotel salon, Graham came back as promised. Simon had been growing more and more impatient as the evening wore on. A long dinner with your arch enemy, who was artfully playing the victim, did little to quell his nerves.

He nearly yanked Graham down into his chair when he arrived and wasted no time on preliminaries.

"Did you see him?" Simon asked.

"Ripper?" Graham said, gesturing for the waiter to come to the table as he took his seat. "No."

Simon clenched his jaw. What the bloody hell was going on?

"Sherry," Graham said. "Harvey's, if you have it."

"What happened?" Simon asked.

Graham sat back in his chair and tugged at his cuffs. "I take it you had no luck either?"

Simon grunted out a no.

Graham crossed his legs casually. "I'm starting to think the universe doesn't want us to know."

Simon, and Victor, had both said the very same thing. "What happened?"

"Vigilance. Vigilantes more like it. I'd barely even gotten to Whitechapel before they cracked me over the skull," he said, gesturing to the back of his head. "By the time I came to, it was too late."

Damn vigilance committee. They were doing more harm than good, even if they didn't know it.

"I suppose it's just as well. Kat's headache kept her home," Graham said. "What kept you away? Did they stop you, too?"

"No, we ran into other trouble," Simon said, hoping Graham wouldn't push.

Graham shook his head and frowned. "Curious thing, isn't it? I'm starting to believe it's no accident no one's ever discovered his identity."

"You mean like a conspiracy?" Elizabeth asked.

"No, not necessarily that. It's just, well," he smiled, a small shared secret smile, "time has a funny way of taking care of itself. Perhaps we're not meant to know."

Simon hadn't considered that; that their knowledge of who Ripper was could be a change itself in the time continuum.

"Not that I'm going to stop trying," Graham said, taking his drink from the returning waiter.

"To better luck next time," he said, holding up his glass.

Simon drank, but he did not want to rely on next time. Whether it was the universe, or a man, or just plain bad luck that was keeping the secret, he was not planning on waiting three weeks to find out.

"Did you see anything that might help? Any leads at all?" Simon asked.

Graham took another sip of his sherry and put it aside. "I did hear a rumor. It's only that though."

"What?" Elizabeth asked.

"About your doctor. Supposedly, and I'm getting this second hand mind you, he was in Whitechapel last night. Helping deliver a baby."

"A baby?" Elizabeth frowned. "That doesn't sound like Dr. Blackwood."

Graham shrugged his shoulders. "They could be mistaken. I just thought it a bit odd." He turned to Simon. "And you? No other leads?"

"I'm not sure," Simon said. "Possibly, but…"

It was maddening having so few leads and so many obstacles.

"I think you're right to keep on the doctor's scent," Graham said. "I'll do a little poking around myself. See what I can turn up."

Simon let out a heavy breath. It wasn't what he'd wanted to hear, but better another pair of eyes than not.

"So," Graham said, eyeing them both with a curious smile. "A husband and wife team? That must put a strain on your relationship."

Simon laughed. "It puts a strain on my blood pressure, but the other," he added looking fondly at Elizabeth, "no."

Graham breathed in deeply through his nose. "I wish I could say the same. I thought this would help bring us together, but…I'm not sure she's cut out for this life."

Simon managed to keep a straight face and took a drink of his scotch. "It's not for everyone."

"I envy you," Graham said. "Having a partner. An equal," he added with a deferential tilt of his head toward Elizabeth.

Simon nodded.

"Well," Graham said. "Perhaps there's hope for Katherine. Who knows, she might just come around yet."

CHAPTER NINETEEN

$\int$ LEEP WAS AS ELUSIVE as luck in this cursed place. Victor scrubbed the grit from his eyes, wincing slightly as he was reminded of the bruise he sported under one them. He would do no one any good sitting in his room trying to force what would not come, though. He'd left just a few hours after the Crosses, and his mood was as gray as the sky.

The morning fog had refused to lift and blanketed the city with heavy, wet air. Victor walked through the murky streets toward Ten Bells. He wanted a drink, a sure sign he shouldn't have one.

The pub was still filled with angry East Enders, and Victor knew that with the frenzy over the murder, things would only get worse. Once the yellow press sank their teeth into the story, sensational head-lines would keep it on the front page for months to come. As a man hawking the latest edition passed the front door of the pub, he knew the newspapers would make a killing off the killing. The paper even promised pictures of the murderer. Of course all that amounted to was a cartoon of a ghoul floating through the streets of Whitechapel. Not that that was all that far from the truth, Victor thought. This man was flesh and blood, of that he was certain, but he was as elusive as a ghost. Not that any of that mattered to the papers. What was true and what sold papers were seldom the same. What they didn't know, they made up, and everything they printed fed the growing mania.

The hysteria would only make his job more difficult. The vigilantes from last night were proof enough of that.

Feeling more sullen than usual, Victor found an empty table on the edge of the room and settled in to watch and wait. He nursed a warm beer for nearly an hour before the two men who'd ambushed him last night appeared. The only way he wouldn't get caught in their net again was to become one of them. And it was possible, he realized, that the killer himself could well be thinking the same thing. Was one of the men sworn to protect the city the very one stalking it?

Victor started to stand to approach the men when he heard a familiar voice.

"Ye look terrible," Marie said.

He hesitated and then gestured for her to sit down, waiting until she did before doing so himself. It was a small, inconsequential act of politeness, but apparently they were so rare here that she paused, unsure for a moment and then smiled as though he'd given her a dozen roses.

He could not bring himself to return the smile.

Her kind eyes scanned his face, frowning at what she saw. Even without a mirror, he knew well what he looked like. The beating last night had done his looks no favors, but Marie didn't seem to mind.

"You've got quite a shiner there," she said, reaching out to touch the skin above his cheek.

He wanted to pull away, but he didn't. It wasn't that he missed the soft touch of woman's hand, he told himself. She was an ally. She could help him infiltrate the Vigilance Committee. He needed her.

"I could make ye a poultice," she said as she deftly touched the wound. "Or you could get some arnica. Tincture's best for bruises like that."

"You seem to know a lot about these things."

She smiled a little shyly. "Had an aunt who was a nurse. She worked with Florence Nightingale at the Crimea."

"Impressive," Victor said, and actually meaning it.

Marie's smile gave way to sadness. "I learned a few things from her, but that sort of life weren't never in the cards for me."

"You are too young to believe such a thing."

She shrugged, but he could see that she was pleased by what he said. "You really think so?"

Victor finished his beer. "I do."

Marie looked at him with hope, clearly hungry to believe him, but she shook her head. "I'm too stupid."

He leaned forward and put his hand on her forearm. "You can be anything you want to be."

An argument erupted near the bar, quickly devolving into a short-lived fistfight; the loser tossed, quite literally, out on his ear.

"If you left this place," Victor added.

Marie leaned forward, her eyes getting watery with coming tears. She looked down at his hand and then back into his face. "You almost make me believe it."

What was he doing? Idiot. Victor pulled his hand away and leaned back in his chair. His discomfort was not lost on her.

A man at a nearby table belched loudly and won a round of laughter.

She laughed lightly to cover her embarrassment. "Wot? And leave all this?"

SIMON ENJOYED THE COGNAC and little else. He and Elizabeth hadn't had two minutes alone with Dr. Blackwood all night. They'd been pleased, and a little surprised, to receive the doctor's dinner invitation. The mystery of why hadn't lasted long.

"There you are," George Roxbury said as he strode toward them with a broad, welcoming smile on his face.

"So you're the one behind this," Elizabeth said, holding up the invitation card. "I didn't think the doctor had suddenly been wooed by my charms."

"Or mine," Simon added, winning a laugh from Roxbury.

He kissed Elizabeth's cheek and shook Simon's hand. "My family is a somewhat important benefactor for London and Bethlam Hospitals. The doctor and others might be foolish, but they are not fools."

"I'm glad you've come," he continued. "Things have grown a bit dull around here," he said with a mischievous smile. "I was hoping you might liven them up."

Sadly, he was going to be disappointed. Elizabeth was on her best behavior and they were both focused on something other than Roxbury's amusement. Dr. Blackwood was their leading suspect and he'd invited them into his home. It was an opportunity they couldn't pass up. Unfortunately, the dinner party was rather large and the doctor, never one to be miserly with the gift of his presence, gave it out freely to one and all. Even Elizabeth's best attempts to persuade him to give her a follow-up interview were brushed aside with a distracted wave as Blackwood hurried to mix and mingle with his more important guests.

Elizabeth made a sour face as she watched Blackwood's stout backside depart. "If you were an earl or something he'd listen to us. But no, you're just a lousy baronet."

Simon laughed, but it was true. His title was near the bottom of the barrel. To most here, anything short of peerage was barely noticeable.

"You shouldn't have married so far beneath you," Simon teased.

She stretched to her toes and scanned the crowd. "There's probably a dotty old duke around here somewhere. Maybe I can upgrade."

"Don't even joke about it," Simon said.

Elizabeth laughed and then turned to look around the party. "Well, we're not going to learn anything interesting standing here together. If we split up, we can cover more ground."

She was right, of course. "Just don't stray too far, all right?"

"Never," she said squeezing his arm before slipping off into the crowd.

Simon watched her easily glide into a group and join the conversations as if she'd been there all along. She was a marvel. But admiring his wife was not why he was here, he reminded himself, and turned his focus to the doctor. He was in unusually good spirits. His typically dour expression had been enlivened. Perhaps he simply enjoyed being the grand host, but there was a noticeable change in him.

Other than his mood, the only other thing of note that caught Simon's attention was the small wound the doctor had on one hand. Word around the Great Hall blamed it on an overzealous patient, but it niggled at Simon.

It was scant evidence to hang anything other than a prayer on, but it was another potentially damning sign pointing toward the doctor. Due to the violence and frenzied nature of the murders, some surmised that the killer might have small wounds on his hands, his own knife cutting him as he rushed to butcher his victims.

For dinner, Simon and Elizabeth had been seated with George, who, Simon had to admit, was far better company than he'd thought he'd be. But however much he'd enjoyed watching the others at their end of the table clutch their pearls over some of the things Roxbury said, it wasn't getting them closer to their goal. Although, the evening hadn't been a total loss, Simon thought, as he sipped his drink from a chair by the fireplace in the grand salon. Mrs. Blackwood's appearance was intriguing.

Too ill to join them for dinner, she arrived afterward for the entertainment. Wheeled out of the bedroom with the assistance of a nurse and the doctor's ever-present and overly dutiful valet, Roderick, she smiled at her guests. Her lap covered with a crocheted blanket and her face pinched in a look of chronic discomfort and fatigue, she looked quite elderly, but was apparently no more than forty, ten years the doctor's junior. Though clearly, she had once been a very beautiful woman.

The doctor doted on her. For a man who appeared as self-centered and self-aggrandizing as the doctor, it was a shock to see him defer to his wife. If his reverence weren't apparent enough, the evening's entertainment certainly was.

Adelina Patti was arguably one of the world's great sopranos and, without argument, its most expensive. Although this was a few years past her prime when she commanded a $5,000 a night fee, this private concert must be costing the doctor a bloody mint.

She began the recital with Violetta's aria from *La Traviata*. Her voice was beautiful, like crystal. Simon allowed himself a few indulgent minutes of pleasure. It was one of the perks of time travel he relished the most, to be able to see and hear art that had been lost to the ages. He listened to the aria, his eyes seeking out Elizabeth across the room. She smiled and waved, and then fell back into whatever muttered conversation she and George were having behind her fan. She didn't share his love of opera, no matter how hard she tried; she always fell asleep.

When Adelina Patti moved on to the turgidly sentimental popular ballad "The Song that Reached My Heart", Simon felt free to move on as well.

He turned his focus away from the show and onto the spectators. Mrs. Blackwood was enraptured. Her husband stood the stalwart at her side as he pompously enjoyed the spectacle.

Simon moved around the back of the gathered crowd. Behind them another show was going on as footmen quietly went about removing empty glasses and setting out a new tray with port and sherry. A young, pretty maid, no more than fifteen or sixteen came into the room. From the state of her apron and dress she clearly wasn't a parlor maid or even a house maid, but a scullery.

To the upper class in England, scullery maids should never be seen, and certainly not during a party. It was a breach of etiquette and if she were found out, she'd be severely punished. Despite that, the girl tiptoed toward the fireplace and Simon realized why. She'd left one of her brushes.

She crept along the far wall and then stopped in mid-step as she realized he was watching her. He smiled slightly and shook his head, silently promising he would not give her away. She smiled in return and hurried to the hearth, and bent down to pick up her brush. Unfortunately, Simon was not the only one who saw her.

Roderick, Blackwood's omnipresent valet, appeared at her side and gripped her arm, pulling her to her feet. The fear in the girl's face was plain to see. However, it went beyond fear of the usual repercussions for a breach of etiquette. It was something else.

She looked at Roderick, her face pale. His gaze moved meaningfully to where Blackwood stood and the girl blanched. Simon leaned forward, ready to move in if the girl needed his help. What on earth was going on here?

Roderick yanked her arm and pulled her toward the door. Blackwood turned just then and frowned deeply in displeasure. The girl struggled one last moment, silently pleading, before Roderick moved her through the door. That was when Simon noticed the change in Blackwood's expression—from angry to pleased. It was as though he'd just gotten something he wanted very much. Simon realized what that must have been, as Blackwood's eyes lingered—the girl.

SIMON WAS ODDLY QUIET on the carriage ride back to their hotel. Not that he was ever a chatterbox, but there was quiet, the content kind, and then there was quiet, the dark brooding kind. This was definitely the latter.

"Did something happen?" she asked.

He looked up, pulled from whatever reverie he was in, and started to answer, but closed his mouth with a frown. He looked up at the roof of the cab toward where the driver was sitting and shook his head, silently telling her that it would have to wait until they were away from potentially prying ears.

Although the cabbie was just for hire and probably wouldn't have any idea what they were talking about, it was wise to be cautious about what they said and where. After all, she'd overheard a few juicy pieces of gossip herself tonight.

Happily, it wasn't long before they reached Brown's Hotel. Simon helped her down and paid the driver. Elizabeth started up the front steps, but he didn't follow.

"How about a walk? I think I could use some air," he said.

The air was manure-scented, but honestly, she was so used it now she hardly noticed. She nodded and came back down the steps, winding her arm through the elbow he offered.

The night was oddly clear, and felt clean and crisp. It had a little nip to it, but between Simon and the fifty layers of clothing she had on, it was not a problem.

They walked toward Berkeley Square and one of the most elite neighborhoods in all of the West End. Enormous houses like Landsdowne and Devonshire were mini-palaces sheltering in the shadow of the real thing. It was early enough that few other people were out walking, and the only sounds were their footfalls on the sidewalk and the occasional carriage or cart.

"What happened at the party?" Elizabeth said as they turned up the block toward the park.

"I'm not sure."

"Simon Cross is always sure," she teased.

He gave a small laugh, then sobered and told her about what he'd seen go on between the maid, the valet and the doctor.

"You think he beats them?" she asked, feeling the anger growing inside her.

"Or worse."

She swallowed down the bile that rose up at the image of the doctor forcing himself on the girl.

She trusted Simon's instincts, but that was a lot to glean from a single look.

As if hearing her doubts he said, "I know it's a bit of a stretch, but it was the way she looked at him, and more so, the way he looked at her. It was indecent."

"That doesn't make him a killer though," Elizabeth said, master of stating the obvious.

"No, but it does make me wonder. He isn't having a sexual relationship with his wife. If he were to find that elsewhere—"

"With the servants?"

"And others," Simon prompted her.

"Prostitutes."

He nodded. "It's possible."

"Maybe that's why Elizabeth Stride was at his office the other day. That didn't seem to be hospital business."

"No," Simon agreed. "It did not."

Elizabeth considered the new information. "Ok, so the doctor might be one of those madonna/whore types. Worships his virtuous and untouched wife, and gets all lecherous with his 'lessers'—the servants and prostitutes."

"He wouldn't be the first."

She knew he was right, but the whole notion was disturbed. Then again, so much here was.

"I learned a little tidbit about the doctor tonight. Guess who went to see him yesterday?"

Simon arched an eyebrow and waited.

"None other than our own little Miss Katherine Vale."

He was duly surprised by the news. "And how did you find that out?"

Elizabeth laughed. "George. He's a worse gossip than any woman I know."

Simon hmm'd softly.

"He said that her headaches are getting worse. I didn't add that it's probably just the crazy breaking off in there and scrambling everything up."

Simon snorted.

Elizabeth shrugged. "I'm not sure what it gets us, but Vale plus doctor who specializes in crazy, well, it's something to keep an eye on."

"A close eye," Simon said. "I've been wondering if we haven't paid enough attention to our Miss Vale. I'd be shocked if she weren't at the crux of whatever changes her old self made to history here."

"We've been so busy, chasing our tails and missing opportunities," Elizabeth said, knowing it sounded bitter.

"It's frustrating, isn't it?"

It was more than that. Elizabeth was a woman of action. She would have come with her own kung-fu grip if she'd had anything to say about it. So far, the only action they'd seen was their own darn fault. And now they had three weeks until the next opportunity. It was maddening.

Simon must have sensed her anxiety because he tucked his elbow in a bit closer, pulling her toward him. "We have to be patient."

"How can you be so calm about it?"

"You think I'm calm?"

His equanimity was one of his most infuriating traits. "Yes."

Simon pulled up short. "What would you have me do? Make him kill faster?"

Shocked at his sudden temper, Elizabeth leaned away from him. He looked poised to fight, but just as quickly the set of his shoulders softened.

"I'm sorry," he said and let out a deep breath before looking up to the heavens for strength. "I hate this. I hate every moment of it. The very thought of having to watch a woman be brutally murdered and do nothing…"

He stopped and closed his eyes briefly. When he opened them, he'd gathered himself again. "I may appear calm, but I assure you, I am not."

Elizabeth felt foolish. Of course, he wasn't taking this in stride. He was just better at not acting like a jackass about things they couldn't change.

"I'm sorry," Elizabeth said and stepped closer to him, putting her hands on his chest and needlessly smoothing out the lapel of his waistcoat.

"It's like being forced to wait to watch a snuff film only to be told to come back and do it again tomorrow," she said. "Sometimes I think the waiting for things is worse than the thing itself. Except this time," she continued looking up into his handsome, worried face, "it's not. They're both unbearable."

Simon gently touched the side of her face, and she closed her eyes and leaned into his palm.

"And yet we will bear it," he said softly, and then gently tilted her head back, urging her to open her eyes. "The price is too high not to."

He looked at her with such love, such faith, it made her chest hurt.

"I would walk through fire for you," he said.

Elizabeth let out a shaky breath. "Let's hope it doesn't come to that."

Simon laughed. "Agreed."

He kissed her lightly, and started them down the street toward their hotel. Elizabeth felt better and worse at the same time. Simon's strength and conviction revitalized her and yet she knew, while it might not be fire, they would both walk through something a lot like Hell before this was over.

Chapter Twenty

After the revelation last night that Katherine Vale was seeing their prime suspect, Dr. Blackwood, Elizabeth and Simon had agreed that they needed to find out more about what Vale was up to. What they didn't agree on was how. They didn't want to separate, but somehow the idea of Katherine Vale spilling her guts, metaphorically, to Simon was hard to picture. If Elizabeth could get her alone, she might let something slip.

In the end, Elizabeth's logic had won out—a rare victory and one to be relished when married to Simon Cross—and so she went alone to Hyde Park Hotel. Well, alone-ish. Simon was not willing to let her stray too far from him, and planted himself in the park across the street where he could see the hotel entrance clearly. A few days ago, Elizabeth would have thought he was being overly cautious, but that had been before she'd run willy-nilly through the streets of Whitechapel with no idea what the holy heck was going on.

Elizabeth looked across the street, nodded once to him and then turned and walked up the steps to the lobby. As she did she focused on Vale, trying out various, potential tacks. *Feeling crazier than usual? Are you hearing voices? Seen any good doctors lately?* But they all seemed a little too direct. This Vale might be younger and less experienced, but she was no fool. Elizabeth would have to tread carefully and hope Vale gave her some information without realizing she'd done it.

Elizabeth entered the lobby and headed for the front desk. She was planning on getting her room number and surprising her with an invitation to lunch, but Elizabeth was the one who was surprised. Vale was already standing at the front desk, either returning her key or getting it.

Just as Elizabeth was about to approach her, a young man appeared at the front desk next to her. He asked the clerk something and that something must have been for Katherine Vale's room because she turned in surprise and the man laughed lightly and then smiled.

Elizabeth wasn't sure what it was, there was nothing odd about the man, but something, instinct, told her to wait and watch. But she couldn't just stand there and gawk. The lobby was busy, but if Vale turned, Elizabeth would easily be seen. She needed cover. It was probably silly, but she edged behind a potted plant and watched between the fronds, trying her best to read their lips as they spoke.

The man, who was not much more than a boy, smiled eagerly back at Vale and fished into his jacket pocket for something. He was well-dressed, but not fancy, a conservative dark suit, maybe in banking or some other Serious Occupation. He pulled out an envelope and held it out to her. She looked at it suspiciously and shook her head. He said something, Elizabeth's lipreading wasn't very good, but it looked like he was saying her name, confirming she was the one he should deliver this to. She nodded and he inched the envelope closer with a smile.

Well, this was interesting development. Who, other than Graham, would send her a note? And if it had been Graham, why not just leave it at the desk or use a messenger boy? The man standing across from her was young, but he was not just a messenger. Elizabeth supposed it was still possible it was from Graham, but…

Frowning, Vale took the envelope from him, but waited until he'd tipped his hat and left the lobby before she made any move to open it.

She turned the envelope over in her hands, curious, but wary. She chewed her lower lip and seemed to be deciding what to do with it when Graham appeared near the stairs. He called out to her and instead of turning to face him, asking or telling him about this odd letter, she stuffed it hastily in her reticule to hide it from him.

Whatever it was, it wasn't from Graham and it was a secret. At least, Elizabeth added silently, until she got her mitts on it.

"Are you all right, Miss?" a man said at Elizabeth's ear.

She turned in surprise and he nodded toward the plant. "Are you…stuck?"

Elizabeth laughed nervously as she shimmied out from behind the plant. "No, I just…I thought I'd lost my bag back here."

"The one on your wrist?" he said trying not to sound like he was talking to an imbecile.

"Ah! So it is. Always the last place you look, isn't it?" she said. She widened her eyes and twisted her hands in a swirling motion near her head. "A bit featherbrained today, I'm afraid."

He smiled and took a step closer as his eyes made a quick run up and down her body. "Not at all."

Elizabeth laughed again. "My husband certainly thinks so."

The man stepped back and cleared his throat. "Oh."

Realizing that there was no room for advancement here, the man tipped his hat and wished her a good day. As she turned back to Graham and Vale, she thought it might just be one after all.

VALE HAD WANTED TO go back to her rooms to lie down and rest. Elizabeth knew it was really because she was anxious to read the mysterious letter. But Graham put the kibosh on the idea, saying that a day out would do her good. Amazingly, she demurred to his wishes. The older one would have laughed in his face and then killed him, or maybe vice versa just for kicks. This Vale was young and unsure, and didn't want to upset Graham, so she agreed to join Elizabeth for an outing. And hopefully a little purloining of the purse, Elizabeth thought to herself.

Graham put them in a cab for Regent Circus, and the look of what seemed to almost be relief at being shed of Vale for the day wasn't lost on Elizabeth. It might have been her imagination, but she didn't think it was lost on Vale either.

Elizabeth craned her neck as she got into the carriage, trying to see if Simon was going to follow, but she couldn't find him. She felt a tightening in her stomach and did her best to ignore it. He was there somewhere, she told herself. He was fine.

She had to follow this clue, or whatever it was. The list of who might send Katherine Vale a letter was a short one. It clearly wasn't Graham. Dr. Blackwood or George, perhaps, but why be so secretive? Another man? From the way Vale looked at Graham that didn't seem likely. Who else could it be?

Vale leaned back into the seat as the cab pulled away from the curb and sighed. It wasn't exactly a fake sigh, but a little forced, dramatic, a sigh people used as a lure to get someone to ask them what's wrong.

Elizabeth was curious and willingly took the bait. "Everything all right?"

"Everything's…all right," Vale managed half-heartedly.

Elizabeth had to keep from smiling. She so obviously wanted to talk about something, but didn't want Elizabeth to know she did. She waited for more, but Vale apparently wanted her pull it out of her.

"Just all right?"

Vale offered her a small, sad smile. "I don't know."

Elizabeth knew this game. *I can't say it, but if you ask me…* She bit the inside of her mouth and then said, "I'd like to think we're friends. If something's bothering you…"

Vale nodded, relieved that some sort of amorphous permission to speak freely had been granted. "I'm worried about Charles."

Worried you're going to grow to hate him with the fiery passion of ten thousand suns? "In what way?"

Vale leaned back in her seat and looked lifelessly out at the city. "I think he might be seeing someone else."

She looked at Elizabeth to judge her reaction and then laughed, embarrassed at having admitted such a thing. "I know it's silly."

"I'm sure whatever's going on," Elizabeth said, "that's not it."

"He's just been so distant since we've been here. Going off by himself, secretive." She shook her head and raised her eyebrows in puzzlement. "I can't blame him if he's tired of my silly headaches. I know I am."

Elizabeth forgot herself for a moment and laid a comforting hand on top of Vale's. "I'm sure he doesn't blame you for those."

"I'm really not usually like this," Vale said.

How well Elizabeth knew that. The woman was made of ice, permanently frozen, unforgiving ice.

"We all have our bad days," Elizabeth said.

Vale smiled genuinely and squeezed her hand. "Thank you. I suppose Charles was right. A day out is just what I need."

A few minutes later their cab pulled up to the corner of Regent and Oxford streets. Elizabeth, hoping for a chance to separate Vale from her purse for a few minutes, had suggested they spend the afternoon shopping in the bazaars.

Elizabeth doubted they were anything like the ones she'd seen in Cairo, but if they were crowded, and loud and busy, she might find an opportunity to borrow Vale's purse to get a peek at that letter.

They turned around the corner, unsure of which way to go when Elizabeth saw it. There was no mistaking the tall long building with the ceiling of glass she'd read about the in Baedeker's Guide she'd found at a shop near their hotel.

She'd heard of the Crystal Palace, built for one of London's Exhibitions, and this bazaar was styled after it. Nestled between two buildings, the Crystal Palace Bazaar was an oddity. They walked through the large, open doorway and into a wide, vaulted hall with an arched ceiling that had to be forty feet high. Iron and glass shaped into stars and diamonds made up the coved ceiling and two tiers of enormous iron columns painted in oddly bilious colors—blue, red, and white—held the entire thing up. There were two levels, with vendors displaying their wares inside large wood and glass counters and lines of shelves that ran the length of the building.

Definitely not like Cairo, but bustling and loud just the same.

They looked at jewelry and pewter work, art and ladies' gloves.

"You should try these on," Elizabeth said holding up a pair of kid gloves for Vale.

She took them and ran them through her fingers, admiringly. "They are nice, aren't they?"

"I'll hold yours," Elizabeth offered.

Vale took off her gloves and handed them to her.

"And your purse," Elizabeth said, "so you can really see them."

"Oh, that's all right," Vale said, holding out her hands in front of her. "What do you think?"

"Nice." So much for plan A.

In the end, Vale decided against them, although she did purchase a handsome black pair for Charles. As she paid for them, Elizabeth caught a tantalizing look inside her purse. There wasn't much inside it, just a small compact, a few coins and the letter. No watch, Elizabeth noted. And while the letter was right there, it might as well have been in a vault. She couldn't exactly snatch and grab it. That would be difficult to explain.

And so she tried to be patient. But that was never her strong suit and what little she'd had had been spent the first week they'd been here.

"How about a new purse?" Elizabeth suggested as they neared a stall with embroidered handbags.

"There's nothing wrong with this one," Vale said, starting to move on.

Elizabeth quickly picked a bag up. "But does it sparkle?"

She wiggled the bag back and forth and Vale laughed, and came back to the stall.

"They are attractive."

"This one is you," Elizabeth said. "It even matches your dress."

She held the bag up against Vale's blue silk dress.

"Try it on," Elizabeth suggested. "There's a mirror over there."

Vale looked at the purse and then nodded. "I'm sure it's ridiculously expensive."

She slipped her reticule off her wrist and handed it to Elizabeth.

"Live a little."

Vale smiled conspiratorially and put the bag on her wrist, and moved to the mirror.

Elizabeth edged around to the other side of the display table, lowered her hands so Vale couldn't see them, and eased open the draw string. Inside the little letter waited.

Making sure no one was looking Elizabeth started to reach inside. She had no idea what she was going to do when she got it. How could she read it and reseal it? If she out and out stole it, wouldn't Vale know she was the one who took it?

Dang.

Elizabeth let the letter slip out of her hand and back into the bag. She'd have to come up with something better than that. Maybe they could get Freddie to hire some of his little pals to steal it?

But when? How?

She needed help and looked around the Bazaar. *Simon, where are you?* He was nowhere to be seen. Elizabeth swallowed the lump of worry that left in her throat.

"Too much for me," Vale said, suddenly reappearing at her side and putting the bag back on the counter.

She held out her hand for her purse and with a forced smile, Elizabeth gave it to her. They window-shopped for a little while longer, before having a cup of tea and heading for home.

They both rode in thoughtful silence until Vale called out for the driver to pull over. He did as instructed and pulled the cab over near the Marble Arch.

"I think I'll walk the rest of the way," Vale said. "Fresh air."

Elizabeth nodded, what else could she do? "It was fun."

Vale climbed out of the carriage. "See you soon?"

Elizabeth nodded again and cursed herself. She'd finally had a chance to do *something* and all she'd managed was to end up full of tea again.

The cab pulled away and drove around the circle. Across the street, Elizabeth could see Vale had stopped. She had the letter out of her purse and was tearing open the envelope.

"Pull around the corner and stop," Elizabeth told the driver.

She paid him and quickly got out and hurried back to the arch. She could just see Vale across the busy street. If she hadn't read the letter yet, Elizabeth might learn something from seeing her face as she did.

Creeping as close as she dared, Elizabeth hid behind a man selling baked potatoes from a large cart. Vale read the letter, slowly shaking her head as she did. She looked around nervously and Elizabeth ducked down behind the large copper warmer. The heat escaping from the boiler pushed against the left side of her face.

"All right, Miss?" the vendor asked, concerned.

Elizabeth waved her hand at him. "I'm not here."

"Right," he said as if women hid behind his cart daily. " 'ot taties!"

Vale turned the letter over to see if there was anything written on the back side. There wasn't. But she opened the little envelope again and pulled something else out. It was flat and square and white on the back, but Elizabeth couldn't make out more from where she was.

Vale looked shaken. She clutched the letter and envelope to her chest and looked around again in a near panic. She hurried over to a coster who was just setting up to sell roasted chestnuts to crowds that evening. He'd built a good fire in his brazier and turned away to see to his stock.

Elizabeth watched helplessly, knowing her chance to know what was in that letter was nearly gone.

Vale looked one last time at the contents of the envelope and then tossed them all into the fire. Elizabeth's heart sank as Vale watched them for a moment to make sure they'd caught and then hurried down the street.

Elizabeth watched her for a second and then overcome with the need to not fail again, she leapt from her hiding place and ran across the busy street.

She was nearly hit by not one, but two horse-drawn carts as she wove through traffic to the other side. She must have looked like a mad woman, but she didn't care. She had to know what was in that letter. Somehow it had become the poster child for this whole darn mission and she just couldn't let it all go up in smoke.

She dashed over to the brazier in time to see the last bits of the letter curl and turn into ash. She was too late. Again.

Feeling sick, she started to turn away when she saw the telltale white edge of a small square piece of paper. It must have slipped between the grates and fallen to the ground, half-burned.

Elizabeth stepped on it, crushing out the remaining sparks. She bent down to pick it up. Somehow, she wasn't surprised by what she saw.

"Good God," Simon said breathlessly as he came to her side. So, he had been following. Dear Simon.

"Are you *trying* to give me a heart attack?" he panted out.

She barely heard him as she stared down at the paper in her hands.

"Elizabeth?" Simon asked, turning her toward him. "You look like you've seen a ghost."

She looked up to see his worried face. "I have."

She held up the burned bit of paper for him to see. It was a photograph. A photograph of the older Katherine Vale.

Chapter Twenty-One

Victor took a long drink of his beer to wash away the taste of the eel pie he'd managed to keep down. Now if there was just something to wash away the taste of the beer.

The pub was crowded, as it always was, but he did his best to listen for anything that might be helpful. It was the beginning of another long night. Time here traveled painfully slowly, inching along like the wretched people that were sometimes called the crawlers—old women so weak and infirm that they literally dragged themselves along the street. He'd seen them huddled together on the steps of the workhouse, in a knot of misery, waiting for the end to come. Some called them "dossers" because they lived in a state of perpetual dozing, stuck between waking and sleep, never finding either. And instead of mercy, they found only more misery. Even death ignored them.

Victor had seen a great many horrors in his life, but the conditions of those women would stay with him forever. Not that it would do him or them any good, he thought as he drank the last of his beer and signaled for another.

"Oi, wot ya got there, Collie?" Fanny, a local prostitute with a shrill voice called out to her friend who'd just come into the pub.

"You know I 'ate that name. It's Colleen," the woman said, putting on airs as best she could.

She would have been able to pull it off if she'd many teeth left. In a sea of mousy brown and bleached blonde, she stood out with almost silver hair and pale, freckled skin.

"Oh, all hoity-toity today, ain't we?" Fanny said, swishing her skirts about her legs.

Colleen lifted her nose in the air and sashayed over to the bar, winning a derisive laugh from Fanny.

"Look at her," Fanny said and then gave an exaggerated imitation of Colleen and flounced her way to the bar as well.

A few onlookers gave hearty laughs, but Colleen was not amused. She said something to the barkeep that Victor couldn't hear before turning to glare at Fanny.

The barmaid dropped off Victor's beer and he took a long drink from it.

"You get somethin' good this time?" Fanny said, leaning in to try to sneak a peek at the small bundle Colleen held close to her bosom.

"If I did, you ain't seein' none of it. I earned it."

"On your back," Fanny said, winning another laugh from the men at the tables nearby.

One of the men reached out and grabbed Colleen by the skirt and pulled her into his lap. "Why don't you share it with me, Love?"

"Get off me," Colleen said, struggling to get up.

Victor set his beer down, his teeth on edge. Things like this happened daily, hourly, in the Ten Bells, but Victor was spoiling for a fight tonight and if these idiots wanted to oblige…

"Don't worry," a voice said from nearby, Marie. "It is like this every time she comes in."

Victor eased, but only slightly.

"All right, all right," the barkeep said, coming around to the table. "Let 'er go, Paulie. It's hers. She's got the right to keep it."

Colleen wrenched herself away and hugged the small parcel even more protectively than before.

Marie sat down at Victor's table.

"What's in it?" Victor asked, curious in spite of himself.

Marie looked at the woman with sympathy. "She sleeps with the baker and he pays her in sweets. It's probably a tart," she added, turning back to Victor. "He thinks that's funny."

Victor clenched his jaw and nodded. Why not add insult to injury?

Marie smiled at him. "Don't feel too bad for her. She does all right. Better than most."

"And you?" he asked, not sure why he wanted to know.

She shrugged. "When I've got a man, I do all right."

She watched Colleen leave the pub before leaning back in her chair and smiling sadly at Victor.

"But you never stay put, do you?" Marie added.

Victor knew she didn't mean him in particular although it was true enough for him as well. All he could do was nod and take another drink of beer.

A small group of men led by George Lusk came into the pub then. Victor had been waiting for them. The Whitechapel Vigilance Committee had finally been officially formed. They'd sent letters to the Powers That Be asking for more police, more attention and so far they'd gotten little in return. The only real change was that the marauding bands of vigilantes had turned into marauding bands of organized vigilantes.

While George Lusk was conservative and, from what Victor had heard and seen of him, a peaceful man, the men under him were not. They'd much rather hit first and not bother to ask questions later, as the lump on the back of his head proved. With Victor's mood as dark as it was today, joining a group of thugs who were bound to find trouble whether it was real or not, sounded just right.

"You'll excuse me," Victor said as he stood and started toward Lusk.

He'd nearly gotten there when he felt someone tugging on his sleeve. He turned, expecting to see Marie, but instead found young Alfie, Freddie's little brother, panting and holding out a note.

Victor frowned and read it quickly. His mood grew that much darker. Vale had contacted her younger self. That witch was still pulling the strings, even from her jail cell.

"No reply," he muttered softly as he folded up the note and slipped it into his pocket.

The boy nodded and looked around the pub, his eyes unerringly finding a rather well-endowed woman.

"Ay," Victor said, tugging on the boy's shoulder to get his attention.

Alfie spun around, fear he'd done something wrong in his eyes.

Victor let out a sigh. "You're doing a good job."

The boy smiled proudly and puffed out his chest. "I know."

Victor couldn't help but smile. "Now, get out," he said, spinning the boy around and giving him a nudge toward the door.

The boy fought his own smile and, with one last cheeky look at the woman's bosom, slipped out the door.

Lusk banged his fist against the bar to get everyone's attention. "I'm looking for men."

"I know a few that swing that way down in Croydon," Fanny said, earning a roaring laugh from the crowd.

Lusk let them have their laugh and then held up his hands. "All right, all right. We're waiting to hear back from Inspector Aberline about adding men to the patrols in Whitechapel. But until we do, we're going to do it ourselves."

That won him a loud cheer and some vitriol aimed at the police.

He held up his hands for silence again. "If you're able bodied—"

"Able to what?" Fanny said again, earning another laugh.

Lusk glared at her.

"All right. Just 'avin' a bit of fun."

He frowned, but turned back to the crowd. "If you're able bodied and want to join up, come see Frank here."

Victor joined the men who moved over to the bar.

The little man who'd been one of his captors earlier frowned at him.

Victor smiled back.

"THE BETTERMOST DOLLS' EYES, they're the natural ones. Made in a superior way, you understand?"

Victor did not reply. He did not need to. The man needed no audience, no reaction; he supplied them all himself.

"Lovely. Fourpence a pair, they are, but no one wants them anymore. They all want common eyes."

Victor sighed and he and his companion continued down the street on a tour as endless as the man's conversation. The men of the Vigilance Committee were sent out in pairs to patrol. Victor was sure it was some sort of punishment that Frank had put him with Old Tuck. The man simply never stopped talking.

"The missus and I, we also make human eyes. I've got two cases; in the one I have black and hazel, and in the other blue and grey.

And for the ladies' eyes we put a little more sparkle in 'em, just to make 'em shine a bit more than the gents'."

Victor tried to ignore the endless prattle, but it was like a bee buzzing in his ear.

"The French makes eyes as well," Tuck said, snatching a sideways glance at Victor. "But, if ya don't mind my sayin' so, they're low quality. Don't move right. Just sort of sit there, starin' at ya."

He held up his hands in front if his face like a mesmerist and wiggled his fingers before letting his hands fall to his sides again. "Quite unnervin'."

There was a blessed pause after that and they walked a few steps in silence. Victor relished the quiet, but it was short-lived.

"I had a lady customer once," Tuck said, launching himself yet again. "Husband didn't even know. That's how fine that eye was. I thought—"

"How about a drink?" Victor said quickly.

He'd noticed Tuck's eyes had lingered on every pub door they'd passed.

"You must be thirsty," he added. After your ceaseless talking.

The man swallowed and licked his lips before pursing them in thought. "A pint would go down easy."

One good thing, perhaps the only good thing, one could say about Whitechapel was there that there was always a pub close by, and Victor nodded toward one just up the street.

Tuck rubbed his hands together and grinned. "Just one. Just to quench the old thirst."

As Victor had suspected, one quickly led to two, and Old Tuck was just as happy to stay put in the pub for just a bit longer, "to rest my poor old weary bones."

Victor left him there and set out on his own. The streets were busy; they almost always were. This part of the city was so overcrowded that the people seeped out of buildings and onto the streets like water through cracks in a bursting dam.

His rounds took him up Wilkes and back around the Black Eagle Brewery. As he turned East, the train and Shoreditch Station to his left, he noticed a cab. A rather nice cab. A rather familiar cab.

He crossed the street and found the cabbie taking off a feedbag from his horse. It was the same man he'd seen outside of the hospital the day Elizabeth Stride had paid Dr. Blackwood a visit. The same man he'd seen drive past Annie Chapman's boarding house the night she was murdered.

"Have a light?" he asked, pulling out his pipe and holding it up.

The man nodded and put away his feedbag. He dug into his pocket, pulled out a pipe of his own and a match. He lit it and held it for Victor to get his pipe going and then did the same for his own.

"It's a nice carriage," Victor said. "You own it?"

The man pushed his shoulders back. "I do."

"Think I saw it the other night."

"I get around," he said, with a shrug.

"The night of the murder."

The man's jaw set.

"Not far from it," Victor added with a thoughtful puff from his pipe.

The driver narrowed his eyes and cocked his head to the side. "Look, I ain't got nothin' to do with any of that."

Victor eyed the small man. "You drove a doctor into Whitechapel that night," he said, hoping he was right.

The driver's face went a bit pale. "How'd you know that?"

"That coroner said that the murderer might be a doctor," Victor said.

The man's eyes went wide with fear and he chewed at the inside of his mouth.

"I'm with the Committee," Victor said, standing a little closer to the smaller man. "If you know something, you should tell me."

The man's eyes fluttered nervously. "I took the doc 'round to Pelham near Hobson. Said he was helpin' a babe be born. Nothin' to do with that other business."

"Dr. Blackwood?"

The man paled visibly. "I didn't say that."

Victor smiled slightly. "Of course not."

So Blackwood *was* in Whitechapel the night of the second murder, and possibly the first.

"Look, I can't afford to lose that job. I just got it last week."

"I'm sure it is nothing," Victor said, and the man relaxed.

Victor nodded genially and then clapped his hand down heavily on the man's shoulder, feeling the cabbie's legs give just a little beneath him. "But if it is not..."

"I just drive. I don't know what he does. He gets out and likes to walk. I don't even know where he goes really."

Victor's gaze did not flinch.

The man swallowed nervously and shook his head. "He just walks."

"Did you drive him here on the morning of the first?"

"The first?"

Victor leaned in. "The first of the month."

"I told ya. I just got the job a week ago."

"Is he here tonight?"

He shook his head. "I ain't seen him in two days."

Victor stared into the man's eyes. He saw fear there, but no deception.

He released his grip and patted the man's shoulder. "I'm sure it is just as you say."

The driver took a nervous step back and massaged his shoulder. If Victor found out he was lying, that he had a part in what was done here, he would need more than a massage to ease his pain.

"What's your name?"

"Netley. John Netley."

Victor regarded him for a moment. "Have a good evening, Mr. Netley."

Victor started down the street and said over his shoulder, "and thanks for the light."

It did not take Victor long to find the house the doctor had visited the night of Chapman's murder. There was no baby born there that night though, although not for lack of trying.

The whorehouse had six girls working and one room that could be rented by the half hour. It seemed the doctor was a frequent visitor there until he'd been asked not to return. Apparently, he tended to take things a little too far. His last time with Lizzy Stride had been one too many times. He'd "damaged the merchandise."

The doctor had come back that night and been turned away. Where he went after that, no one knew.

Finally, the pieces were beginning to fit together, Victor thought. And the picture they made was not very pretty.

Chapter Twenty-Two

It was a Punch and Judy show. These so-called sitters were no more than Blavatsky's puppets and they danced when she told them to.

Simon hated events like this. Lies and deception, preying on people's fears. The "séance" took place in Blavatsky's home in St. John's Wood which doubled as headquarters for the Theosophy Society. The main parlor had been prepared with a table and chairs for the "sitters", the people who would channel the spirits, and several rows for the paying spectators.

Of course, having the performance in a place she could rig with any number of tricks was wise, and every one of her stunts played well to the audience—except for Elizabeth, who seemed transfixed by the taxidermy baboon Blavatsky called Mr. Fiske. It stood in the corner of the room ironically holding a copy of Darwin's *The Origin of the Species*. Apparently, Blavatsky was not a fan of science.

Simon shifted impatiently in his seat. As if having to listen to a mad woman conjure spirits weren't enough, he was forced to sit next to Katherine Vale for the duration of it.

After he'd seen the photograph Elizabeth had salvaged from the fire, the cold fist that had held his heart since they'd come here tightened its grip. They'd half expected Vale to cancel the invitation, but she hadn't. In fact, other than being a little more nervous than usual, she hadn't behaved differently toward them at all. Simon had anticipated some change. It was almost worse that there wasn't one, or at least not one they could observe. As Elizabeth had said, "Secret crazy is the scariest kind."

Simon definitely agreed. It was possible Vale's letter hadn't done whatever she'd intended it to do, that their very presence had changed things and Vale's plan was already thwarted just by them being there.

Was he so far gone that wishful thinking was now a viable option? Simon snorted softly at his own folly. The small noise he'd made earned him a reproachful glance from Elizabeth. He arched his eyebrows in an insincere apology and they turned back to the show.

"The room is too cold," Blavatsky kept saying. "The spirits are shy."

Simon bit his tongue to keep from shouting out, "Then just turn up the damned heat."

Not that it would have done any good. He would have been escorted out and Blavatsky, clever woman that she was, would turn it to her advantage. People like her always found the angle.

Tonight, she found it for the princely sum of £2 per person. With roughly thirty people in the audience, it wasn't bad for a night's work.

In spite of the "challenging" conditions, Blavatsky pressed on, trying to summon the spirits of Annie Chapman and Polly Nichols. The sitters channeled all manner of dead persons from a poor Cockney boy to Fredrick Chopin, but the victims were too traumatized to communicate. Unsurprisingly, neither Chopin nor the boy knew who Jack the Ripper was.

Despite the evening being a complete farce and generating not a shred of evidence toward the crimes, it was deemed a huge success by all in attendance, Vale included.

As the séance ended, she turned to Simon, a strange look in her eye. Gone was the guileless young woman they'd known here, and in her place was something else.

It was the look of someone who knew something he didn't, of someone who had the advantage and took pleasure in that. It was an expression he'd seen in her before. In the other, older Katherine Vale. Suddenly, the room did feel cold.

He held her gaze, keeping himself as steady and unaffected as he could, and like a spark that was snuffed out, whatever had been in her eyes vanished.

She smiled, excited, seemingly unaware of the moment that had just preceded. "Wasn't that fascinating?"

Simon nodded. Perhaps Elizabeth was right and bits of crazy were breaking off. The duality she presented was not a good sign.

"Rubbish," Graham said.

He'd not bothered to hide his feelings about Blavatsky before the performance and clearly wasn't going to sugar coat them now. Simon could see that the jibe struck Vale, but she shrugged it off and turned back to Simon and Elizabeth.

"I could introduce you, if you'd like," Vale offered. "She's very busy, but she's taken a bit of a shine to me."

"I'll wait out front," Graham said, giving Simon a look that said *and if you were smart, you'd follow my lead.* Simon was tempted to follow, but before he could, Elizabeth accepted her offer.

Madame Blavatsky sat in a large reading chair and looked very much the queen holding court as people came to pay their compliments for the evening.

When Vale arrived, Blavatsky smiled. "Ah, my dear child, what did you think?"

"You're amazing."

Blavatsky shook her head. "The room was not conducive. But I tried," she added with a put-upon sigh.

"I'd like to introduce you to someone," Vale said.

Madame Blavatsky nodded tiredly and turned her gaze to Simon and Elizabeth.

"This is Simon and Elizabeth Cross."

Blavatsky eyed them briefly before turning her attention back to Vale. "Help Peter with the pamphlets, would you?"

Vale smiled, happy to be of service and hurried to hand out literature about Theosophy as people lingered.

Blavatsky watched her for a moment before turning back to them. She looked at Simon briefly and then her gaze slid to Elizabeth.

"It's nice to meet you," Elizabeth said.

Blavatsky stared at her, her eyes squinting slightly, her expression unreadable. She tilted her head to the side and then pushed herself out of her chair and took a step toward Elizabeth to close the distance.

Elizabeth looked uneasily to Simon and then back to Blavatsky.

The older woman took Elizabeth's hands in hers. "I am sorry for your loss."

Elizabeth laughed nervously. "What loss?"

If she didn't have Simon's attention before, she definitely did now.

Blavatsky's eyes searched her face and then darted over to Simon. "Your child."

That fist around Simon's heart clenched. Elizabeth looked over at him, near-panic in her eyes.

They'd had this conversation before, but somewhere else and with someone else. Old Nan, the blind seer in Natchez, had said the same thing to them and it had haunted them both ever since.

Elizabeth shook her head and Simon heard the way she struggled to keep her voice calm. "We don't have any children."

Blavatsky smiled, a little sadly and a little something that made Simon's skin itch. "Perhaps it has not come to pass."

The words took Simon's breath away. He stood transfixed for a moment, stilled by the shock of a conversation repeating itself decades later and thousands of miles away. Forcibly, he pulled his mind under control. This was not right.

Gentle, but insistent, he pulled Elizabeth away from her, breaking the contact.

Her face had gone pale and she looked up at him with large, frightened eyes. As much as he wanted to pull her into his arms and comfort her, he couldn't. Not here. Not now. Instead, he shook his head and shifted his eyes quickly to Vale across the room.

Elizabeth seemed to understand and forced a smile to her face, and turned back to Madame Blavatsky. "Well, let's hope you're wrong about that."

Blavatsky raised her eyebrows and gave a small, indifferent shrug. "I see what I see."

"Yes," Simon said, and had to clear his throat to continue. "It was a fascinating evening."

She lowered herself into her chair and waved a regal hand, dismissing them.

Simon took Elizabeth by the arm and led her across the room. "Simon…"

"I know," he whispered, his voice sounding strained even to his own ears. God, he had to get out of here. He had to get some air in his lungs.

She nodded and let out a shuddering breath. They found Vale and quickly begged off dinner.

"Are you sure?" Vale asked.

Elizabeth touched her forehead. "I think it's my turn to have a headache."

"I'm sorry," Vale said kindly and then frowned. "It wasn't anything to do with this evening, I hope?"

It could have been Simon's imagination, God knows it was working overtime just now, but it almost sounded as though there was a hopeful note in Vale's question. And for a moment he saw in her face the older version of herself, her eyes calculating the depth of their misery and enjoying every nuance of their suffering.

If Elizabeth noticed it she ignored it and shook her head. "Just overtired."

"Of course," Vale said. "Well, we'll see you later this week?"

"I'm sure," Simon said, already easing Elizabeth away. "Give Charles our apologies."

Vale smiled and nodded, and they made their escape. Although, Simon thought with a horrible sinking feeling, perhaps from some things there was no escape at all.

Victor's patrol had been much as everything else here, pointless. He'd talked to people, but, unsurprisingly, no one had seen anything. For reasons he didn't want to examine too closely, he stopped back by the pub before heading to his rooms for the night.

Marie was nowhere to be seen. Just as well, he thought. He was in no mood for company. He settled into his hard wooden chair to drink his lukewarm beer when Lizzy Stride came in. She sported a fresh bruise under her eye and the remnants of a fat lip. After a stop at the bar, she slid onto a chair at the next table where two of her friends sat drinking.

"Oi, that's a new one," one of them said.

Stride snorted loudly. "It'll be the last, I'm tellin' ya."

She reached over and took her friend's beer and finished it in one long, sloppy drink. Wiping the dribbles off her chin with the back of her forearm, she continued, "I was paid a little visit last night. Not a gentleman caller."

One of her friends leaned forward, her eyes red and glassy. She tried to put her elbow on the table, but missed and she sloshed forward before catching herself. "Who was it?"

"Berk named Roderick," Lizzy said. "Chi-chi valet, he is, thinks he and his master can do wotever they likes."

That caught Victor's attention. Roderick was Dr. Blackwood's valet.

"Think they can shut me up with a little beatin'. I've had worse from people I like!" she said.

Her friends nodded, dumbly.

"No one's gonna stop me from gettin' mine," Lizzy said. "Not after what he done. Ain't right."

She shook her head slowly and then seemed to suddenly remember she hadn't gotten her beer and screamed like a banshee at the bartender for one.

"All right, Lizzy, all right," the barkeep said with a tired shake of his head.

Lizzy snorted again. "I ain't no pushover. I gots a plan. And that rich doctor," she said, leaning in whispering loudly, "he's gonna pay."

"They should all pay," Victor said, raising his beer in solidarity and hoping he could get more information from her.

"You're right about that," she said without thinking and then her eyes narrowed at him. "Who're you?"

"Victor. Friend of Marie's."

She squinted her eyes even tighter as she tried to remember who that was. "Marie? Oh," she said and then gave a short laugh. "Right. Marie."

"Did the doctor hurt you?" Victor said. "No man should hurt a woman."

She nodded, her head heavily flopping up and down. "He ain't wot he seems," she said, and then leaned over conspiratorially. "None of them is."

Her breath was fetid, but Victor nodded and leaned in. "What did he do?"

She smiled, a secret smile, pleased with herself and then started to open her mouth to talk, but like drunks so often do, her mood changed in an instant and she shook her head. "Naw, then you'll be in on it."

She shook her head more dramatically now. "You ain't hornin' in. None of ya is!"

She stood then, knocking her chair back and sending it nearly clattering to the floor. "You'd like that, wouldn't ya?" she said, addressing the whole bar, none of whom had any idea what she was on about or cared.

She stood there swaying for a moment, before flopping back down into her chair. She turned to Victor. "It's a secret, see? And I ain't supposed to be talkin'." She put a dirty finger to her lips.

"It'll be just our little secret," she said to the top of the table as her head drooped forward. "Shhh...be as silent as the grave."

She nodded to herself and laid her head down and fell asleep.

"HELP ME UNDO THIS," Elizabeth said tugging at the waist of her dress. "I can't breathe in this thing."

Simon closed the door to their rooms and turned up the gaslight.

He moved behind her and unhooked the back enclosures of her dress. "It's going to be—"

She pulled away and turned to face him, her cheeks flushed with anger and emotion. "Don't say it. Don't tell me everything is going to be all right."

Simon closed his mouth and nodded slowly.

Elizabeth looked at him, her anger ebbed quickly and her face fell. "I'm sorry. Maybe you should say it. I think I need to hear it."

Simon took hold of her arms, lowering his head to see eye to eye with her. "It *is* going to be all right."

She hesitated and then looked at him with love and a little admiration. "How can you be so sure?"

He let her go and took off his jacket. "Because I won't allow it to be anything else."

Elizabeth laughed lightly, but it wasn't unkind. "When you say it like that, I almost believe you."

He turned back and caught her eye for a moment before turning away and hanging up his coat on the wooden valet. He wanted to believe it, too.

"How did she know?" Elizabeth said, voicing the one question that plagued them both.

Simon pulled down his bracers. "Vale, I suspect."

Elizabeth paused as she undressed. "What do you mean?"

He pulled off his boots and set them aside. "Vale's letter could have easily included information about us. What better weapon to use against us than," he said, pausing as he imagined their future child, "our most vulnerable area."

"She did needle us about that in Cairo," Elizabeth admitted. "But I'm still not sure how she knew."

"She might be mad, but she's clever and, unfortunately, very astute."

"True," Elizabeth said and then added with a look of apology. "I let her push my buttons. And all that did was let her know that I had them."

He nodded and undid his cuffs. "We're both guilty on that front."

Elizabeth sat down on the edge of the bed. "So you think older Vale told her younger self how to hurt us?"

Simon let out a breath. "And she told Blavatsky. It made for fine theater, after all, didn't it?"

Elizabeth pursed her lips. "But those words? Those exact words? How could Vale know what Nan said? She wasn't there."

"I don't know," he admitted, "but she's…motivated and—"

"Hates our guts?"

Simon frowned. "Yes. With the ability to time travel, there's no telling if she found out where we'd been and went there herself."

"Time stalking?"

"I wouldn't put it past her," he said.

"Well then it's a good thing future her is in the Council jail and her younger self will be in Bedlam soon. Unless we screw this up."

Simon walked over to Elizabeth as she tossed her corset aside.

"Which we will not do," he said.

She nodded, but he could see the fear in her eyes. Fear not for herself, but for their child.

Gently, he pulled her to her feet and against his chest. "I wish I could take you away from all of this, somewhere safe. Where this couldn't touch us."

"It already has touched us," she said, looking up at him, resigned to it, but not beaten by it. "And unless we stop whatever it is she's up to here…"

Simon kissed her forehead. "We will."

Elizabeth sat back down on the bed heavily. "What *is* she up to? It obviously has something to do with Jack the Ripper's death. Do you think she kills him?"

Simon sat down next to her. "Possibly."

"But why? What would she get out of that?"

Simon shook his head. "I don't know. Maybe she's somehow realized that's a focal point in Council history and is targeting it because it unravels so much, alters her path."

Elizabeth leaned against his shoulder. "Maybe. I mean, managing not to be sent to Bedlam is a pretty good motive to change things. It's just that…"

Simon leaned away from her to get a look at her face. "Just what?"

She shook her head as she thought out loud. "It seems impersonal. Everything she's done so far has been *very* personal, with us at the center of it."

"Or Graham," he said, realizing that while they bore the brunt of her vengeance, it was only because they had been there and he hadn't. "She was out to destroy Graham in San Francisco and in Cairo. We were just in the way."

"And Graham's here this time."

"And looking for the Ripper."

Elizabeth shifted to face him. "Maybe she finds him first and kills him."

"Or has him killed," Simon suggested. "Or has them both killed."

Elizabeth nodded and chewed her lower lip in thought. "Maybe."

"Either way, I think we should warn Graham. Whatever she's up to, you can be assured he'll be a target."

She nodded, but looked worried. Not that he blamed her. He was damned worried himself.

He ran a hand down her now bare arm until he reached her wrist. It was so slender he could reach around it with his thumb and forefinger. So small and fragile. He lifted her hand to his lips and kissed it.

She smiled back at him, but the unease remained in her eyes. No words of assurance would take it away. It would stay with her, with him, until this mission was over. One way or the other.

Chapter Twenty-Three

Simon leaned back in his seat as their carriage made its way out of the city and into the country, but he did not relax as he watched the city disappear into the distance behind them. It would hardly be the respite George had painted when he'd invited them. With Dr. Blackwood and both Graham and Vale also in attendance for the weekend, there would be little rest and no relaxation.

After the revelation of Vale's letter and the disturbing encounter with Madame Blavatsky, Simon had been waiting for the proverbial other shoe to drop. Every time they'd seen Vale, he'd been prepared for the worst, prepared for her to strike like the viper she was. But, if anything, she'd been calmer than before, kindness and pleasure in their company oozing out of every pore like a noxious perfume.

The nervous energy she'd exuded when they'd first seen her here in London was nearly gone. Frankly, he'd rather she'd have ranted and raved and foamed at the mouth. Her quiet confidence and unnatural grace were far more unnerving.

Coupled with the new and far from improved Katherine Vale, their investigation had stagnated. After Victor had told them about what he'd overheard from Lizzy Stride, they thought they'd finally caught the break they needed. If she were blackmailing the doctor, that meant he'd done something worthy of it. It also gave him a motive for killing her. With her connections to the other victims, it seemed like they were finally onto something. The doctor was looking more and more guilty. But after that night, Stride clammed up and the doctor kept to himself. Every attempt Victor made to get more details about her "plot" and the reason for it came up dry.

And so, instead of things coming to a head, they simmered, slowly, their reserves burning away. Each day moving achingly, painfully, slowly forward toward the next murder, but bringing nothing of use with it. And all the while the words Blavatsky echoed from their past still lingered. The fear of them coming to pass was cancerous.

The days stretched into weeks. The dinners and luncheons and parties all ran together in his mind. Nothing stood out. No more clues, no more revelations. Everything and everyone seemed to settle into a slow, relentless rhythm; each day grinding past, melting into the next, drawing them inexorably toward their fate.

He looked across the carriage at Elizabeth as she leaned toward the window soaking up the green landscape and fresh air. He knew that despite her indomitable spirit, she was feeling the strain as well. Her beautiful blue eyes were rimmed with dark circles from lack of sleep. Her laughter was less frequent. Her smile dulled just enough to break his heart a little.

He would have given anything to take it all away from her, to shoulder her burden. But even if he could have, she wouldn't have let him. And that just made him love her all the more.

Roxbury's estate, Larkridge Manor, was an imposing Elizabethan country house with gothic pinnacles and a vast array of mullioned windows.

Elizabeth gave a soft, impressed whistle as their carriage turned down the lane toward the main house.

"And I thought Grey Hall was swanky."

Simon chuckled. His family estate was actually quite modest compared to many, including, it seemed, Roxbury's. Larkridge was impressive.

The butler, a small man with keen eyes and an implacable expression, greeted them.

"Good afternoon, Sir Simon," he said, bowing slightly. "Lady Cross."

Elizabeth didn't quite manage to stop her snort of amusement at her title.

The butler's right eye twitched slightly, but that was the only chink in his otherwise impenetrable social armor. As the butler of a grand house should be, he was precise in every way, from his flawless livery to his ramrod posture.

"Sir George is out at the moment, but should be back shortly. If you'll allow me," he said, gesturing to the large entry hall behind the immense front door.

"Thank you," Simon said, giving him a lingering, questioning look.

"Jeeves, sir."

Elizabeth tried to cover her sudden burst of laughter with a coughing fit.

"Is the lady all right?" Jeeves asked, oblivious to the reason for her outburst.

Simon fought down a smile of his own with a pressing frown. "She's fine," he said with a glare that Elizabeth happily ignored.

"I'm fine," she said. "Thank you, Jeeves."

Simon could see her struggling to keep from laughing again. "Perhaps some rest before dinner?"

"Very good, sir. Dinner is at eight, the gong will ring at seven."

"Have the other guests arrived?" he asked.

"You are the first," Jeeves said.

Simon nodded and Jeeves waited to make sure there were no other questions before he waved his hand and a tall, slender footman appeared and escorted them to their rooms—a rather expansive and very elegant suite.

"My name is Edward," the footman said as other servants deposited their ridiculously overstuffed trunks in their room. "I am at your service as your valet for the duration of your stay. Simply ring for me here," he said as he gestured toward a velvet rope that hung near the doorway.

"And if Lady Cross should need a lady's maid or anything at all," he continued, "Eleanor will be pleased to serve."

Simon thanked him and the young man bowed. George had thought of everything. He knew they hadn't traveled with a valet and maid, as would be customary for a couple with his status, and had delicately given them the option.

Elizabeth came back into the sitting room from the bedroom holding a bottle of champagne. "Good ol' George."

Simon met her halfway and took the bottle. It was a fine vintage, but he set it aside.

Elizabeth pouted and he took her in his arms. "Two glasses of that and I'll have to carry you down to dinner."

She laughed. "George would like that."

"I'm sure he would, but we have to pace ourselves and cannot let—"

"Our guard down," she finished for him. "I know."

He kissed her forehead. "It won't be long now."

She hmm'd against his chest. "When this is all over, we are going to Hawaii or Tahiti or somewhere and sleeping on the beach for a week."

"Agreed."

He let go of her and pulled out his pocket watch. It was just now four. "We still have a few hours before we need to dress for dinner. Why don't you lie down? I'll keep watch."

Elizabeth nodded and took a step toward the bedroom before turning back to him. "I sleep better with you next to me."

He wanted to protest, but the words wouldn't come.

She held out her hand. "They're not even here yet. You're watching an empty house."

He hesitated, but realized she was right, and stepped forward taking her hand.

"For a few hours," he said.

"Just you and me."

ELIZABETH WOKE WITH A start and sat up in bed. Next to her, Simon did the same. They'd fallen asleep in their clothes nearly as soon as they'd lain down, but something had startled them both awake.

Simon checked his pocket watch. "Quarter past seven. Slept right through the gong. We'd better dress."

Elizabeth nodded and slipped off the bed, and as she did, they both heard the door to the suite next to theirs close with a bit too much force. Elizabeth went toward the door to their rooms to investigate, Simon close behind.

In the hallway, they could hear raised voices. Elizabeth cracked their door open and listened.

"Then you should have stayed in London," Graham said, his voice choked with anger.

"You'd have liked that, wouldn't you?" Vale bit back.

Graham took a quick step toward her, but Vale held her ground defiantly. Graham paused and her eyes shifted away from him, catching sight of Simon and Elizabeth. Graham's gaze followed hers.

He cleared his throat and smoothed down his dinner jacket before shooting Vale a final look.

Caught watching them, Simon and Elizabeth stepped out into the hallway, apologetic expressions on their faces.

Graham plastered on a smile and for the first time Elizabeth felt uneasy with him. It wasn't that he'd tried to cover their argument and pretend everything was all right. Everyone did that once in a while. It was how *well* he did that. His smile was effortless. He shifted from anger to pleasant nonchalance in a heartbeat, as if he could just flip a switch.

"Sorry about that," Graham said, striding toward them, hand extended. "I heard you two would be here. I'm so glad."

Simon shook Graham's hand.

Vale's expression remained icy and her eyes darted to Graham, clearly not finished with their argument.

Graham eyed Simon and cocked his head to the side. "Is dinner casual?"

"Oh," Simon said, looking down at his clothes. "No, we're running a bit behind."

"We won't keep you then," Graham said and turned to Vale. "Shall we?"

She glared at him, and then back to Simon and Elizabeth before nodding and leaving without him.

"We'll see you downstairs," Graham said as he caught up to Vale and headed down the hall to the stairs.

Simon and Elizabeth slipped back into their rooms.

"Now what do you think that was all about?" Elizabeth asked.

Simon looked back at the door. "I don't know. But things are starting to look a bit frayed around the edges, aren't they?"

Elizabeth nodded. "I'd be more than frayed if I were Graham."

Simon began to unbutton his shirt. "I wish he'd taken our advice and left here when we told him about Vale's letter."

"I know I wouldn't spend a minute more with her than I had to."

Simon sighed. "He's obsessed with the Ripper case. Beyond all good sense."

"I'm starting to think he's as crazy as she is," Elizabeth said, and then added off of Simon's curious look. "Well, not that crazy. She's cornered the market on that brand of nuts."

Simon looked thoughtfully back toward the door. "Let's hope so."

Marie ate her food as she always did, as if it were the last she'd ever see. She washed down an enormous mouthful of fried haddock with the last third of her beer.

It would have been impressive, Victor thought, if it weren't so very sad. The meals they shared together were some of the few she got, he was sure. The rest of the time it was stale bread and bits of cheese. Meat was a luxury and vegetables non-existent.

He watched her as she scraped the last bits from her meal into a pile, not willing to waste even the smallest crumb.

He pointed at her plate. "Another?"

She grinned and spoke with a mouth half-full. "I couldn't."

She swallowed and put her hands on her stomach. "Stuffed like a Christmas goose."

She eyed her glass though and he knew the silent request. He took her glass and his, and moved to the bar for two more. She drank too much. They all drank too much, but it was the only pleasure here, leaden though it was in the end.

Victor leaned his elbows against the bar as the barman drew two more pints. The pub was busy as usual, but the noise and the stink didn't bother him anymore. He barely noticed them.

That was a bad sign, he thought. But hardly surprising considering he'd been there almost a month. He'd been on long assignments before. The greatest risk was always complacency. Becoming comfortable, accustomed, meant losing his edge, not seeing the things he needed to see. Not being the man he needed to be.

He'd learned that lesson the hard way just outside of Paris during the war. It was easy to become one of them, to forget why he was there. Their cause was just and they were the sort of men and women he could fight alongside and be proud to die with. However, despite sabotaging convoys and tapping phones, he was not there to fight their enemy. He shared their food, he smoked their cigarettes, but he was not one of them.

He'd lost sight of that then and it had nearly cost a good man his life. He vowed that that would never happen again. And in the years since, he'd kept that promise. With everything at stake here, now was not the time to break it. He was not here to interfere in their lives or to become part of them.

The barman placed two beers in front him, he took them and turned back to their table. Marie smiled at him.

No matter how much they might need him to.

SHE WAS NEVER EATING again. The dinner had been equal parts amazing and disgusting. The sole was delicious. The calf's head would fuel nightmares and indigestion for days to come. Elizabeth could still see it staring at her.

Her stomach burbled again and she turned her head to see if it had woken Simon. His eyes stayed closed though and his breathing was deep and rhythmic.

Poor him. She could only imagine how tired he was. He'd only been half-joking earlier when he'd said he'd stand guard. She knew he did that most nights. Unwilling to leave them as vulnerable as they would be in sleep, he allowed himself only cat naps. Even for a master of the sleepless night like Simon, doing that for several weeks was a few weeks too many.

From the looks of it, his body had finally convinced his mind to shut the heck up and let it rest. Afraid she might wake him and needing something to settle her upset stomach, she carefully slipped out of bed. Simon rolled his head to the side, but didn't wake. Elizabeth grabbed her robe and tiptoed out of the room.

The house was dark except for a few low-burning gas lamps in the halls. She managed to get downstairs, but had no idea where the kitchen was. One of the grandfather clocks sounded three chimes. Her stomach gurgled in response.

It was late, but maybe someone would still be up in the servants' quarters and could help her find something. Of course, she had no idea where the servants quarters were either. But she'd seen enough Masterpiece Theater to know they were downstairs. Somewhere.

Quietly, she padded along through the halls. The house was enormous though and the servants' quarters were well hidden. She started to backtrack when she noticed a light coming from a doorway. The distinct odor of cigar wafted down the hall to her. Maybe it was George. He'd help.

She retied the sash to her robe and made her way toward the light. She peeked inside, but couldn't see anyone. Easing the already ajar door open a bit more, she stuck her head in.

All she could see was a curl of smoke drifting up over the back of a large wingback chair near the fireplace.

"George?"

Dr. Blackwood's large, mustached face appeared around the edge of the chair. His bushy eyebrows shot up and after a moment's surprise, he stood. "Lady Cross."

"I'm sorry," Elizabeth said, already starting to back out of the room.

"No, no," he said, a sleepy, indulgent smile coming to his face. "I see I'm not the only one who can't sleep."

He held out his glass in question.

"No, thank you," she said.

His eyes took her in, quickly, clinically, before he finished his drink in one long draw. "You don't mind if I indulge, do you?"

He didn't wait for an answer and was already moving toward the drink cart.

"It might not be the best medicine for sleeplessness," he said as he poured himself another glass, "but it is the most pleasant."

He turned back and eyed her again. "Or the second most," he said softly, almost to himself as his eyes drifted over her. They were heavy with drink and something else she couldn't name and didn't quite want to.

Although her robe was as tightly wrapped around her as possible, and her nightclothes thick, she still felt naked under his gaze. She tugged at the edges of her robe and wrapped her arms around her waist.

His gaze drifted back up to her face then and he seemed to come back to himself and cleared his throat as he looked away.

Elizabeth repressed a shiver. She'd overheard two maids talking about the doctor the other day, one warning the other to avoid being alone with him, and here she was doing just that.

He walked slowly, and bit wobbly back to his chair. "You're not suffering from one of Miss Vale's headaches, are you?"

The way he said headaches made it sound like a euphemism. But for what?

Despite her fear, Elizabeth stepped further into the room. He was drunk, which was creepy, but it was also good, she realized. Between that and his weight, she could get away from him if she had to, as long as she kept a safe distance between them.

She walked around to stand behind the chair opposite his.

"Did you give Katherine something to help with her headaches?"

The doctor looked down into his glass. "She's very clever, that one."

Oh, she is that, Elizabeth thought. But what made the doctor think so?

His head lolled slightly to the side and he caught it, jerking it back up into position. His eyes were getting glossier, his focus waning and Elizabeth eased around to the front of the chair.

She moved closer to him and leaned down slightly. "Has she done something?"

Slowly, he lifted his gaze up to her. "Why are women such vile creatures?"

Taken aback, Elizabeth took a step away.

He looked at her and whispered hoarsely, "Why do we need you so badly?"

Elizabeth couldn't stop the shiver that overtook her body. The doctor looked at her again, and started to reach out for her, but was interrupted by a voice at the door.

"Doctor?" It was Roderick, the doctor's valet, standing in the doorway to the study.

Elizabeth tensed, but tried to look casual. If Lizzy Stride were to be believed, Roderick was not above doing the doctor's dirty work and she didn't want to give him any cause to do any now.

He came in, shooting Elizabeth a cold look, and addressed the doctor the way one would a child.

"I've been looking for you," he said. "Time for bed, I think, sir."

The doctor grunted. His eyes shifted to Elizabeth briefly as Roderick helped him out of his chair.

They stopped at the entrance to the room and doctor turned and bowed sloppily. "Good night, my dear."

With an imperious wave, he stumbled down the hall. Roderick paused before following after him and shot her a look that said in no uncertain terms—*whatever happened here, you'd be wise to keep your mouth shut.*

Her stomach churned again, but this time it wasn't because of dinner.

CHAPTER TWENTY-FOUR

Simon's lungs burned. His legs ached and his mouth was bone dry. He hadn't felt so damned good in ages. He'd nearly forgotten how good it felt to run himself ragged on the pitch. Simon had been reluctant to play, but between Elizabeth's encouragement and George's refusal to accept any other outcome, he'd finally agreed. And now, he was glad he had. He'd been a tolerable cricket player in his youth, and it was nice to know he hadn't forgotten everything.

Of course, that was twenty years ago, as his aching back would testify and re-testify with vigor tomorrow. Even as out of practice he was, he'd done fairly well. He was no match for young Almovar and the twins from Brighton, but he held his own.

Despite his pride, he was relieved when the final wicket of the morning was taken. Due to a general lack of fitness and perhaps too much alcohol the previous night, the next innings, and the match, were called off. It was just as well. He wasn't sure he could have made his ground for another run if his life depended on it.

Sweat trickled down his forehead into his eyes and he wiped it away with the back of his hand.

"Excellent stuff!" a tall, gangly man called Masters said as the teams shook hands. "You have the makings of a fine batsman."

Simon smiled his thanks. The day had been pleasant. Blackwood was blessedly absent. Apparently, he was spending the morning recuperating from his evening.

The thought of Blackwood though soured Simon's mood, and he instinctively sought out Elizabeth. She looked very much at home and quite lovely in her white dress and broad-rimmed sunhat. She waved to him from a spot in a canvas recliner in the impromptu stands that had been set-up on the edge of one the estate's lush lawns.

As he grew near, she grinned up at him, handing him a towel and a glass of lemonade.

"Did we win?" she asked.

Simon laughed. "It's not over. I doubt it ever will be. Roxbury's team was trouncing us."

George passed by and clapped Simon on the back. "Well, to be fair. I think without Lord Willingham you never had a chance."

Lord Willingham was a round little man who'd given up in the first innings and taken a nap by a large oak tree somewhere in the general vicinity of his cow corner position.

"Someone go make sure he's alive, will you?" Roxbury called out, pointing to the still napping Willingham.

Simon wiped his forehead and neck with the towel, and drank half of his lemonade without taking a breath.

Elizabeth's smile grew even broader. "We should do this more often."

Simon snorted. "A pick-up game of cricket?"

She stepped close to him. "It's been a long time since I've seen you this relaxed."

He nodded and flipped the towel around his neck. "I wish I—"

"Good game," Graham said, coming around to shake hands.

"Match," Simon corrected him.

Graham shook his head. "I'm afraid I'll never get it all straight. I was never much for team sports."

"You did very well," Simon said with a smile behind his lemonade glass. "For an American."

Graham laughed and then turned back to where Katherine Vale had been sitting. She'd left barely an hour into the contest.

"She's been getting worse," he said quietly. "Katherine."

Simon felt fresh tension join the soreness in his muscles. "How so?"

Graham frowned and shook his head. "It's like she's a different person somehow."

Simon and Elizabeth exchanged worried glances.

"What do you mean?"

Graham sighed. "At first I thought it was because of those memory lapses."

Several weeks ago, Graham had asked Simon if he'd been experiencing any peculiar omissions in his memory. He'd considered lying, but Graham was astute and if Vale was suffering from them, it could work to their advantage. She was, and so was Graham.

"But it's more than that," Graham continued. "It's the way she looks at me sometimes. I'm not the nervous type, but it's unsettling."

Simon could well imagine.

They'd kept the details of his and Vale's futures from him. It was a difficult decision, knowing the jeopardy he was potentially in, but they couldn't risk affecting the timeline by telling him. Knowledge of the future was a dangerous thing.

If only they could send her away for the duration. But with no cause, they couldn't exactly tie her up somewhere for the next

month, as tempting as it was. She had a part to play in this, the star-
ring role in the final act, locked up in Bedlam if all went well. And
for now, all they could do was watch and wait.

"Tea is being served in the tent," Roxbury called out.

Those who'd lingered started toward to the large white canvas
tent that had been erected not far from the pitch. The three of them
slowly made their way toward it.

"I see that the doctor was indisposed this morning," Graham
said.

"I'm guessing he's busy taking some of that headache powder
he's been giving to Katherine," Elizabeth said.

Graham pulled up short. He cocked his head slightly to the side.
"What?"

"She went to him for her headaches," Elizabeth said.

"Oh," Graham said, having clearly been in the dark about that.
"Of course."

He frowned in thought.

"Something wrong?" Simon asked. He could think of no above-
board reason as to why Vale had kept her visits with the doctor a
secret from Graham.

Graham arched an eyebrow. "Well, it is a bit troubling that she's
sought help from our prime suspect, isn't it?"

And if she were the one who killed Jack the Ripper and changed
time, that made it a little more than troubling, Simon thought. He
nodded in agreement.

"Any progress on that front?" Graham asked. "Any clues linking
him to the murders?"

"Just a feeling," Elizabeth said, keeping her late-night adventure
to herself.

"And you?" Simon asked Graham. "You've found nothing else?"

He shook his head. "About the doctor? No. Nor anyone else. Whoever our Jack is, he's quite clever."

"You almost sound like you admire him," Simon said.

Graham sighed. "I wouldn't say that, but he's avoided being seen so far. No ordinary man could do that."

"Not without help," Elizabeth said.

Graham rolled down his shirtsleeves and began to button the cuffs. "The partner theory? Possible."

"You're sure you didn't see anyone else suspicious the night of the murders? Anything that might help," Simon asked.

"No, it's as I told you. The first night I was too far to see anything, and the second I was rudely interrupted by the Vigilance Committee. They locked me up before the night even began. I'd just arrived in Whitechapel when they said hello," he said, rubbing the back of his head where they'd knocked him unconscious.

Some niggling sensation took root in Simon's mind. Something about that wasn't right. "What time was that again?"

"Couldn't have been past midnight," Graham said. "I'd barely even gotten there."

"You're sure?"

Graham looked at him in confusion. "I'm certain."

Simon nodded. "Of course."

After a few more paces, he stopped walking and made a show of patting his pockets. "I think I left something."

He took hold of Elizabeth's arm to keep her with him and added, "We'll catch up with you later?"

Graham nodded and kept on toward the tent. Simon watched him, wondering what had just happened. And, more importantly, why.

"What did you forget?" Elizabeth asked.

Simon stared after Graham, a troubled feeling growing in the pit of his stomach.

"Graham just lied to us."

Elizabeth looked back at Graham as he neared the tent. "What do you mean?"

"Victor said he saw Graham *just* before Annie Chapman's murder. Minutes before. He made a point of it."

The light dawned in Elizabeth's eyes. "That was close to four in the morning."

"Certainly not before midnight," Simon said.

"Why would Graham lie about that?"

Simon clenched his jaw. "I don't know. But it makes me wonder just what else he's has been lying about."

THAT NIGHT AFTER DINNER, the company didn't split into two groups—men and women—as was the custom, but instead all gathered together in the grand salon. Simon was glad of that for many reasons, not the least of which was he needn't be separated from Elizabeth.

They'd gone from having an ally to, well, frankly, Simon wasn't sure what Graham was anymore. Perhaps they'd been fools to trust him at all. He was, after all, still with Katherine Vale despite their, albeit vague, warnings. And now the lie. How many others had he told?

Simon glanced around the room. Graham stood near the piano, smiling amiably as the evening's entertainment continued. Roxbury and Masters' wife were singing a song from Gilbert & Sullivan's *HMS Pinafore*, "Things Are Seldom What They Seem." Willingham had even recited some poetry earlier. The evening was veering dangerously close to becoming an amateur talent night. Thankfully, it stopped just shy of that.

Katherine Vale sat with Doctor Blackwood on the far side of the room. The two of them weren't exactly what one would call cozy, but there was an attachment. An unwilling one, perhaps. But on whose part? Was Blackwood the one who was responsible for Vale's ending up in Bedlam? It was an intriguing possibility and made Simon even more curious about their current relationship.

Graham offered sherry to Vale and the doctor. Both accepted, but neither happily. Also, Simon noted, neither drank, putting the untouched glasses aside as though they were filled with poison and not sickly sweet sherry. Whatever divide existed between Graham and Vale earlier, it had grown.

Meanwhile, Elizabeth was busy talking with Almovar. And while she was keeping an eye on the other players as well, the young man she was talking to was keeping a close eye on her. A very close eye, Simon thought with a tightening of his jaw.

Elizabeth, absolutely stunning in a new gown she'd purchased just for this, chatted away, oblivious to the intensity of the man's gaze. Spaniards. Simon ground his teeth and looked away. He couldn't afford to be distracted by Elizabeth, no matter how distracting she might be.

He took a sip of cognac and as he turned to set it aside, his head swam. The momentary vertigo passed quickly, but he still had to steady his hand as put his glass down on the end table. He pinched the bridge of his nose and closed his eyes briefly. What the devil had come over him and who the devil was Elizabeth talking to?

Wasn't it bad enough that she had that idiot Maxwell following her around San Francisco like a damned puppy? Did she really need to be flirting with some swarthy, dark haired man who looking at her with undisguised appreciation? What game was she playing at? God, did he have to keep watch over that woman every minute? His neck grew hot with his increasing jealousy and anger.

Clenching his jaw, Simon stood and strode toward her about to slice into them both. If she thought she could—

All at once, barely two strides in, the room tilted again and his memory came back. Simon drew up short, understanding now that he wasn't in San Francisco and it wasn't 1906, but 1888 London.

Elizabeth came to his side.

The concern in her eyes made him feel all the worse for the thoughts he'd just had. He forced a smile to his face and brushed his lips across her cheek.

"No worries," he assured her. "Just going for some air."

She nodded, but clearly didn't believe him. Blessedly, she didn't pursue it. He would explain later, he thought. Right now, he just wanted to be alone.

Simon found the back veranda and took a long pull of cool country air. What an ass he'd been about to make of himself. What an ass he'd been. It wasn't just the memory loss, the disorientation; it was the cold, clear reminder of who he'd been.

It was one thing to remember your previous self; gilded by selective memory, it was never quite right. But to experience it, to feel the loneliness of that man, the unsettled worry always nagging; it was immensely discomfiting.

He did not want to be that man again.

He looked out into the darkness of the expansive back lawn. It was still and quiet. He let out a breath. He was not that man anymore. He would not be that man as long as he had her.

"Simon?"

He smiled to himself, and closed his eyes for a moment in contentment.

"Are you all right?" she asked as she came to his side.

He put his arms around her. "I am now."

"WHEN'S IT MY TURN, Jolie?" a man said with a leer, as Victor walked into the Ten Bells.

The object of his lewd remark was a woman sitting at a nearby table nursing a baby. It was incongruous, to say the least, to see a nursing mother in a place like that god-awful pub. But then again, she wasn't likely to have a sitter, if she wanted to go anywhere the baby went with her. Or it stayed home alone. Apparently, she fancied a drink. Hopefully, the baby did too. He was sure by the way she downed her pint that her milk had to be half beer.

Marie waved to Victor and he joined her at what, despite his intentions to keep it otherwise, had become their table.

She noticed his staring. "Ain't ye seen a baby before?"

Victor frowned. "Of course. Just not in a pub."

Marie shrugged. "Most don't bring 'em. Too noisy."

On cue the table next to theirs erupted into raucous laughter and appreciative screams.

"How would they notice?" Victor asked.

Marie smiled and he was reminded again how much he liked to see it and how rare it was.

"She and little 'un almost didn't make it. Been laid up ever since. No work, can barely take care of the other little 'uns," Marie said.

Victor made a sound of agreement, but he was barely listening. As he always did when he came in, he searched each face in the bar for some sign of the monster they sought. And, like every time before, he didn't find anything.

"Gabriel," Marie continued, "that's after an angel, ye know, that's what she calls him. Cause he was like an angel, bringing life on a night filled with death."

Victor arched a questioning eyebrow.

"He was born the night Annie Chapman was murdered. Her soul left and his came. Some think it's unnerving, but I think it's kinda magical."

"He was born the night of the murder?"

Marie nodded. "It's kinda beautiful, innit?"

"And you say she had a hard time of it?" Victor asked, something working its way from the back of his brain to the front.

"Even a midwife couldn't help, had to call a doc. One just happened to be nearby, I hear. Both of 'em woulda died without him. Was there all night. A saint, he is."

Victor looked over at the mother and child. "That was very fortunate." He turned back to Marie. "You don't happen to know the doctor's name, do you?"

"Blackwood."

Victor's heart sank. "And he stayed with her all night?"

She nodded. "Midnight till past sunrise."

Blackwood hadn't been lying about where he was on the night of the murder. Graham had told the Crosses that he'd heard Blackwood was delivering a baby and damn if it weren't true. If he'd really been with this mother and child all night…Victor leaned back in his chair. If he'd been with them, he couldn't have committed the murder. Annie Chapman was murdered close to four in the morning. There was no way he could have done it.

Blackwood was not Jack the Ripper.

CHAPTER TWENTY-FIVE

"**M**ORE WINE?"

"None for me," Elizabeth said with a shake of her head.

Graham turned to Vale next and while she smiled and nodded, there was a noticeable iciness in it. The young, naive woman they'd met just a few weeks ago was transforming before their very eyes into the freakshow they'd left back in the present. It was incredibly disturbing to see. The changes were small—a slightly different mood, a look in the eyes, her posture—but all together they were a seismic shift in personality. And none of it for the better.

They'd both tried to put on a smiling face, but neither could manage it for the whole evening. Early on in the dinner, they began sniping at each other with increasing frequency and bitterness. Both of their masks had begun to slip, and more and more, Elizabeth had to wonder just what was behind Graham's.

It seemed everyone here was lying, except the one person they thought surely was, the doctor.

When they'd returned from the country, they'd been met by Freddie and a note from Victor. It was not the news they wanted to hear. Their main suspect, Dr. Blackwood, was no suspect at all. He had an airtight alibi for the night of the second murder. Victor had even managed to find other witnesses to corroborate the truth behind the doctor's whereabouts.

So much for that. So much for all of it. They'd been chasing the wrong man for weeks, and now with just three days to go before the next murders, they were back to square one.

Simon laid a hand on her forearm. "All right?"

She smiled and nodded at him, but he looked worried. Then again, these days, he always looked worried. And with good reason. If they didn't find Ripper and save him....

"I saw Madame Blavatsky yesterday," Vale announced, winning a grunt of derision from Graham.

Her eyes narrowed. "She said that things are going to get worse. Far worse."

She stared at Graham for a long, meaningful moment. "The murders, I mean. She said there'd be more. That's very perceptive of her, don't you think?"

"It's very something," Graham said, taking a sip of wine.

Vale ignored him and spoke to Elizabeth and Simon. "She also said that it's no coincidence that the victims are prostitutes and not normal women."

"Really?" Simon asked.

Graham set his wine glass on the table. "Normal women?" His voice was tight.

"Well, those were her words, not mine," Vale said, not the least bit contrite, and then gave an expression of forced surprise. "Oh, that's right. I'd nearly forgotten. That's a sore spot with you, isn't it, Charles?"

He blanched slightly and she seemed to delight in his discomfort. She smiled sweetly before turning back to Elizabeth and Simon. "You see, his mother was a whore."

It was all Elizabeth could do not do a spit take with the water in her mouth. From awkward to crazy awkward at the speed of light. Simon and Elizabeth exchanged glances. Nervous, whoa, what the Hell just happened glances.

"I beg your pardon?" Simon asked, as if he couldn't believe his ears. Elizabeth knew she couldn't.

Graham's face tightened. He clenched his jaw and then looked to Simon and Elizabeth, weighing his words carefully when he finally spoke. "We were poor, and she did what she had to do. I'm not ashamed of it. Or," he added, looking back at Vale, "of her."

Although, he clearly was.

His dark eyes glittered a promise of something unpleasant as he looked at Vale. However, she wasn't frightened by his anger; if anything, she seemed to revel in it. Her smile only grew broader as Graham excused himself and made quick work of leaving the dining room. She watched him go and then returned to her meal as if nothing had happened.

"I highly recommend the veal," she said and took a delicate bite from her fork.

It was quite the revelation. "By the way, my lover's mother was a whore," wasn't typical dinner conversation. And considering they were there investigating a man who killed prostitutes, alarm bells didn't just go off, they went off like crazy.

Maybe his mother's...occupation had been what made him so fascinated by the Ripper case. It certainly struck close to home. It was one possibility, Elizabeth thought. She glanced at Simon and could see him weigh what this new bit of information could mean. And judging from the look on his face, he did not like the conclusion he came to.

"You don't really think…" Elizabeth said, her voice trailing off as if saying the words would make them real.

Simon looked at her and frowned. "That Graham is the Ripper?"

He didn't want to consider the possibility, but given what they knew, it was impossible not to.

"I think it's possible," he said.

Elizabeth flopped down in a chair in their hotel room. "I am never trusting anyone again. Present company excluded."

Simon smiled wanly.

"And Jack. Wells, I mean," she said. "I miss him."

Simon nodded. "I'm sure he's fine. Probably romancing some Russian spy."

Elizabeth smiled and then sighed. "I still can't believe Graham could the Ripper."

"It is a disturbing prospect."

"He seemed so nice. He was so helpful."

Simon sighed and walked over to the window. He pushed aside the curtain and looked out, but his mind was elsewhere.

"Was he really helpful?" he asked, turning back around to Elizabeth.

Elizabeth thought for a moment and the frown on her face matched the feeling in Simon's gut. "He pointed us toward the doctor."

"Misdirection?" Simon suggested.

She nodded and continued. "Vale told me she thought he was having an affair. He was going off by himself, being secretive. I didn't think much of it at the time, I'd be doing everything I could to avoid spending time with crazypants, too, but now…"

"His past certainly puts things in a new light, doesn't it?"

Elizabeth tucked her legs up under herself, a sign she was settling into not just the chair, but into an idea. "Do you remember when we first met him?"

"At the party," Simon said, nodding.

"He had a bandage on his hand."

Simon pushed out a breath and shook his head. "I'd completely forgotten that."

"And Vale had that bum ankle," Elizabeth continued, "so she couldn't go with him to the first crime scene, and then she had a headache for the next."

"Convenient that she's out of commission on both nights." Simon sat down heavily on the edge and ran a hand through his hair. "After the bad luck we'd had, I didn't think much of them having it too."

Elizabeth made a *pfft* sound and walked over to sit next to him.

"I didn't make any connections either. After losing Jack and Victor being…"

"French?" Simon said with a smirk.

Elizabeth shook her head with a laugh. "Not very warm and fuzzy."

Simon snorted.

Elizabeth ignored him and went on. "After all that, I was so relieved to have someone on our side that I didn't even think that he might be…"

She shook her head. "It's still hard to believe."

Simon had to agree. "We certainly don't have any hard evidence."

"No, but he did lie about where he was the night of the second murder, and now this. Not to mention, that of all the suspects, he's the one Katherine Vale would like to see dead."

"True," Simon said, but there was still doubt. "I worry we're so desperate for a suspect after losing Blackwood that we might be jumping to conclusions, just to have to something to hold onto."

Elizabeth took hold of his hand and squeezed it in solidarity. "We'll just hold onto this, right?"

Simon squeezed her hand in return and kissed it. "Right."

VICTOR'S MOOD WAS AS sour as old milk. Ever since learning about Dr. Blackwood's alibi, he'd found the skies a little darker and the streets a little filthier. Not that either needed his help, the city was pesthole and he was just one of the pests.

He took out his pipe for a smoke, but even that prospect didn't entice him and he shoved it back into his pocket and glared around the room. They laughed and they drank and they had no idea that in three days time two of their own would be dead, butchered and bleeding.

While it had only been weeks since they'd washed Annie Chapman's blood off the sidewalk, in a place like this where the days blended together in misery, weeks were like months. Time passed and life, such as it was here, moved on.

But it didn't for Victor. It lingered, and the vile stench of what was and the worse that was yet to come permeated everything. He reached for his beer, but it was empty. Apt, he thought.

If he and the Crosses didn't find and save this animal, he thought as he looked around the room trying to see each man's true guise, then his role in this horror would not come to pass. And God help them all then.

"Hello, Victor," Marie said, offering him a smile as she came to his table.

He did not return it.

"All right?" she asked as she sat down next to him.

He looked at her, really looked at her. She was tired and worn. He noticed a small bruise on her neck.

She touched it self-consciously and tried to pull her collar up to cover it, but it did no good. Her fingers lingered over it, fluttering uncertainly.

He started to wonder how she'd gotten it, but pushed the thought from his mind. He'd let himself be too distracted before. He couldn't afford that now. None of them could.

He gave her a curt nod and turned back to watching the crowd.

He could feel her eyes on him, feel her nervousness, but he ignored it. He should have just ignored her from the start. She was not why he was here.

He watched a man at a nearby table. He kept to himself and pulled nervously on his hands. It was difficult to say how tall he was, but his build was close to what they were looking for. Victor snorted to himself. Yes, he was an average man, of average height. As were half the men in the Ten Bells.

He heard Marie shift nervously in her seat and turned to see what bothered her. Her eyes were across the room. A man with a broad mustache and wearing a faded bowler cap had come in, and he stood in the doorway, his eyes scanning the crowd.

Marie stood quickly, nearly knocking her chair over in the process and tried to hurry across the room. The man saw her and his eyes narrowed.

"Joe," she said, her voice tight with anxiety. "I thought you'd gone to Billingsgate."

He glared at her and then at Victor. "Billingsgate. No license, no work. You don't need no license though, do you?" he added looking meaningfully at Victor.

She turned back to Joe. "It ain't like that. He's just a friend."

Joe took a step toward Victor and jutted his chin out as he stood over him. "He's just a friend," he repeated and then, without breaking eye contact with Victor, jabbed his thumb toward Marie. "She's my girl. Don't need no friends like you."

Victor leaned back in his chair casually, and didn't say anything.

That bothered Joe, who started to take a step closer, but Marie grabbed his arm. "He's been good to me."

"He's been good to me," Joe repeated again, almost mechanically before his eyes flared and he tore his arm from her grasp. He shoved the sleeves of his jacket up. "Has he now?"

Victor remained unmoved.

"He's been kind," Marie said, her voice starting to waver.

Joe glared at her. "Kind. I'm off finding work, trying to keep you off the streets, and you crawl into the lap of the first man you see."

"There ain't nothin' between us," she said and then cast a quick apologetic look at Victor.

The glance was not lost on Joe. "Ain't nothin', I see."

It took Victor a moment to realize the repetition was a verbal tic, like Tourette's.

"I can't turn my back on you before you're whorin' yourself out," Joe said angrily.

"It ain't like that," Marie protested, but Joe would have none of it.

He grabbed her arm and pulled her close. "Ain't like that. You know what it does to me."

Marie struggled in his grasp, but Joe just held her tighter and she winced in pain.

"Let her go."

Victor said the words quietly, calmly.

Joe glared down at him. "Go. Mind your own business."

He jerked Marie toward the door.

Victor stood. "And if I do not?"

Joe seemed surprised both at Victor's response and his size, but he was the sort who was used to fighting for everything he'd ever gotten and wasn't about to back down.

Joe started to push his jacket sleeves up again, and made a show of it. It was an obvious feint and when he threw a quick punch, Victor dodged it easily, not even having to move his feet.

Enraged and embarrassed, Joe took another swing. This one, Victor did sidestep and Joe's momentum sent him stumbling forward. When he caught himself and turned around, Victor delivered a sharp jab that sent his head rocketing back.

Joe recovered quickly, shaking it off faster than Victor had anticipated. His jaw was iron and Victor's hand stung. Joe grinned, his gap-toothed smile crooked and smeared with blood.

By now the crowd was cheering them both on, tables sliding out of the way for the night's entertainment. Joe balled his fists and raised them in front of him. He was no novice.

"Four brothers," Joe said in answer to Victor's unasked question. "And none of us likes to share," he added and then followed it with a quick combination. The right landed and Victor's head snapped back.

Joe laughed.

Despite being able to take a punch and land an occasional blow, Joe was still no match for Victor. If he didn't pull his punches, he would probably kill the idiot.

Marie begged them both to stop.

"Shuddap," Joe spit back at her.

"Please, Joe?" she said.

"Please, Joe. I'll teach you when we get home," Joe promised.

The look on Marie's face told the story. A story of a woman who loved a man who beat her. Who would beat her again.

Her expression was all Victor needed to see.

Joe grinned broadly. Victor wiped the grin off his face with his fist. The time for games was over. Victor ducked a slow loping roundhouse from Joe and as he stumbled forward, Victor hit him hard in the belly. He heard the air shoot out of Joe's lungs, and he delivered two more tight uppercuts to the ribs in quick succession.

Joe wheezed and doubled over, falling to his knees. He leaned forward on his hands, a long string of of blood and saliva dripping from his mouth toward the floor as he gasped for breath.

"Oi," the bartender said, as he stepped forward. "That's enough."

Joe stayed on his knees, trying desperately to get air into his body.

Victor stood over him, adrenaline, anger and disgust coursing through his veins. He looked over at Marie who stood half in shock, half in wonder.

Two men stepped forward and helped Joe to his feet. He was still having trouble breathing, but he managed to stand. He glared at Victor, but his real anger was saved for Marie.

"This ain't over."

Marie stepped close to Victor for shelter and held onto his arm.

Joe panted for breath. "Just you wait," he said with a nod. "I gets what's mine. And you're mine, Mary Jane Kelly."

Victor froze. Time stopped. He was sure the earth stopped spinning.

Mary Jane Kelly?

"Come on, Barnett," one of the men said as they helped Joe toward the door.

Dear God. Victor's heart stopped in his chest. Joe Barnett? Mary Jane Kelly.

He turned to Marie, to Mary, and lifted a brow. "Mary?"

She shrugged. "Marie sounded better. And you bein' French and all, thought you'd like it."

Victor's head spun. Not only would he not be able to protect her from the likes of Joe Barnett, he would not be able to protect her at all.

Mary Jane Kelly was the Ripper's fifth and final victim.

SIMON'S EYES STRAINED TO see in the dim gaslight. "Where?" he asked.

Freddie pointed into the distance and Simon could just make out something leaning against a building.

"He's pretty far gone," Alfie said. "I tried to lift him, but he's too heavy."

Simon sighed and the three of them walked over and stood looking down at Victor, pissed drunk and nearly unconscious. Simon sighed heavily again. He should just leave him. Bastard deserved to sleep it off in the street if he was fool enough to drink himself into such a state when they needed him. And that was the rub, they needed him; unfortunately, alive and in one piece.

"Dammit."

"I hope I done right," Freddie said. "I didn't mean to—"

"No," Simon said quickly. "You did well to come get me. Thank you."

Freddie's head bobbed. "I hope he's all right."

Simon shook his head. What the bloody hell had gotten into him?

"He'll be fine," Simon said as he dug out a few coins and gave them to Alfie. "Help me with him."

Alfie pocketed the money and the boys went around to the other side.

"Renaud," Simon said as he knelt down next to him, his eyes nearly watering from the stench of him. He must have literally fallen into the gutter.

Simon squeezed Renaud's face and his eyes opened just a slit before closing again. He hit his cheek gently, mostly, with the back of his hand a few times to rouse him, but the man was insensate.

"Idiot," Simon grumbled.

It took all of his effort, but he managed to lift up the man's dead weight and wedge him against the building before dipping down and picking him up in a fireman's carry. Freddie and Alfie tried to help, but they were barely ten stone between them.

"Dear God," Simon muttered as he gained his balance. He hefted Renaud up into the air to shift him into a better position on his shoulder.

Freddie stuffed Renaud's fallen cap into his pocket and led the way back to Victor's flat. Simon was sure the stairs multiplied on the way up. Each groaned under their combined weight.

Alfie opened the door to the rooms and Victor's head banged against the doorjamb as Simon carried him over the threshold. The boy winced in sympathy, but Simon didn't care. His back was about to go out, and the git deserved it and more.

Simon unceremoniously dropped Victor onto the bed.

Freddie put his cap on the dresser. "You need anything more?"

Simon shook his head. "No, thank you both."

The boys nodded and slipped out, leaving Simon alone with Victor. He watched Victor, trying to think of a reason that would drive the "French Super Ninja" as Elizabeth called him, to throw off his responsibilities and get pissed drunk just when the eleventh hour was nearly there.

He fumed silently for a few minutes and then gave up trying to figure it out. There was no reason for him stay. Victor would sleep it off and Simon could find out what had happened in the morning. And it had better be good.

Simon flipped Victor onto his stomach so he wouldn't choke on his own vomit and glared down at him for a moment before starting for the door.

"Cross?" Victor's voice was thick.

Simon sighed and turned around. "Yes."

Renaud managed to open one eye and pushed himself up onto his elbow. "What are you doing here?"

"That's just what I'd like to know."

Victor looked confused.

"What the bloody hell, Renaud? Thought it was a good time to tie one on, did you?"

Victor winced and squeezed his eyes shut. "Apparently."

Simon's temper flared. "Maybe you don't give a damn about what's going to happen if we fail, but I assure you I do. I have every-thing to—"

Victor lifted a hand to stave off the rest of Simon's rant. "Yes, yes. I know. Your precious wife."

Simon clenched his jaw. It took every ounce of strength not the throttle the man.

Victor forced himself to sit up and cradled his head in his hands. He groaned softly. "I am a fool."

"Clearly."

Victor lifted his head and eyed Simon, but instead of a parry, he nodded. Slowly, he shuffled over to the water basin, poured some from the pitcher and splashed his face.

"Are you going to tell me what prompted this," Simon said crisply, "or do you want me to guess? Or is this merely typical for you?"

"It is not," Victor said, as he toweled off his face. "Not in a long time."

"Hardly comforting."

Victor grunted, but again, didn't argue. He sat down heavily on the little chair at the table and looked up at Cross. After a long moment, he nodded his head toward the bed. Simon's impatience was growing, but he sat down anyway.

Victor frowned in thought and leaned back in his chair. "Do you know why I'm here? Why they sent me?"

The question was odd. He was there to help them find and save the Ripper. But, judging from the man's expression, that wasn't what he meant.

"I wasn't sure if Travers told you or not," Victor said finally. "You never know with him."

"What do you mean?" Simon asked, tension beginning to fill his stomach.

"The timeline is fragile," Victor said. "A life here or a death there. You and your wife," he said, with an almost wistful smile, "you save lives, yes? A man must live or the timeline will fall apart."

Simon nodded. "Yes."

"Sometimes…" Victor said and looked down at his hands for a moment before continuing. "Sometimes it is not a life that must be spared, but a life that must be lost."

Simon frowned.

Victor looked up at him, his expression flat. "You save lives and I take them."

"You kill people?"

Victor nodded. "Sometimes. Others I am there only to make sure."

Simon had a sinking feeling as he began to realize what Renaud meant.

"To make sure that the right person dies at the right time," Victor continued. "They call me Faucheuse."

Simon's French didn't fail him, although he wished it had. "The Reaper."

Considering all he'd dealt with before on missions, vampires and ghosts, and quite possibly the Devil himself, Simon felt very nervous. "You're not *the* Reaper, are you?"

Victor laughed, but it was humorless and short. "I am flesh and blood. Just a man. And right now, I'm a man who must make sure an innocent woman dies at the hands of madman."

Simon finally understood. He and Elizabeth were there to save Ripper, but Renaud was there to make sure his last victim died.

Victor shrugged sadly, resigned. "It is what I do."

"And tonight?" Simon asked. Not that Victor's job alone wasn't reason enough to drink, but what made this evening different from the rest?

"I found that I have gotten to know her." He looked at Simon with acute pain in his eyes and not just from tonight or for tomorrow, but the past as well. "It is more difficult when you know them. When you have grown to care for them."

Simon couldn't imagine. Victor's mission was grotesque, but necessary. Simon understood that. Life and death were two sides of the same coin. It went a long way to explain why Renaud was the way he was. How could a man live with that? Watching, ensuring that people died, time after time? And yet, he needed Renaud to do just that. To make sure an innocent woman died.

"I do not envy you."

Renaud looked at him sadly. "And I envy you with all my heart."

Chapter Twenty-Six

WHEN SIMON RETURNED TO their hotel he found Elizabeth deep in thought. That was never good. He told her what had happened with Victor and she didn't seem surprised.

"I didn't know that's what he did," she said, "but it makes sense in a way. He's so…broken."

Simon had to agree. "I just hope he can pull himself together. We're running out of time."

"Speaking of time," Elizabeth said in a way that made Simon instantly worry.

"Yes?" he said, bracing himself.

"Katherine Vale still has her watch."

Simon stared at her dumbly. "I suppose."

"She's supposed to lose it soon," Elizabeth explained. "It's part of what made her go 'round the bend. She lost her watch and Graham didn't use his to save her. That's how she ended up stuck here and shipped off to Bedlam."

Simon nodded. "Perhaps she loses it herself or Graham takes it."

"Or…" Elizabeth said with a look that promised he would not like the option. "Or we take it."

"Elizabeth—"

"Hear me out," she said, scooting forward on her chair. "We know she loses it. That has to happen. And I don't know about you, but I don't think any of us wants one of the watches just floating around out there."

Simon hadn't thought about that. It would be potentially catastrophic to have a watch in the wrong hands, Vale's aside.

"I wouldn't be surprised if Graham takes it from her," he suggested.

"But we don't know he will. We can't rely on that happening."

"No," he said, with a sinking feeling.

"The only way we can make sure what's supposed to happen, happens—she loses her watch—and that the watch doesn't fall into the wrong hands, is if we take care of it ourselves."

"Steal it."

She sat up straighter. "Yes."

It was dangerous and foolhardy, and she was absolutely right.

"Besides, how do we know we aren't the ones that took it in the first place?" she offered.

Simon frowned. Vale's past was part of their future. It was possible their future selves had taken her watch and that's what caused her to lose her watch in the first place. He sighed heavily. Time paradoxes were migraine-inducing.

"I know," Elizabeth said, and then added, with wriggling fingers above her head. "It's all twisty, but a good kind of twisty."

"And how do you propose we steal her watch? You couldn't get ahold of her purse to read the letter and that was before she was on guard."

Elizabeth smiled. "I did get a sneak peek inside it and the watch wasn't in her purse. She must not carry it around with her. I'd guess she's got it stashed in her room."

Simon narrowed his eyes at her. "This isn't just a plot concocted so you can do a little breaking and entering, is it?"

"No," she said. "But, bonus!"

Simon shook his head. "God help me."

ELIZABETH MADE EASY WORK of the hotel room lock and they quickly set about searching for Vale's watch.

"Laudanum," Elizabeth read as she picked up a bottle from the bedside. She held it out for Simon to see. "Crazy *and* drugged. Awesome."

"Elizabeth."

"I know, I know. Shut up and look."

She put the bottle back on the table and went through the drawers. Nothing.

Elizabeth frowned. She wouldn't just leave it out in plain sight. She'd hide it somewhere. But where?

Simon was busy looking through the small writing desk, in and under lamps, and anyplace an object the size of the watch could possibly be stashed.

"Think, think, think," Elizabeth said in her best Pooh.

She looked around the room and noticed the two chairs and small table by the window, and walked over to them.

"I looked there."

"Did you look inside?" Elizabeth asked. "My daddy used to stash his cash, when he'd had a good day, inside the chair cushions.

She picked one up and felt around. Nothing. With the second though she hit pay dirt. "Ah-ha."

She could feel something hard stuffed into one of the corners. Sure enough, when she flipped it over, there was a small slit. Shoving her hand inside, she pushed the stuffing around until she felt it.

She worked her hand out and held up the watch in triumph. "Got it!"

"Score one for Eddie West," Simon said, winning a broad smile from Elizabeth.

Elizabeth put the cushion back and they rearranged things as best they could and started for the door. Just as they'd crossed from the bedroom into the sitting room, the front door opened and they heard Vale and Graham and come in.

Simon grabbed Elizabeth's hand and pulled her back into the bedroom. He looked out of the window, but she knew it was no use. No balcony and three stories up.

The voices grew louder and Elizabeth dropped onto the floor next to the bed. Waving for Simon to join her, she squiggled under the bed. She got halfway under when her bustle got stuck.

"I'm stuck," she whispered.

Simon pushed down so hard she thought she might go clear through to the suite downstairs, but it did the trick and she slid the rest of the way between the floor and the mattress. Simon slipped in next to her just as the door to the bedroom opened all the way.

Graham and Vale were mid-fight.

"You need to shut your mouth," he said, his voice low and tight.

"Do I?" Vale said on the edge of hysterical laughter. "Your pretty little secret isn't much of a secret anymore."

"I don't know what you think, Katherine, but you're wrong."

"Am I? I know where you go at night."

Elizabeth could see Graham's feet just under the edge of the dust ruffle. He paced across the room. "I don't know who's been feeding you these lies, but you've got to get control of yourself."

"I know so much more. I know the past and the future."

Graham laughed. "That sounds like that witch you've been seeing. Blavatsky. Are you really fool enough to believe her? She's a con."

There was a pause and when she spoke again it was almost pity. "Oh, Charles. You're so wrong."

"The Crosses warned me about you. They—"

"Did they?" Vale interrupted. "That was kind of them."

Elizabeth's heart raced and she glanced over at Simon. He squeezed her hand as they both tried to keep their breathing shallow and quiet.

Now, it was her turn to laugh. "You're such a fool."

"I was a fool to care about you, to bring you here with me."

"Yes," she said calmly, "you were. Too bad only one of us will be leaving."

"Yes," Graham said, now as calm as she was. He walked over and stood in front her, their shoes nearly toe to toe. "Tell me. If I'm what you say I am, why shouldn't I just kill you?"

"Because you're a coward."

The words hung in the air for a split-second before the sound of his hand hitting her face made Elizabeth jump. She nearly hit her head on the underside of the bed.

She looked at Simon, his breathing coming faster now.

One blow was followed quickly by another. And then Vale's body crumpled to the floor at the edge of the bed, her face just inches from Elizabeth's.

Elizabeth held her breath. The moment stretched out painfully. Vale's eyes stayed closed.

"Fool," Graham muttered. Elizabeth wasn't sure if that was directed at Vale or himself.

Graham knelt down next to Vale. Elizabeth looked frantically to Simon. Was Graham going to finish her off? What would they do then? What if she was already dead? Time would change.

Before Elizabeth could follow that horrible line of thought, Graham stood. A moment later she saw him walk toward the door and then heard his footfalls in the other room. As soon as they heard the outer door close, she and Simon wriggled out from under the bed.

Elizabeth looked down at Vale. Was she dead?

Simon knelt down and checked her pulse. "Alive."

Elizabeth exhaled, both relieved and confused. What had just happened?

"Come on," Simon said, taking hold of Elizabeth's wrist and urging her toward the door.

They hurried to the front door and Simon eased it open and peeked out. They stepped out into the hallway and rushed toward the stairs.

"Where are we going?" she asked.

"Wherever Graham is."

THEY ARRIVED OUT FRONT of the hotel just in time to see Graham step into a cab. Knowing they couldn't afford to lose him now, Simon waved another one over and said the words Elizabeth had always wanted to.

"Follow that cab."

They did and it was no surprise where it was headed. Whitechapel.

"Do you really think…?" Elizabeth asked, unable to even say it out loud.

It was horrible to even conceive of, and yet, yes, he did really think that Graham was the man they'd been after the whole time.

Simon kicked himself for not having seen the signs earlier. Dear God, he'd shaken hands, had meals with the man. It turned his stomach.

Before long, Graham's cab pulled to a stop.

"Pull over here," Simon ordered and the cabbie obliged.

Simon dug into his pocket for payment as he watched Graham climb out of his carriage and hurry down a street.

Once he was far enough away, Simon threw open their cab door and leapt out. He paid the driver and helped Elizabeth out, keeping his eyes on Graham's back as he did.

As Elizabeth gathered her voluminous skirts, Simon realized then how much they were going to stick out in Whitechapel. But there was nothing to be done for it and Elizabeth wasn't about to be left behind.

Together, they hurried to catch up with Graham.

He walked quickly ahead of them, furtively looking around him, but trying not to draw too much attention. He, too, stood out in his fine gentleman's clothes amongst the wretched poor of the East End.

He turned a corner, and then another before stopping to look behind him. Simon and Elizabeth ducked into a small butcher's shop and prayed he hadn't seen them. Waiting as long as he dared, Simon stuck his head back out just in time to see Graham step into a doorway.

"Come on," Simon urged needlessly as he grabbed Elizabeth's hand and they hurried down the street.

The building was a three story tenement building. There was no telling where Graham had gone inside. Carefully, Simon opened the front door and they nearly crashed into a man coming out.

"Oi, watch it," he blustered before pushing past them and down the front steps.

Simon held the door for Elizabeth and they both slipped inside. The interior was dark and dank and quiet except for the sound of a baby crying.

They paused and Simon heard footsteps on the creaking stairs above them. He looked at Elizabeth, unsure, but she just nodded, urging him to go on. Careful not make any noise, they crept up the steps. They'd nearly reached the first landing when the last step creaked under Simon's foot, traitorously giving them away. They paused and so did the other footsteps.

But only for a moment; then they could hear a door open. Simon held up a hand for Elizabeth to stay put, praying for once she would, and crept halfway up the second set of stairs. Peeking his head over the railing he just caught a glimpse of Graham's back as he stepped inside a room. Simon ducked down just as Graham turned to look behind him.

Simon held his breath, not daring to breathe or move and finally heard the door close. Very slowly, he made his way back downstairs to Elizabeth who arched her eyebrows in silent question.

Simon nodded and led her out of the building.

"3B," he said as they found a secluded spot across the street to wait.

"Why did he come here?" Elizabeth asked.

Simon shook his head. "I don't know. But it must be important somehow."

They waited in their little spot for Graham to come out again. Barely fifteen minutes later, he did. He seemed much more calm than he had when he'd gone in, but he still looked around apprehensively before starting down the street and back the way they'd come.

They waited until he'd gone from sight before hurrying back into the tenement. The door was locked, but Elizabeth made short work of it. Her breaking and entering skills were disturbingly quick.

They stepped inside and Simon closed the door behind them. It was a small, thoroughly nondescript room. A small bed, a chair and rough-hewn table, and a very old, decrepit armoire.

Simon and Elizabeth shared a confused glance. What was so important here?

Simon stepped over to the window and eased back the ragged curtain. He could barely see through the filthy glass, but it did afford him a decent view of the street below. He kept watch as Elizabeth started to search the room.

She opened the armoire and he heard her gasp.

Letting the curtain fall back, he hurried over to her. "What is it?"

"I'm not sure I want to know," she said, her voice quavering. "Dear God."

Inside the armoire were rows of jars and each held something more grotesque than the last. Intestines, parts of organs, pieces of flesh. The wave of revulsion was so overpowering, it took Simon a few moments to recover himself.

"It's his trophy case."

"I feel sick," Elizabeth said.

Simon nodded. He'd known that the Ripper had taken things from his victims, but to see them, to know that Graham was the murderer…it made his head spin.

He turned away and started back toward the window. "We should go," he said, and then as he turned back he saw a pair of black gloves on the table. Dread made his nerves spark. "Now."

Elizabeth looked at him in confusion, but there wasn't time to explain. He reached for her and they turned to the door just as it opened.

"Well," Graham said. "Aren't you clever?"

Chapter Twenty-Seven

Elizabeth stared at Graham, at Jack the Ripper. He was surprised to find them there, to say the least, but as he'd done before, his mood changed on a dime. He smiled at them, genuinely impressed.

He closed the door behind him, took a step into the room, and reflexively Simon stepped between her and Graham.

Graham chuckled softly to himself. "Forgot my gloves."

He picked them up off the table and ran them through the circle of his fingers. "Careless."

He turned back to them and as he did his eyes landed on the door to the armoire that stood slightly ajar.

"I see we've no secrets anymore." He raised an eyebrow. "It's not what I thought it would feel like, you know, being caught out. A bit anticlimactic really."

"Katherine knows what you are," Elizabeth said.

"She suspects," he admitted, and then spread his arms, "but you...you *know*."

The way he said the last word sent a shiver up Elizabeth's spine. He shrugged and sat down in the small wooden chair. "So, now what?"

For a serial killer who'd just been caught, he seemed terribly calm.

"I'd very much like to kill you," Simon said, meaning every word.

Graham crossed his legs. "I'm sure. But you won't, will you?"

Simon didn't answer and Graham smiled.

"You can't. You can't risk changing time can you? I've work yet to do, and you know it."

It was horrifying. He was right. They might know who he was, but they couldn't stop him. Worse still, they *needed* him to do what he did.

"So, why are you here?" Graham puzzled aloud. "The Council wouldn't send someone else to discover who the Ripper was, that's why I'm here," he added with a grin.

"Something else. Something important," he mused and then sighed. "If you want my help you're going have to give me something more."

"Your help?" Simon bit out.

Graham nodded. "You know who I am, and yet you can't do anything with that information or risk the timeline. I know I escape. Handy bit of information to have. So what are you doing here?"

Elizabeth and Simon looked at each other. There was no use in keeping it a secret any longer. His knowing might just make the difference.

"We're here to save your life," Simon said, choking on every word.

Graham laughed. "Save me? Oh, that's unexpected. But a pleasant surprise. From dear Katherine, I'd imagine. I wouldn't worry about that. If she tries, she fails. It's her lot."

"Maybe not," Elizabeth said. "Those memory lapses you've been experiencing—those are time shifts. She's already killed you."

Graham's face hardened. "What do you mean?"

"Time is in flux between our reality and the one she's altered," Simon explained.

Graham leaned back in his chair. "I underestimated her." He narrowed his eyes at them. "Why not kill her before she kills me? Simple enough."

"And another alteration to the timeline."

Graham frowned in thought. "We don't want that, do we? Too unpredictable. Well then," he said as he stood, "we'll all just have to hope you can do your job."

He straightened his back. "I suppose I'll have to find a new hotel. Any recommendations?"

Simon ground his teeth. Graham smiled and shrugged.

How could Graham be so casual about it all? She tried to make sense of it. How this man, this man she'd actually liked could be such a vicious killer.

He must have read her expression. "Why?" he said, echoing her unasked question.

His insight surprised her, but he shrugged. "It's the one thing everyone wants to know, isn't it? I'm not sure I can give you a satisfactory answer. It's simply who I am."

He walked over to the armoire, Simon and Elizabeth edging away as he did.

He closed the door and turned back to them. He fiddled with the loose gloves in his hands. "I found my mother murdered. I didn't do it," and then added, "but I wished I had."

He shrugged, as if confessing such a thing were like ordering a soft drink. "I was fourteen when I first read about Jack the Ripper. Fascinating. So clever not to get caught. So, I studied him. Learned everything there was to know, but it was just words in a book. Ancient history or so I thought, until I joined the Council. It took years, but I finally convinced them to send me back to study him, and find out once and for all who he was. And to tell him how much I admired him."

Elizabeth shuddered. Graham was terrifying.

If he noticed her reaction, he ignored it and continued. "Imagine my surprise when I showed up to the first crime scene and no one else came. Except for Mary Ann Nichols, of course. I looked at her and wanted her dead. Needed her dead. That's when I knew. I felt it inside," he said, tapping his chest. "*I* was Jack the Ripper."

Elizabeth swallowed. "So you killed her."

He nodded. "I've done everything exactly as it's supposed to be. I know it all by heart. Where they'll be, how I'll cut them. I'm simply a tool of destiny."

Holy crap, Elizabeth thought, what was with the crazies and their destinies?

"And as you know," Graham said, "I'm not quite finished."

"Not yet," Simon said, emphasizing the last word.

Graham smiled at the implied threat and then shrugged. "Everyone dies. But I don't die here and I don't die now. And since I need your assistance…you don't either."

It was a horrific stalemate. They knew what he was, what he was going to do, and they couldn't stop it. And Graham couldn't kill them because he needed them to help keep him alive so he could kill. It was the worst kind of Gordian knot, and Alexander and his sword were nowhere to be found.

Simon looked around their new hotel room. It was significantly smaller than their previous suite, but it had one added benefit.

Neither Graham nor Vale knew where it was.

The first thing they'd done when they'd left Graham's hovel was return to their hotel and get the hell out of it. It was bad enough when one murdering psychopath knew where they lived, but two…. The second thing they'd done was find Freddie and send a note off to Victor.

It had been several hours now and they'd had no reply. Simon knew Renaud could take care of himself, when he wasn't pissed, but he felt a worry take root in his stomach and grow with each passing hour.

A knock on the door interrupted Simon's gloomy train of thought.

"Who is it?" he asked before opening the door.

"Freddie."

Simon opened the door and there stood young Freddie, looking tired and unwell.

"Are you all right?"

The boy nodded and swiped at his nose with his forearm. "Got a message."

Simon held out his hand, but the boy shook his head.

"Ain't writ down."

"All right," Simon said. "What is it?"

Freddie looked down and squinted as he tried to remember it. "Important news. Need to see you. London Bridge 4 a.m."

"That's all?" Simon asked.

The boy nodded but he seemed nervous.

"Is something wrong, Freddie?" Elizabeth asked as she joined Simon at the door.

"No, miss," Freddie said quickly. "It's just I needs to get back to me brother."

"If there's anything we can do…"

The boy nodded quickly and hurried down the hall.

Simon closed the door and turned to Elizabeth. "Why no note?"

Elizabeth shrugged, but said, "Maybe he didn't have time to write it down?"

"Perhaps." Changes to the usual methods and Freddie's odd behavior had him worried. "I don't like this."

Elizabeth sighed. "It's a little weird, but…"

"We go," Simon agreed. "But we don't go unprepared."

ELIZABETH WRAPPED HER COAT more snugly about her as they waited in the shadows on the shore at the far end of the bridge. They'd gone early and found a good vantage point to watch the diminishing traffic. But even from there, they couldn't see more than halfway across. The darkness and distance were too great. The bridge spanned almost 100 yards across the Thames.

Simon took his hand from his pocket where Elizabeth knew it had been wrapped around a gun, and checked his watch. "Ten past."

He frowned and put his watch back in his vest pocket.

"What do we do now?" she asked.

"Wait."

And so they did. Ten minutes turned into twenty and then thirty. Finally, she saw someone walking across the bridge, alone.

"There," she said, pointing.

"I see him."

Whoever it was, stopped in the middle and waited. From so far away it was impossible to see who it was, but he was far too short to be Victor. Whoever it was stood near the balustrade and waved his arms in the air.

"Hallo?"

The voice was small, but one they knew. Freddie.

Simon looked at Elizabeth warily.

"What's he doing here?" she asked.

He frowned and slipped his hand back into his pocket with his gun. "Stay close."

It took them a few minutes to get to the edge of the bridge and they started the long walk toward the center. It was an oddly vulnerable feeling. They were so exposed, but they had to find what was wrong.

A few lone carriages made their way across, the sound of the wheels and horse's hooves loud in the quiet and stillness of the night.

When they got close enough, Simon called out in a hoarse whisper, "Freddie?"

The boy kept his eyes trained on the river beneath them.

"What's wrong?" Simon asked. "Where's Victor?"

Freddie sniffled and then finally turned to face them. "I'm sorry."

"What's…"

Elizabeth knew they'd been trapped. It wasn't a sound, but the lack of one. A carriage that had been passing by stopped and they all turned toward it.

Simon had his gun out and pointed it at the driver.

Even in the darkness Elizabeth recognized him. Roderick, Dr. Blackwood's valet.

"Now, now, don't do something foolish," a woman said from inside the carriage. Elizabeth knew that voice as well.

Simon didn't move and kept his gun trained on Roderick.

The carriage door opened and a small boy, Alfie, stepped out. Behind him came Katherine Vale, a small pistol pressed against the boy's temple.

Elizabeth instinctively took a half-step forward, but stopped herself. Next to her, Simon's hand remained amazingly steady.

"Let the boy go," he said.

"It's all right, Alfie," Freddie said.

The smaller boy shivered with fear.

Elizabeth edged in front of Freddie to shield him.

"Katherine," she said, hoping she could still reach the young woman she'd gotten to know. "Please—"

"Put down your gun or I'll blow this boy's brains out," she said calmly. "I think you know I will."

Both the words and the cold way she said them sent a chill through Elizabeth. Simon glanced at her once, but they both knew he had no choice and lowered the gun.

"On the ground," she instructed him.

He dropped it to the pavement.

"Step back," she told them.

The three of them did as they were told and took a step back and then another, until they were standing up against the edge of the bridge and touching the balustrade.

"Get the gun," Vale ordered and Roderick climbed down from his perch atop the carriage.

"And his watch," she added after Roderick had picked up the gun. "I seem to have lost mine."

The valet looked at her oddly, but she didn't take her eyes from them.

"Just do it," she said.

Roderick stepped forward in front of Simon. "Easy way or the hard way, makes no difference to me."

Simon grunted in frustration and handed his watch to him.

Roderick slipped it into his pocket and then moved back next to the coach.

Vale smiled. "Don't worry, you won't be needing it."

"Let the boy go," Simon said again.

"I think I will," she said. "But I need one more thing."

Her eyes drifted over to Elizabeth and her smile grew.

"No," Simon said.

Vale pulled Aflie closer and pushed the gun against his skull.

"It's okay," Elizabeth said, stepping forward.

She looked at him sadly. What could they do? She couldn't let Vale kill Alfie. She might kill them all anyway, but if there was something, anything Elizabeth could that might save his life, she had to do it.

"It's all right," Elizabeth said to Alfie as she raised her hands in front of her and slowly stepped forward.

"Elizabeth," Simon said in an anguished voice, but she knew he wouldn't argue with her; couldn't argue with her.

Elizabeth crossed the final few steps to stand in front of Vale and Alfie. She knelt down. "Go to your brother," she said with a pleading look to Vale.

Vale released him and he hurried to Freddie's side.

Roderick came up behind Elizabeth and stuffed a kerchief in her mouth, jerking it tight and then tying the ends behind her head. The coarse fabric dug into the corners of her mouth and she gagged.

Simon took a half-step forward, but Vale raised her gun.

Elizabeth looked at Simon, willing him not to move, not to do anything stupid. If they were both alive, they had a chance.

Roderick pulled her arms behind her back so hard that Elizabeth let out a small gasp. He bound her hands so tightly they were already beginning to tingle.

Her heart raged in her chest and her mind whirled. What was Vale doing? Where was she taking her?

She looked at Simon again and forced a small, brave smile to her lips. I'm okay, she tried to tell him, but they both knew it was a lie.

"Inside," Vale ordered and Roderick shoved Elizabeth up the step and into the carriage before climbing back up to the driver's seat.

"What do you want?" Simon asked, desperately.

"This," Vale said and she pulled the trigger.

As the gun went off, Elizabeth screamed and her heart leapt into her throat.

Out of the window, Elizabeth could see the bullet had hit Simon in the chest. Shocked, he stumbled back from the blow, but there was no room, nowhere to go. He lost his balance against the balustrade and fell backward off the bridge, and plummeted into the night.

Chapter Twenty-Eight

Elizabeth screamed, but the sound was hoarse and muffled by the gag stuffed into her mouth. She tried to push her way forward out of the cab, but Vale shoved her back and leveled the small double-barrel derringer at her.

"I have one more bullet," she said.

Elizabeth didn't care. Simon was dead. What did it matter?

And then a little voice inside her head called to her. No, he wasn't dead. He couldn't be dead. He would find a way, she told herself. It's what they did. She had to believe.

The carriage pulled away and Elizabeth moved back in her seat as far as her bound hands would let her. She had to stay alive. She had to stay smart. Simon would need her and she wouldn't let him down.

Vale smirked. "That's a good girl."

She reached into a small doctor's bag and took out a syringe.

Elizabeth cringed back and Vale shook her head.

"Don't worry. It's just a little something to calm your nerves."

Elizabeth doubted that and kicked at Vale, nearly knocking the syringe from her hand. But Vale was stronger than she looked and had the advantage of not being hog-tied. She pinned Elizabeth back into her seat.

Elizabeth felt the sting of the needle piercing her skin and stopped struggling. She tried to say something, but whatever was in the needle was already working on her. Her head began to swim and her eyes droop.

"That's it," Elizabeth heard as she started to slip away. "Just close your eyes. It'll all be over soon."

HE WAS COLD. So damned cold his mind was numb from it. And tired. All he wanted to do was sleep. To let go and sleep. With Elizabeth.

Elizabeth.

It was deep and dark where he was, but the thought of her pulled him up. Finally, he took a gasping breath and choked on a mouthful of water. He lifted his head and spit out the fetid water.

He was in the river. And, he realized, looking around him, moving downstream quickly. With all the strength left in his body he started to swim. His shoulder screamed in protest and his ribs ached. He vaguely remembered being shot. And falling. And Elizabeth.

He saw the silhouette of the bridge disappearing behind him and the wharves on the shore slipping past. In the distance he could see the construction for the Tower Bridge. How far had he drifted? His mind couldn't make sense of it. He must have blacked out at some point. It didn't matter, he told himself. He had to get to shore. He had to get to Elizabeth.

He swam and swam, but the current carried him away. He dug in harder, ignoring the searing pain in his side and shoulder. Slowly, he made progress. It was small, but it was something. He could just make out the muddy shore near the wharves. He swam harder and harder and the world grew darker and darker with every stroke. Until, finally, everything went completely black.

ELIZABETH'S HEAD THROBBED AND her tongue was thick and coated. She tried to swallow, but couldn't, her mouth too dry. She opened her eyes and the bright light that shot into them was so painful, she closed them again immediately. More cautious now, she opened them, and the light dulled, but the world around her wasn't right. It blurred along the edges, every image smeared slightly.

She blinked a few times and tried to focus, but her mind was just as blurry. Vaguely she remembered what had happened. She'd been drugged and—

"Simon," she said in a coarse voice as she tried to sit up. He'd been shot and she had to get to him. There was still time, there had to be, but she had to hurry.

Part of her body listened to her, but the rest ignored her, and all she could manage to do was roll her head to the side. It ached and she lifted a hand to it, but her arm wouldn't move.

She looked down at it. It stretched out impossibly far along the bed. She was lucid enough to see that she was bound. It wasn't with the ropes, but leather cuffs attached to a bed.

She rolled her head to the other side and tried to concentrate. The walls and the floor were white tile and the room was empty except for a metal tray and her bed. Was she in the hospital? Why would Vale take her there?

Elizabeth coughed and her head felt like it was going to snap off her neck. She used the pain to focus, to center herself. She was still groggy, but the blurriness was slowly fading.

As the fog in her mind began to thin, she realized that her room wasn't just a room, but a cell. There were iron bars on the one small window and a heavy metal door. The bright light that had assaulted her earlier was a dim gas lamp and it flickered high above her.

She looked again down at her wrist and tried to wriggle it free from its bond, but it was no use and she laid her head back down. A chill ran through her and she realized the layers of clothing she'd been wearing were gone. All she had on now was a thin white cotton shift. Even her feet were bare.

Then she heard a scream. A terrifying, soul-wrenching scream. It echoed down the hallway. Another, lower in pitch, followed and then another and another, like a pack of animals calling out, a chorus of screams came.

Elizabeth closed her eyes. She tried to shut them out, but they kept on. Kept on screaming.

Finally, she heard someone yell. A deep, male voice, and the cries stopped. And she shivered in the silence.

A few moments later, she heard metal on metal, a key going into a lock. She lifted her head and watched the door open. Katherine Vale stepped inside.

A familiar, stout man wearing a white lab coat and holding a clipboard walked in with her and closed the heavy door to a long corridor behind him. Blackwood. Elizabeth's shock turned to horror and she knew. She knew she wasn't in just any hospital.

She was in Bedlam.

Chapter Twenty-Nine

Simon slowly opened his eyes. The world around him was murky and he was so cold, so tired, so willing to close his eyes again and embrace the peace that the nothingness offered.

"Please, sir," a small voice said and it tugged Simon back up through the haze.

A small, dirty face looked down at him with big round eyes. A boy. He knew his name, but couldn't find it. His mind was swampy and slow.

But one constant, one solid thing remained—Elizabeth.

Simon tried to sit up, but the boy protested.

"You should stay down," he said.

Simon shook his head and instantly regretted it. The world swirled around him and he nearly collapsed back onto the ground. The hard ground.

Just a moment to rest, he thought. He needed a moment.

Slowly, he lay back down and turned his head. The river rolled past. Small boats and large floated along the surface like thoughts he could not grasp. And the darkness came again.

When consciousness came the second time, Simon's mind was sharper, but his body ached even more.

Alfie, that was the boy's name, looked down at him with big, worried eyes.

"I thought you was dead," he said.

"Not yet," Simon said, and then coughed. More river water worked its way up and he turned his head to spit it out. The sun was just beginning to rise.

"What time is it?"

The boy shrugged.

Simon had to get to Elizabeth. Vale had taken her God only knew where. He swallowed down the urge to vomit and slowly sat up.

Every part of his body ached. His head throbbed, his shoulder was stiff, and his ribs protested every breath he took. He tried to stand, but his head spun. He had to get moving, had to start looking, but his body was not ready to move quite yet.

"Where are we?" he asked looking around.

Alfie looked up from the muddy shore toward the wharf above them that was busy with men loading and unloading. "Stanton's."

One of the men looked down at them as he and another lifted a heavy crate. But he turned away and continued with his work. Perhaps a near dead man on the shore was a common occurrence here.

"How did I—"

"Me brother and I fished ya out," Alfie said with profound pride. "Biggest thing I ever caught."

He owed his life to them. "Thank you," he said, knowing it was poor payment for what they'd done. How the two small boys had managed to get him to shore, he couldn't imagine.

"Where's your brother?"

"He's gone to look for your friend. He's been gone hours," Alfie said, sounding worried.

"My friend? Do you mean my wife?"

"I think he means me," Victor said as he appeared on the muddy shore, young Freddie running along side.

Simon hated to admit it, but he was very glad to see Victor. He needed the man's help. Now.

"Elizabeth—" Simon started.

Victor nodded. "Freddie told me what happened." He looked down at Simon. "He said you were shot."

Simon frowned. He'd almost forgotten about that. "I was," he said and then looked down at his chest, expecting to see blood.

He patted his chest with his hand and felt the hole in his jacket and something beneath it.

He reached into his breast pocket and pulled out his journal. Embedded in the pages, mushroomed from the impact was a small caliber bullet. Beneath it, the ink smeared but still legible were the words he'd written a lifetime ago: *She loves me.*

He felt a lump form in his throat and swallowed it down.

Victor shook his head in disbelief. "You have an angel on your shoulder, Cross."

"Let's hope he's got one more miracle in him," Simon said.

"Can you stand?"

Simon wasn't sure, but nodded. With Victor's help he managed it. He looked up into the sky, squinting against the light. It had to be past noon.

"Do you know where she is?"

"Roderick was there," Simon said.

"Blackwood's man?"

Simon nodded.

"What's Blackwood's connection? Do you know where he lives?" Victor said.

Simon straightened his back and took a deep breath. Pain shot through him and he grunted, but he could deal with it. He would have to.

Victor sensed that he was testing himself, testing his body.

"You are in no condition to do this. Tell me where to go."

Simon looked at him, one man to another. "If it were your wife…"

Victor looked like he was about to argue, but closed his mouth. Instead he shook his head. "All right. But we only have a few hours."

Simon frowned, confused. "A few hours?"

He looked around and realized that it had gotten darker, not lighter. The sun he'd seen rising had actually been setting. He'd lost nearly an entire day.

"It all happens tonight. We cannot afford to miss it. It will be Vale's best opportunity to kill Graham. And that must not happen, no matter the cost."

And that cost would be Elizabeth's life. "You do what you have to," Simon said, willing to risk the fate of the world. "I'm going to find my wife."

"WHAT'S GOING ON?"

That's what Elizabeth had intended on saying, had tried to say, but all that had come out was mumbled gibberish. She tried again, but her mouth wouldn't form the words.

"Here's our patient," Vale said as she smiled down at Elizabeth.

Blackwood looked up from his chart and arched an eyebrow. "Your cousin?"

Vale shrugged. "As good as any lie."

She looked back at Elizabeth with mock pity. "Poor woman is lost to us. Simply gone mad. And you, Doctor," she added turning back to Blackwood, "are our only hope."

Blackwood's eyes narrowed. "We're moving too quickly. Drawing too much attention—"

Moving where? Elizabeth thought.

"We have an agreement, Doctor," Vale said coolly and then smiled sweetly. "You have a problem that I can solve and I have one you can solve. It's a mutually beneficial arrangement."

"You're blackmailing me," he said.

She shrugged again. "Incentive for you to hold up your end of the bargain. I will take care of Miss Stride, and you will take care of her."

Vale looked down at Elizabeth as though she were preparing to savor a special meal.

Elizabeth shuddered involuntarily and Vale's smile grew.

Somehow, Vale had discovered Stride's blackmailing plan and stepped in to take over. The Ripper would kill Stride tonight and Vale would get the credit. That was sick enough, but it was wondering what the doctor was going to offer Vale in return that made Elizabeth's stomach ache.

"It hasn't been easy to meet your timeline," the doctor said with a frown.

"But you have?"

Blackwood looked down at Elizabeth. "It's unusual, but we're scheduled for this evening."

Vale's smile broadened. "Don't fret, doctor. You're going to be famous."

She looked back down at Elizabeth. "The world's first lobotomy."

Elizabeth felt a surge of honest to goodness panic. A lobotomy? She struggled more, but she could barely move. She tried again to cry out for help, but all that came out was a strangled sort of moan.

"Psychosurgery," Blackwood corrected her. "It's risky, untried."

"Do your best not to kill her," Vale said. "I'd rather she was simply…hollowed out. But if your hand slips…"

Elizabeth's heart raced and she struggled against the cuffs that held her down.

"She's becoming agitated," the doctor said needlessly.

"Is she?" Vale said, clearly enjoying every minute of her pain.

Blackwood looked down at the chart. "I'll make sure she's given more morphine."

Vale shook her head. "No. I want her to feel this. To know her world is slipping away."

Elizabeth shuddered and swallowed hard. Dear God. This woman was evil.

The doctor looked at her with something close to fear in his eyes. "A local anesthetic then."

"Yes, that sounds perfect," Vale said, clearly picturing the horror in her mind's eye and relishing in it.

After a moment, she turned back to the doctor. "I'm going to stay with her for a few minutes."

It was a dismissal, and the doctor cast one last look at Elizabeth. She tried to plead with him with her eyes, hoping there was some spark of humanity left in him, but he looked away and then closed the heavy metal door behind as he left.

Katherine Vale smiled and sighed a sigh of pure delight. "Oh, how the tables have turned, haven't they? Your husband is dead, and you're about to wish you were."

Elizabeth's wrists strained against the restraints so hard that her hands shook.

Vale practically purred. "I know who you are, you see. What you've done. And now it'll be your turn here, not mine. I'm doing you a favor really," she added, touching Elizabeth's temple, "with this. You won't even know who you are once they're finished. You won't know how awful and empty your life is."

Elizabeth fought the tears that welled in her eyes. She would not give this witch the satisfaction of seeing them.

Vale tugged needlessly on the edges of her kid gloves and walked around the edge of the room, running her hand along the stones. "This will be your whole world," she said. "These four walls. Twelve years, I would have spent here. In this very room."

Vale stopped in the corner and lingered there for a moment before continuing. "But now, you'll be the one to hear the screams at night, wondering when they'll stop."

She walked back over to Elizabeth and looked down at her. "Until finally, you realize that you're the one screaming."

Elizabeth struggled against her bonds, fought back the tears and wished this woman to Hell.

Vale knocked on the door. A moment later an orderly opened it and with one last cruel smile Vale said, "Not all stories can have a happy ending now, can they?"

CHAPTER THIRTY

CROSS BANGED HIS FIST against the door. "Blackwood!"
People walking down the street turned to look at the disturbance.
Victor sighed. He was a fool to be here. Cross could barely stand
and would surely waste time being noble getting the information he
needed. He was too soft.

And at this rate, they would surely get themselves arrested for
their troubles, and that Victor could not afford.

"Cross—"

The door to the doctor's townhouse opened and a butler scowled
at them both. "Please sir, some—"

Cross pushed him back into the residence and scanned the entry
way. "Where's Blackwood?"

The butler straightened his slightly askew tie and stiffened his
back in defiance. "I'm afraid I'm going to have to ask you to—"

Cross grabbed the man by the lapels and shoved him against the
wall. "Where is he?"

Perhaps, he would not waste time after all, Victor thought.

"I'm afraid—"

"What's going on here?" Roderick said as he appeared at he top of the stairs.

Cross tossed the butler aside and strode to the bottom of the stairs.

Roderick stopped mid-step and raised a surprised eyebrow, clearly surprised at seeing a man he thought dead.

"Where did you take her?" Simon said, his breath coming in short bursts now. His hand gripped the newel post for balance.

Roderick looked to the butler and the two maids who'd come curiously into the foyer and jerked his head to the side, indicating they should go.

Cross caught his breath painfully, his ribs were probably broken and glared at Roderick. "Where's Elizabeth?"

The valet was unimpressed, more the fool he, and came down the stairs. Victor stood aside and let Cross do what he must.

Roderick stopped two stairs above Cross and regarded him coolly. "I don't know what you're talking about."

Cross lunged forward, catching Roderick off guard, grabbing him by the coat and throwing him to the bottom of the stairs. Impressive.

The valet crashed into a coatrack that fell down on top of him. Cross kicked it away as he stepped forward and loomed over the man. "Where..." he said, barely able to find a breath, "is she?"

Roderick smirked up at him.

Cross leaned down and pulled him up, groaning loudly as he did. Roderick fought back, but Cross found strength somewhere and held on. He hit him twice, knocking the man back against the wall.

"She's gone by now," Roderick said with another smirk through the blood that trickled down from his nose.

It was a mistake.

Cross punched him once in the gut, and then again before pressing his forearm into the man's throat, slowly choking him. "Where?"

Victor stepped forward then and pulled out his knife. He pressed it to Roderick's neck, just above Cross's arm.

"No more games. Where is she?" Victor demanded.

But Roderick held firm. He looked at them defiantly. Victor knew the type, he was not going to talk. They could torture him and he would not betray his master.

They were wasting time here. He put his knife away and Cross glared at him, before pressing so hard against the man's neck, his face started to turn purple.

"Kill him or don't, we are wasting time."

Cross hesitated for a moment, seeing the truth in what Victor said. He looked back at Roderick, barely conscious now, and let him slip from his hands. The valet slid to the floor.

Cross stood lost, staring down at him.

"Bethlam," a soft voice said behind them.

They both turned to see a young maid, who couldn't have been more than fifteen, standing just inside the hall. She looked nervously at Roderick and then back to Cross. "I overheard something the other day and I think that's where they went."

"Thank you," Cross said, his voice hoarse with effort and emotion.

The girl smiled and looked down again at Roderick. She would clearly pay for betraying him.

Victor strode over to her, dug into his pockets. He handed her all the money he had left. "Get as far away from here as you can."

She looked down at the coins, grateful, and nodded quickly.

Victor walked back over to Cross who was already heading for the door. Victor grabbed his arm.

"Let go of me," Cross bit out.

"If she's there, we can't just walk into Bedlam and take her out."

Cross glared at him again, but Victor could see he knew that he was right. Iron bars, guards and dozens of people stood in their way.

"We're going to need help. Any ideas?"

Cross grimaced as he straightened his back. "Perhaps," he said. "Just one."

THE METAL WHEELS OF the gurney squeaked as Elizabeth was rolled down the long corridor and into the surgery. Her eyes were beginning to focus more, and she could see that it was a teaching amphitheater. A handful of curious onlookers dotted the gallery. She couldn't believe Blackwood was really going to go through with this. But he was. He wasn't the Ripper, but he was just as much a monster.

She tried to call out for help, but the words still wouldn't come. Her mind, though, was sharper, and her voice couldn't be far behind. If she could just catch the eye of someone, anyone, surely they'd see the truth.

Desperately, she tried to get their attention, but the handful of doctors in the theater chatted busily amongst themselves, only giving her the barest glance as she was wheeled in.

She turned her head and saw a tray with scissors, shaving cream and a straight edge razor and she felt another wave of panic. They were going to shave her head and dig out her brain. She tried to breathe, tried to calm herself, but when she saw the tray next to it, she nearly cried out. On it were what could only be described as instruments of torture—a long metal hook, spike, hammer and hand drill.

A nurse came over and peeled back her eyelids. Elizabeth knew this might be her last chance.

"P-please," she managed to whisper.

The nurse was surprised and stopped what she was doing.

Elizabeth's heart raced and she tried to form more words.

"Help me."

It was barely a whisper, but it was words and Elizabeth's heart soared.

The nurse looked at her kindly and gently patted her shoulder. "We're going to, my dear. We're going to."

"No," Elizabeth said, and turned to look for anyone else who would listen. She caught sight of a young doctor in the front row. "Please help me."

He couldn't hear her, but he was watching her, he seemed to understand. His face grew concerned and he turned to his colleague and said something Elizabeth couldn't hear.

"Please help me," she said again.

"I don't think that's right," the young doctor said. "Your patient is lucid, Doctor."

Blackwood came over to the table and stared down at her. His eyes betrayed a momentary flash of fear, but she could see him snuff it out, leaving them cold and dull.

"Please," Elizabeth whispered.

She knew he'd heard her, but he turned to the gallery.

"It is an involuntary action, I assure you," he said, dismissing the young doctor's concern. "Administer more chloroform, nurse."

A nurse nodded obediently and moved to the table.

"Please don't do this," Elizabeth managed to say just before the wire mask was placed over her face, muffling any more words.

A cloth was placed over the mask and Elizabeth shook her head, trying to shake it loose.

"Hold her," the nurse ordered and strong hands gripped the sides of Elizabeth's head.

She could see the dropper filled with chloroform being handed to the nurse. Elizabeth screamed, but the sound was muffled by the mask and even if they'd heard it, no one cared.

"OPEN THE DAMNED DOOR," Simon said as he tugged impatiently on the locked metal door that led from the main entrance of Bethlam hospital to where the patients were, where Elizabeth was.

The woman behind the desk moved to stop him, pulling up short at the anger in his face. "Sir, I'm going to call security, if you—"

"Open the damned door."

George Roxbury had finally caught up with him. Once they'd reached hospital, Simon had run up the front steps and into the lobby. His entire body ached, but he didn't care. Elizabeth was here. Somewhere.

Next to him, Victor waited quietly like a coiled spring.

"I'm afraid—" she started.

"Don't be afraid, just open the door," Roxbury said, his demeanor brooking no arguments.

Despite that, the nurse did just that. "I can't just—"

"Do you know who I am?"

"Sir George?" a man said, who'd come from a nearby office to see what the fuss was about.

"Yes," George said curtly. He pointed to Simon. "This man's wife is being held here against her will."

"Impossible," the man said. "We would never—"

"You will never do anything again," George said, showing more menace than Simon thought him capable of, "if you don't open that door."

The man blanched at the threat.

George stood a little straighter. "And you'll never get another red cent from me or anyone I know."

That spurred the little man into action and he waved to the nurse. "Open it."

The nurse was clearly shocked, but she did what she was told and opened a drawer, pulling out a large key ring with half a dozen iron skeleton keys on it.

"She was brought in earlier today by a woman," Victor said. "Where would she be?"

"Today?" the man said. "That must be Miss Vale's cousin."

"Where?" Victor demanded.

"Surgery," the man said, as if they should have known.

"Dear God," Simon said, fear of what that could mean shot through him.

The nurse walked over to the door with the keys.

"Quickly," he urged her. He felt sick. He couldn't be too late. He wouldn't.

"What in Heaven's name is going on here?" George said. "If she's harmed…"

"Which way?" Victor asked.

"End of the first corridor on the right."

Victor and Simon ran down the hall and Simon could just hear the man continue. "But you're too late."

His chest burned, his head throbbed and his heart ached, but he would not give up. He would never give up.

They ran down the long hallway and made the sharp turn to the right. Together, they burst through the double doors and into some sort of surgical amphitheater. In the center of the room, Blackwood stood over a patient on a gurney. Elizabeth.

Simon strode forward as the men in the gallery clamored over the interruption. The doctor stared at him, angry at the intrusion, until he realized who it was. And then a very satisfying wave of fear overtook him.

Simon took a long step forward and the doctor edged back away from the table.

Simon looked down at Elizabeth, a mask covering her face, her eyes closed. What had they done to her? He wanted to beat the life out of Blackwood, but he *needed* to know she was alive.

Orderlies stepped forward, but Victor intervened and kept them busy.

He leaned down over the table, his heart firmly planted his throat. He desperately scanned her quickly for any signs of injury. "Elizabeth."

He took the metal mask off of her face and threw it aside. Her face was pale and dirty and her eyes were closed. His heart stopped beating. Gently, he cupped her cheek. "Elizabeth."

Slowly, she opened her eyes and blinked up at him. He held his breath until she smiled and said his name. It hung in the air like an answered prayer.

"Oh, thank God," Simon said as he dipped his forehead down to hers for a moment. She was alive. "Thank you God. Are you all right?"

She nodded, unsure. "I think so."

Her voice was soft and slurred and he looked down at her with worry.

"Drugged," she said.

He nodded, relieved again, and then set to untying her. She was safe, he told himself as he undid the straps that bound her. Safe, for now. Unless they could stop Vale from killing Graham, he realized, he still might lose her.

"What's going on here?" a man from the gallery demanded.

"These men are insane," the doctor said.

"A lot of that going around," George said as he arrived, two constables in tow.

He came over to Elizabeth, disbelief and relief mixing on his face. "Elizabeth?"

She managed a shaky smile and Simon helped her sit up.

Roxbury jerked his head toward the doctor and the two constables moved to his side.

"We have to go," Victor said as he lifted his eyes toward the clock above the doors. It was already well after midnight.

Simon looked down at Elizabeth. She was regaining her strength slowly, but they couldn't afford to delay and he wasn't going to leave her here one more moment.

Simon lifted Elizabeth off the table and cradled her in his arms. His ribs screamed in protest, but he didn't care as he looked down at her.

"I'm all right," she said.

The Hell she was. The Hell either of them were, but their night was not yet through.

Elizabeth safe in his arms, Simon and Victor hurried back down the corridor toward the entrance and Simon prayed they'd make it to Whitechapel in time.

Chapter Thirty-One

B Y THE TIME THEY reached the outskirts of Whitechapel it was nearly one in the morning and a thick fog had rolled in. It would be close, too close, Simon thought with a wincing breath. This was the night of the double-event where Ripper...Graham...killed two women—Elizabeth and Catherine. The coincidence of the victim's names sent a shiver down his spine.

He pushed away the feeling of dread that had sunken to the pit of his stomach as it mixed with the general nausea he'd felt since waking up on the shore. As far as they knew Lizzy Stride was first, killed sometime close to 1 a.m., with Catherine Eddowes following shortly after. They had too much ground to cover and not enough time to do it in.

They'd agreed to split up the murder scenes with Victor heading straight for the second one and Simon Elizabeth to the first. Before the carriage had even come to a full stop, Victor leapt out of it, heading west toward Mitre Square and Catherine Eddowes. Simon didn't like splitting up, but as much as he hated to admit it, Simon knew he would slow Victor down. He cast a glance at Elizabeth. Slow them both down.

Elizabeth had recovered quickly from whatever Vale had given her. If the doctor had given her the anesthesia...If he'd been too late....

"I'm all right," she said, reading his thoughts.

She wasn't, but she was regaining her strength while he was losing his.

Simon paid the cabbie and climbed down to the cobblestone street. Elizabeth, in a hodgepodge of clothes borrowed from the hospital, looked like she'd been through Hell. And she had. And so would they both again before this was all over.

She started to run and Simon struggled to keep up. He just couldn't catch his breath.

"Simon?" Elizabeth said, stopping ahead and then coming back to him. "You should wait here."

The thought of sending her off alone to face Ripper and Vale was unthinkable, and he shook his head. "I'm all right."

Elizabeth clearly wanted to, but didn't argue with him and they pressed on. Simon did well for a few blocks, even managing to run. But he knew before they'd even reached Stride's murder scene in Dutfield's yard that they were too late. People had already begun to gather. A dozen people crowded into the yard and two constables hurried past them.

"This way," Simon said, tugging on Elizabeth's arm and turning back west toward the place Eddowes was found.

He'd considered going there first, but with Vale hunting Graham now, they couldn't expect her to stick to the script. Even though Travers had told them that both Eddowes and Stride were murdered, as history needed, Simon didn't trust Vale not to change her plans. But she hadn't, and they'd wasted precious time. All he could do was pray that Victor got to Graham in time.

They hurried back toward Aldgate and Mitre Square. His chest began to burn in a new and deeply troubling way. Simon's shortness of breath became almost no breath at all and he had to stop and lean against a building. He tried to pull in air, but his lungs wouldn't take it. They were only two blocks away now.

"Simon?"

He shook his head, about to tell her he couldn't go on, when he saw a man crumpled on the ground. He stumbled over to him.

"Victor!"

He was lying face down on the sidewalk. Elizabeth ran to him and knelt down next to him. Slowly, painfully, Simon joined her.

Elizabeth looked up at Simon, worry pulling on her face, before pressing her fingers to Victor's neck in search of a pulse.

There was a long pause before she let out a breath. "He's alive."

Simon knelt down and could see the blood matted in his hair on the back of his head. He must have been ambushed on the way.

"Vale," Simon said. She was ahead of them. She was always ahead of them. According to the woman at the desk, she'd left hospital long before the operation was scheduled to begin. That gave her plenty of time to lay a trap for Victor and take care of Graham.

"We have to go," Simon said, forcing himself to stand.

They'd barely made it to the end of the block when the world tilted.

Simon stumbled to a stop and put his hand against a building to keep from falling.

"Simon," Elizabeth said softly as she came back to him.

She didn't have to say it. He knew what she was going to say, what she was going to do. She looked in the direction they'd been headed and then back to him.

He shook his head, knowing she was right. He tried to walk, but his head was spinning. He must have a concussion he thought with odd clarity as though he were outside of himself.

"We're running out of time," she said.

And he was slowing them down. And if they were too late...

She touched his cheek, forcing him to look at her. "I love you. I'll be back. I promise."

Simon stared at her, his heart breaking. He'd failed her. "I'm sorry."

She shook her head. "I'll be back," she said again and started off, only to turn back and kiss him. He wanted to hold her there, to keep her with him, but she pulled away and ran down the dark street, disappearing into the fog.

ELIZABETH RAN TOWARD MITRE Square, alone. She turned up Mitre Street and saw the entrance to the square, just twenty feet away now. Her heart pounded in her chest as she reached the gateway. She ran into the square, but it was empty. She couldn't make sense of it for a moment, until she saw her, Catherine Eddowes, lying on her back in a puddle of blood.

Elizabeth stumbled over to her and what she saw made her stomach lurch. He hadn't just cut her throat, he'd butchered her. Her face was disfigured, parts of it missing. Her bonnet lay behind her head, soaked in the blood from her slit throat. Entrails had been torn out of her and placed, staged, over her shoulder.

Elizabeth turned to the side and retched. A kind of fear and loathing she'd never felt welled up inside her. This was inhuman.

Even though she had faced demons and vampires, the worst and most cruel things she'd seen were always the work of men.

Forcing herself to look away, she stumbled on. Images of Catherine's face haunted her every step. But the thought of Simon pushed her on. She couldn't lose him.

It seemed like miles, but it was only a short distance to Graham's little hovel in the tenement building. Heedless of what she might find, she ran toward it and threw open the front door.

She ran up the stairs, adrenaline clearing her head with each step and pulled the door to his room open. It clanged against the wall.

She stood in the doorway, gasping for breath, stunned at what she saw. Graham was lying on the bed, Vale standing over him, a knife plunged into his stomach.

Blood dripped off the knife as Vale pulled it out.

Elizabeth's heart stopped. Was she too late? Simon...

The thought of him snapped her out of it. She still remembered him. Their lives together were still part of her. She wasn't too late. Not yet. Vale lifted the knife again.

"No," Elizabeth cried and threw herself into the room.

Vale jerked her head to the side, her eyes were wild, frenzied. Beneath her, Graham groaned in pain and gasped for breath.

As Elizabeth closed the distance between them, Vale turned back to Graham and with a cry raised the knife for another strike.

Panic and fear propelled Elizabeth across the room and into Vale. The two of them crashed into the wall at the head of the bed. Vale screamed, something unintelligible, and swung the knife wildly.

Instinctively, Elizabeth held up her arm to shield herself and the knife sliced into her forearm. It burned and she cried out. Vale lunged for her, but Elizabeth managed to step away just in time and Vale stumbled forward.

Elizabeth started to rush her again, but felt a wave of dizziness. No, not now, she thought fighting it until in that same second she didn't know she needed to.

She lurched forward, disoriented, disconnected. Where was she? She looked up to get her bearings, stopping short at what she saw.

A dark-haired woman turned to glare at her. And, God above, she had a bloody knife in her hand. Elizabeth staggered to a stop and the woman grinned. She started toward Elizabeth and in that instant, the world righted itself. Vale. Elizabeth's memory was back.

She had to get that knife away from her, and now. With renewed energy, Elizabeth tackled her to the floor this time. The knife fell from Vale's hand and skittered across the floor.

Vale tried to reach for it, but Elizabeth gripped her arm and pulled it back. As she did, she lost her leverage and Vale flipped them both over. Her eyes wild and frenzied, she dug her fingers into Elizabeth's neck and squeezed.

Beneath Vale now, Elizabeth struggled to pry her hands off her neck. Vale's eyes were filled with hate and something that could only go by one name—evil. Elizabeth arched and bucked, determined not to give in. Finally, she managed to pry one of Vale's hands away and grabbed her by the hair, yanking her to the floor beside her.

Immediately, Vale rolled over, reaching out with one hand toward where the knife had slid. Elizabeth gasped for breath and Vale moved too quickly to stop her. In the next moment, Elizabeth found herself flat on her back, as Graham had been, Vale loomed over her again, knife raised above her head. She didn't hesitate and plunged the blade downward.

Purely by reflex, Elizabeth caught Vale's arm just before she could sink the knife into her chest, but Vale had leverage and Elizabeth's arms began to weaken. The knife moved inch by inch closer to her heart, until finally she could feel the tip through the thin material of her dress.

Elizabeth pushed against her with every last ounce of strength she had, but Vale was too strong. Her eyes bore into Elizabeth's, willing her to die. The hatred and desperation were so thick, they practically dripped off of her. Elizabeth steeled herself, searching for that last bit of strength. But then, something changed. Vale swayed to the side and her near animalistic rage twisted into confusion.

Hope sprang in Elizabeth's chest. She knew that look, and for the first time, welcomed it. It was happening to Vale! Time was changing for her.

For a brief second, Vale let up, and Elizabeth did not let the opportunity pass. Summoning all her strength, she pushed Vale off her, sending her tumbling to the side and into Graham's armoire of horrors. The doors swung open.

Elizabeth scrambled to her feet and grabbed the only weapon she could. The lapse didn't last long and Vale looked up at her, her memory back, her anger renewed. With a cry that came from somewhere deep inside her, Elizabeth swung the empty glass jar and it collided with the side of Vale's head with a loud, sickening thud. Her eyes still open, she slumped to the floor.

Elizabeth kicked the knife out of Vale's hand and then held the jar ready for another strike. She stood above her ready, panting for breath, but Vale didn't move.

"Elizabeth?"

She hardly dared look away, but she managed a quick glance to reassure herself that it was truly Simon. He stood in the doorway, gripping the door jamb for support.

Elizabeth looked back down at Vale as Simon came in and picked up the knife. Had she killed her? Would time change now anyway? It took her a moment to see Vale's chest rise and fall. She was alive. Thank God.

"Are you hurt?" Simon asked.

Elizabeth shook her head. She was, but she'd live. The question was, would Graham?

She turned back to the bed where Graham lay, bleeding from a gaping wound in his stomach. He groaned as she pressed down on it, and then looked up at her and smiled.

THEY MANAGED TO GET Graham to a hospital just in time. He would live. For Elizabeth, it was bittersweet news. They'd done what they what they had to do; the timeline had been saved, but they'd saved a monster's life. It would take weeks for him to recover, but he would and he would kill again.

Battered and exhausted, Elizabeth and Simon prepared to leave. Once things had been set right, and after they retrieved Simon's watch from Vale's room, they were ready to go home. Boy, were they ready to go home. Elizabeth could only hope things were as they should be there as well, and that Jack, angry and confused, would be there waiting for them.

They offered to stay with Victor, knowing his mission wasn't yet over, but he told them to go. Then he said that they were perhaps not the worst operatives he'd ever met after all. High praise from Victor Renaud.

George had taken care of Blackwood. He would not be practicing medicine, except from a prison cell, for a very long time. And Katherine Vale was where she was meant to be—Bedlam.

"I don't see why we're here," Simon said as they walked down the halls of the asylum. "I'd think you'd never want to set foot in it again."

"I don't," Elizabeth said. "I just want to see her here for myself. To make sure it's really happened."

Simon sighed and winced as he did. He had three broken ribs, a concussion and was more bruise than body.

After all she'd been through, Elizabeth couldn't really explain what made her come back to Bedlam. She just knew she had to. A little voice inside her head told her to, and she always listened to that little voice.

The guard opened the door to Vale's cell. "She's restrained," he said, "but call if you need help."

Simon and Elizabeth walked into the small room and Elizabeth felt a wave of panic. Simon took her hand and it faded. Mostly.

Vale sat in a chair, her wrists and ankles manacled. Her eyes spat venom at them. "This isn't over," she said.

"Looks pretty over to me," Elizabeth said much more calmly than she felt.

Vale's eyes darted away from her and then quickly back to Elizabeth. In that instant, Elizabeth felt the rush of understanding; she finally understood what the little voice had been trying to tell her.

She turned and stepped away from Simon.

"Elizabeth?"

"What are you doing?" Vale said, her voice betraying her worry.

Elizabeth walked to the far corner of the room, the one she'd seen Vale linger in when the tables had been turned. She took off her gloves and ran her fingers over the rough stones. She felt one move ever so slightly.

She took a hat pin out of her hair and used it to help pry the stone loose. Simon was beside her now.

"What is it?"

She reached into the small cubby hole and pulled out a pocket watch.

Behind her Vale struggled against her handcuffs.

"I'll be damned," Simon said.

Elizabeth hadn't known until just then why she'd come back. Older Vale must have hidden one of the watches there that she'd escaped from Cairo with. When she'd come back to 1887, she must have planted it there as a failsafe in case her plan didn't come off. And it almost worked. Or maybe it had. There was still one more watch unaccounted for. What if Vale had hidden that one too? Elizabeth pushed the thought away. The timeline was secure. The memory loss events had stopped. All was right again. All was as it should be. Now, all they could do was hope that it stayed that way.

Chapter Thirty-Two

Victor leaned against the cold stone wall of 13 Millers Court. It had been nearly six weeks since the double murders, since he'd begun waiting for this moment. He watched from the shadows as Marie, Mary, stumbled back to her lodgings. He hadn't seen her since that night in the pub. He could not bring himself to, but tonight that was his job.

He stayed in the darkness as she leaned against her front door and fumbled to open it. He stayed in the darkness as Charles Graham joined her. And he stayed in the darkness as the Ripper butchered her, mere feet away from where he stood.

He could hear the sound of the knife, the sound of her flesh rending under it, the sound of Graham's effort as he worked. Worse than all the previous combined, what he would do, what he was doing, to Mary Kelly, was beyond comprehension. Victor told himself it did not matter. Once dead, what did it matter what happened? But it did matter. It mattered to him very much.

Silently, Victor waited outside, able to see through the broad slats of the shuttered window. He thanked God he couldn't see in clearly, that all he could see was Graham as he moved around the room, committing his atrocity.

Victor did what he was there to do. What only a man like him could do. He watched Mary Kelly die.

And when it was over, when Graham was finished, he strode out of the building, his hands covered with blood, and looked right into Victor's eyes. He knew he was safe from him. He knew he lived. He knew he was free.

Victor could have killed him right there. Part of him told him that he should, but he didn't. History would change and all of this would be for naught. Charles Graham lived. He went back to San Francisco. He was hunted by Katherine Vale. His ending was yet to be written.

Graham wiped his hands on a handkerchief, and smiled at Victor as he walked casually down the street.

In that moment, Victor made a promise that he would write the end for Graham. Somehow, some day, he would find him again and he would kill him. Justice would finally be done. Some day.

THE END

NOTE TO THE READERS

THANK YOU FOR READING *A Rip in Time*. I hope you enjoyed it. Look for the next book in the series soon and a few spin-offs, too!

If you enjoyed this book, please consider posting a short review here: **http://www.amazon.com/Monique-Martin/e/B003Y889M6**

Have an idea for a time and/or location you'd like to see Simon & Elizabeth visit? Would you like to see more Jack? More Victor? Drop me a line or come on by Facebook and let me know. I have quite a few ideas for future adventures, but would love to hear from you! Visit: **http://moniquemartin.weebly.com**

ABOUT THE AUTHOR

M ONIQUE WAS BORN IN Houston, Texas, but her family soon moved to Southern California. She grew up on both coasts, living in Connecticut and California. She currently resides in Southern California with her naughty Siamese cat, Monkey.

She's currently working on an adaptation of one of her screenplays, several short stories and novels and the next book in the Out of Time series. For news and information about Monique and upcoming releases, please visit:

http://moniquemartin.weebly.com/

ALSO BY MONIQUE MARTIN

Out of Time: A Time Travel Mystery (Out of Time #1)

When the Walls Fell (Out of Time #2)

Fragments (Out of Time #3)

The Devil's Due (Out of Time #4)

Thursday's Child (Out of Time #5)

Sands of Time (Out of Time #6)

A Rip in Time - (Out of Time #7)

Visit **http://moniquemartin.weebly.com** to sign up for the new release newsletter and don't miss another of Simon and Elizabeth's adventures.